WOLF

A Reed Security Romance

GIULIA LAGOMARSINO

To all men: You give me so much material for my books.

Chapter One

CRAIG

"Reese!"

I ran to catch up to her outside the school where she taught. I had Becky run a background check on her so I could find out where she lived and worked. I figured it would be a little creepy to show up at her house, but work was good. There were other people around and she would feel safe.

I took in every inch of her as she turned toward me. She was short, maybe 5' 3", but she was so damn beautiful. She was curvy and had blonde hair in one of those pixie haircuts. It looked damn good on her too.

She turned and her eyes widened. She looked around quickly, so I followed her gaze, thinking she saw something suspicious. "What's wrong? Is someone after you?"

"No," she said incredulously. "Why would you assume that?"

"Because you were looking around, like there was danger or something."

"Yeah, *you're* the danger! Why are you here?"

"Because I wanted to talk to you. I feel like we got off on the wrong foot in the coffee shop and you've been ignoring my calls-"

"Because I didn't give you my number."

"Well, I didn't get it on our date–"

"We never had a date. Look, it was nice to meet you, but there's nothing going on between us. We aren't dating."

I scratched the back of my neck, not sure why she was denying what I saw clear as day. "Okay, I can see how you would think that there's nothing between us. I mean, high intensity situations cause stress on new relationships."

"We're not in a relationship."

"But we could be," I grinned. "See, I think you're not really giving me a chance here. We had a connection back in that coffee shop."

"What we had was some banter before I found out that you murder people for a living!"

I shook my head slightly. "See, that's not entirely accurate. First, I told you that I worked in security, and I even told you that sometimes I took out the bad guys. I never lied about that. And second, I never ever murder anyone. I strategically take out people that should otherwise be dead or imprisoned because they're really bad people."

She stared at me dumbfounded and I grinned, thinking I had gotten through to her. "I don't believe it."

"You're starting to come around, am I right?"

"Are you really this...obtuse?"

"Okay, I resent that. I'm not stupid. I'll admit, there are some times that I can be a little...oblivious and it's gotten me into trouble, but I know exactly what happened in that coffee shop and you do too. You can't deny that we had something."

"Yes, I can. We didn't have anything in the coffee shop. See? I just denied it."

"I object your denial," I said firmly.

"What? You can't just...ugh!"

"You're so cute when you get flustered. I could just pick you up and carry you around in my pocket all the time."

She glared at me and stomped past me to her car.

"So, should I pick you up tonight?"

"No!" She spun around, putting her hands on her hips as she stared me down. "I don't want to go out tonight. In fact, I don't want to see you ever again!"

She got into her car and slammed the door. I went over and knocked on her window. "Seven?"

She threw her car in reverse and squealed out of the parking lot. "Hey, this is a twenty mile an hour zone!" I shouted.

I grinned as I walked back to my truck. I had a date for tonight and it was going to be great. I just had to figure out what to wear. And I needed to get in a workout and get rid of some of this pent up frustration that I had. Every time I closed my eyes, I saw that little pixie on her knees, sucking my cock. It made me so hard that I was constantly walking around feeling like I had a pole down my pants.

When I walked into the training area at Reed Security, I was pleasantly surprised to see Alec and Florrie sparring. This was perfect. I needed some good advice, and seeing as how they both just went through a bunch of shit, I figured they would have some good perspective.

"Hey." I gave a chin lift to Alec and pulled Florrie in for a hug. I was feeling the love today, even if she wasn't. She punched me in the shoulder.

"What's with you?" she grumbled.

I spread my arms wide and grinned. "I'm in love."

"What?" Alec spat. "What the fuck are you talking about?"

"Reese," I reminded him.

"Yeah, but I thought you hadn't been on a date with her."

"Well, no, but it's only a matter of time," I said with a smile. "I saw her today and I'm taking her out to dinner tonight."

"How did you convince her?" Florrie asked. "I thought she didn't want anything to do with you after the coffee shop."

"Well, okay, technically, she didn't agree to go out with me to dinner, but I figured that if I showed up at her door, she couldn't turn me down."

They both just stood there and stared at me. I was starting to feel like maybe they didn't think this was such a good idea.

"Are you trying to get arrested?" Alec asked. "I mean, if you show up at her house and she doesn't want you there, she's calling the police on your ass."

I chuckled slightly. He thought he was so smart. "Come on, we have it pretty good with the police. I'm not seeing me getting arrested."

"Okay, I know I'm the only female here and it took me a while to admit that I love Alec, but what makes you think that you really love her? Or that she's going to fall for you?"

"I'm glad you brought that up, because I was wondering, do you think you would have realized how stupid you were being sooner if you and Alec had actually dated?"

"What the fuck are you doing?" Alec growled. "Shut the fuck up."

"No, I'm interested," Florrie said, looking at me intently. "Is that how you think you're going to win her over? By forcing her to date you?"

I shifted uncomfortably at her implications. "I'm not forcing her to do anything. She just hasn't gotten a chance to really know me. See, if I show up enough, she'll realize that maybe I'll just leave her alone if she goes on one date with me. And that's when I make my move."

"You throw her in the trunk of you car and kidnap her?"

"No," I chuckled. "Why would I...I'm not psycho."

"Look," Florrie stepped forward and placed her hands on my shoulders. I looked to my left shoulder and raised an eyebrow. This wasn't like Florrie, so it had me a little concerned. "You can't show up at her house tonight. She's going to freak out and you will end up in jail."

"No," I laughed. "You just don't understand how charming I can be."

She sighed and backed up. Alec held out his hand to me. "Good luck tonight. I'll be waiting for your call."

"My call?"

He turned with Florrie and headed for the ring. "From jail."

I straightened my tie and checked in the rearview mirror for any signs of anything out of place. I looked good. I nodded to myself and picked up the flowers off the seat beside me. I didn't know what to go for, so I picked up something that I thought was pretty. It was a little difficult to get the flowers out of the truck. It was a pretty big arrangement, but it was beautiful, just like my Reese's Pieces. And she deserved the best.

I walked up to her house, appreciating how well she took care of the place. It was one of those older homes that was actually made out of brick and had a nice brick porch with a white wicker set. I could picture her out here in the summer, drinking coffee with her feet tucked up under her.

I slicked back my hair one last time and gave a confident knock on her door. I saw her peer at me through the sidelight by the front door. Her eyes widened and she moved away from the door. I was expecting the door to open, but it didn't. Frustrated, I knocked again and waited. Two minutes later, her front door opened, but she made no move to come out or let me in. In fact, she wasn't even dressed for our date.

"Uh, it's seven."

"I know," she snapped. "What are you doing here?"

"I'm here for our date." I pulled the huge wreath out from behind my back and held it up for her. "I brought you flowers."

"You brought me a wreath," she said dumbly.

I cleared my throat uncomfortably. She didn't seem to like them. "Right, well, I didn't know what to get and they were pretty."

"Lillies are a funeral flower."

"Oh...well..." I scratched at the back of my neck and then pulled at my tie. I was starting to feel a little stupid standing here holding flowers that she apparently didn't like. "So, I made reservations for us at the Italian restaurant. We should probably get going soon."

"That's...not gonna happen. Look, Craig, it was nice to meet you, but I'm not into," she waved at my body and I looked down questioningly.

"What?"

"All that."

"All what?"

"You know, big muscles and scary looking."

"I'm not scary looking," I said, slightly offended.

"Look, thank you for the coffee at the coffee shop, but I'm not interested in more."

"This wasn't how this was supposed to go," I muttered to myself. "I don't understand. I'm talking about one date. I just want a chance to get to know you."

"But I don't want to get to know you."

"That's a little harsh," I grumbled.

"Well, you're the one standing on my porch when I already told you that I wasn't interested in going out with you. I figured that being gentle right now wasn't the way to go."

I heard sirens in the distance and looked down the road. An undercover car with a police light was headed this way. "Did you call the police on me?"

"You showed up to my house. What did you think I was going to do?"

"Go on a date with me," I said foolishly.

"Look, I'm sure you're a great guy, but-"

"But you don't want to find out."

The car pulled into the drive and Sean stepped out. I groaned and turned back to her one last time.

"Please, I'm begging you. I know this guy."

"So do I."

"Okay, so just go get your shoes on and tell him this was all a misunderstanding."

"Is everything okay here?"

I closed my eyes and then turned around, giving Sean a big grin. "Hey, Sean. Nice night."

He eyed me skeptically and looked past me to Reese. "I got a call about a trespasser. Everything okay here?"

"I'm just here to take Reese out on a date. I got her flowers and everything." He looked at the flowers and then looked to me like I was a dumbass. "They looked nice."

"Right. Reese, I can personally vouch for this man, if that's the problem. While his choice in flowers may be terrible, I can tell you that he's a good guy."

"I appreciate that, but I told him that I wasn't interested. I told him that again when he showed up at the school, and I told him again when he showed up at my door." She turned back to me with a suspicious look. "How did you find me anyway?"

"Oh, I asked Becky," I grinned. "She's our IT woman and she's excellent at finding anything or anyone."

Reese looked past me to Sean. "Do you see what I'm dealing with?"

"Yeah..." Sean cleared his throat and motioned for me to come closer. I took a step toward him and leaned in. "I think she's telling you to leave."

I snorted. "Yeah, I know that, but she just needs to get to know me."

"Look, if you don't leave, I'm gonna have to take you in and I really don't want to book you for stalking."

I reared back in surprise. "Stalking? I'm not stalking her. I just went to her school because I didn't get her phone number. And when I got it from Becky, she wasn't answering."

"Because I didn't want to talk to you," she snapped.

"Well, I didn't know that. I thought you probably figured that I was a telemarketer or something. So, I told her that I would take her out tonight at seven. Here I am."

Sean scratched his jaw and jerked his head toward the stairs. I followed and leaned in so he could keep things quiet. "Look, I don't want to do this, but you don't seem to be getting the hint. I won't book you, but you're gonna have to come to the police station with me. I'll call Cap to pick you up."

I turned back to Reese in confusion. "What about our date?"

She shut the door in my face and Sean started pulling me down the stairs.

"I'm gonna have to find a new way to convince her to go out with me."

"Maybe she's not the right woman for you," Sean grumbled. "She's obviously not impressed by your muscles or good looks."

"You think I'm good looking?"

Sean rolled his eyes and opened the back door, shoving me inside.

"Hey, gentle. I'm a big guy. There's no reason to be rough."

I watched Reese as she stood in the window and watched Sean drive me away. There had to be some way to reach her. I knew that she was the one I was supposed to be with. It was clear to me, so why wasn't it to her?

Chapter Two

REESE

I let the curtain drop back in place as Sean pulled out of my driveway with Craig in the backseat. I shook my head in disbelief. I couldn't fathom how he didn't get my message back at the school. I picked up my phone and called Brooke, my best friend. I'd known her since we were kids, and that meant that she knew exactly how much I was freaking out right now.

"What do you want?" she said in fake annoyance.

"He was here."

"Who?"

"The stalker. Craig."

"Seriously? He showed up?"

"I know! I don't understand." I started pacing the floor like I always did when I was nervous. "Sean had to come take him away."

"Isn't Sean a detective?" she asked in confusion.

"Yes, but his wife is a teacher at the high school. We met at the beginning of the school year during conferences."

I was a kindergarten teacher, new to the district. I had been teaching in Pittsburgh, but I found that I really didn't like teaching at such a big school. Our little town had grown a lot since I was a kid, but it was still small enough that the class sizes were manageable. I only had eighteen kids in my class, but in Pittsburgh, those classes were more around thirty kids per teacher. And with kindergarteners, you didn't want that many at once.

"I'm sure that he heard my address and came over."

"I don't know how you work with those snot-nosed kids all day long. I can't imagine wiping my own kid's nose, let alone someone else's."

"And that's why you don't have kids and probably won't ever."

"I'm good with that," she retorted. "Maybe send Stalker Man over my way and he can throw that sexy grin at me."

"How do you know he has a sexy grin?"

"I looked up his profile on the Reed Security website."

I rolled my eyes and sat down in my chair, trying to control my jitters. "It figures that you would be just as much of a stalker as he is."

"Hey, I get my kicks where I can."

"We really need a new nickname for Craig besides Stalker Man. It's not very sexy and it reminds me of a serial killer. Not that I *need* a nickname for him. He's not going to be in my life anymore."

"Sure," she said knowingly. "You want him. Admit it."

"I do not. I mean, sure, it's nice to be wanted. But I want a man that wants me on my terms."

"Why?"

"What do you mean why?"

"Why would you want that? Mr. Boring Man that only comes to you when you call for him? No thank you. You need a man that stalks you like prey in the night. A man that needs to devour you. You need a man that won't back down and lay down at your feet."

"That's...it's not..." I sputtered, trying to come up with a logical comeback. "Not gonna happen." I stood and started pacing again, but I could hear her smug grin through the phone. She had me and she knew it.

"It didn't work out with Daniel. He worshipped the ground you walked on and you were bored out of your mind with him."

"That was different. He lived at home with his mother."

"Mhmmm. And Jason?"

"The man had a tattoo of aliens on his back. I mean, come on. We both knew that wasn't going to work out."

"Yet he was always there for you when you called and respected your boundaries. How long was it before he made a move on you?"

"Six months," I muttered.

"Uh-huh. Yeah, that was a real slow burn. So slow burning that not even the sex could save that relationship."

"That's not a fair-"

"And then there was Thomas, George, Henry-did you plan on dating men that had names like kings? Boring," she said in a sing-song voice. "You need this guy. If only for the amazing sex that you'll get out of it."

"You don't know that the sex will be amazing."

"He's hunting you like a wolf. Trust me, the sex will be so amazing, you'll have multiple orgasms before he even touches you."

"That's not possible."

"You won't know until you try. And you know what my momma always used to say-"

"Can't never did anything. Try killed him," I said mockingly.

"That's right. So, you need to let the Wolf come to you and do with you as he wishes. Let him sink his teeth into you and devour you like the beast he is."

"A clueless beast," I reminded her.

"Doesn't matter. I say that a clueless beast is better than no beast at all."

"I'm hanging up now."

"Why?"

"Because you're going to get me thrown in a trunk and carted off to some cabin in the woods where I'll never be heard from again."

"Okay, one, that would be so sexy with this man. And two, there are worse ways for a date to end."

"Such as?"

"Body bag?"

"The cabin in the woods ends with me in a body bag," I stressed. "We're trying to avoid that."

"Look, he wouldn't work at a security company if he was a guy that went around kidnapping people and killing them."

"That's exactly what he wants everyone to think! He looks like the good guy that protects people until I end up taped to some chair while he looks at me all crazy-like and tells me that this wasn't how it was supposed to go. I can literally hear him saying it now!"

"Reese, you're on the crazy train and it's time you got off. Both literally and figuratively. The man is super sexy and he wants you. Just go with it."

"The only place I'm going is to bed."

"That's right. Go be a cat lady that goes to bed at seven-thirty at night."

"I don't have any cats," I shouted at her.

"Listen, you've had a rough night. I'll take care of this."

"No, I didn't-"

"Yeah, yeah, you can thank me later."

"Don't you dare-"

"Gotta go!"

The line disconnected and I punched her number again, trying to stop her from doing something stupid. But she didn't answer the phone. I dialed again, but this time it went to voicemail. I started pacing around my house. She wasn't really going to do anything. This was insane. I mean, what would she do? Show up at Reed Security? I scoffed and then laughed to myself. That was insane. No way was that happening.

Chapter Three

CRAIG

I waited in Sean's office for Cap to show up. I just didn't understand what went wrong. I brought her a fucking wreath. It was gorgeous, just like her. I showed up in a fucking tie. So, what went wrong?

The door opened and I groaned. Alec walked in with a fucking shit-eating grin on his face. Arms spread wide, he spun around slowly, looking at the room. "I could be wrong, but I believe this is the police station. Didn't I tell you I was going to be hearing from you?"

"*I* didn't call you."

"But you would have if Sean didn't."

"Look, this is all a misunderstanding. She knew we were supposed to be going out on a date. I wore a tie and everything."

"And she still didn't go out with you," he said in amazement. "You're lucky that Florrie went to grab your truck with Cap. If this gets around to any of the other guys, you're in so much shit."

"I don't see why. I just need to talk to her. I think maybe she got the dates wrong or something. Nothing else makes sense to me."

"Did she look like she wanted to go out with you?"

"Well, no, but I think maybe she's a little scared about going out with me. I think she's not into the whole guns and strong man type."

"Then why are you going after her?"

I looked at him stupidly. It was like he wasn't hearing a single word I was saying. "Because we're supposed to be together. Sheesh. Keep up. It's not that complicated."

He shook his head and walked out the door. Assuming I was able to leave now, I followed him out the door and through the police station. Sean stopped me just outside the front doors.

"I think this goes without saying that you can't go see her again."

"Sure," I nodded, though I had no intention of leaving her alone.

"I'm serious. And I'll know if you're bothering her because she's friends with my wife. And I really don't like when my wife gets upset, so don't do anything you shouldn't do."

"Of course," I laughed lightly. I saw Alec shake his head like he didn't believe me, but he didn't say anything. After getting in his truck, I waited for him to start in. I knew I wouldn't have to wait long.

"I know you're not this fucking stupid," he finally said, breaking the silence.

"Here we go."

"What's that?"

"I said 'here we go'. You know, because this is the point where you lecture me about how I'm not giving up on my woman, when it's so clear that you did the exact same thing with Florrie."

"I did not."

"The fuck you didn't. You killed a man because you thought he hurt her. Face it, you chased Florrie for three fucking years and now you're telling me to back away when I meet someone I like. Why can't I have what you have?"

"Well, first off, Florrie and I were already fucking. Your girl doesn't even want to be in the same room with you."

"So, I need to work on that part," I said with a nod. "I know that we're supposed to be together. I just need to make her see that."

Alec sighed next to me, drumming his thumb on the steering wheel. "Fine, what can I help with?"

"I need to figure out how to get her to stay and talk to me. When we were in that coffee shop, we were having great conversation."

"Before three men walked in and held the place up, and you used your ninja skills to take them out."

"Right. But I didn't kill anyone, which I made very clear to her. And I didn't throat punch anyone like I thought I would. With some therapy, those men are relatively fine."

"Yeah, but remember, this isn't Florrie we're talking about. This is a woman that has probably never seen an actual fist fight."

"There are people like that?" I asked.

He nodded and sighed. "This is why I'm not so sure this whole thing is gonna work. Remember the woman I was dating before Florrie? She was terrified of weapons. And I know she would have made me get rid of my cannon. So, you have to ask yourself, are you prepared to be with a woman that won't like your job?"

"I just have to warm her up to it, that's all."

He sighed and pulled through the gates of Reed Security. "Okay, so let's put a plan together. We need a way for her to get to know you when you aren't quite so...brutal looking."

I nodded, liking where he was going with this. "Okay, so nonthreatening locations. There are plenty of those. The gym."

"You could play ball at the park."

"A restaurant."

"If she didn't want to go with you tonight, she's not gonna want to later," he pointed out.

"Right. Okay, so, other locations that I won't potentially kill someone..." I snapped my fingers rhythmically as I tried to come up with something clever. I noticed Alec was quiet on his end too.

"You know, maybe we should just go for running in the park. I'll do some background on her. She looks like she stays fit, so there's a possibility she runs too."

"And if not?"

"We'll go for the gym. I mean, really, what are the chances that something would go wrong exercising?"

"Here's your earpiece," Alec said, handing over the small, black piece. I shoved it in place and checked coms. I held up my thumb, telling him we were good to go. "Alright, she usually runs in town and then down the path through the woods behind the playground."

"So fucking unsafe. Imagine all the psychos that could be hiding in the woods, just waiting to take out someone."

"Right, well, this is a small town. I think she's pretty safe."

I nodded even though I didn't agree. "I really don't think it's necessary that I wear an earpiece. I think I can handle this on my own."

"Relax, I'm not going to do anything unless things start getting out of control."

"You'd better not," I muttered. "You stay in the SUV and you don't come out for any reason."

"Cross my heart," he grinned. I flipped him off and got out of the SUV, stretching for a minute before I took off at a light jog. I didn't want to run too fast and miss her. I was about halfway through my run when I spotted her. She was just a tiny little thing. I could pick her up and haul her away and she wouldn't be able to fight back. Which only fueled my anger even more that she was running alone out here.

I ducked my head and pretended not to see when I plowed right into her. I grabbed onto her arms and pretended to trip. I took us both down to the ground, but rolled so that she fell on top of me.

"I'm so-" Her eyes widened when she saw me and then she was pushing up off my body. "What are you doing here?"

"I'm out running. I have to keep in shape for my job."

"Your job of murdering people?"

"I don't murder people. Not technically. I restrain them and wait for authorities unless they try to kill me first."

"Semantics," she huffed as she shoved to her feet.

"Hey, don't go," I said, grabbing her arm. "This must be fate. We should talk and...I don't know, run alongside each other."

"Smooth," Alec grumbled in my ear.

"Shut up," I spat back.

"What?" Reese asked. "Did you just tell me to shut up?"

"What? No. No, not at all."

"Then who were you talking to?"

"Oh," I chuckled nervously. "That. That was Alec."

She looked around in confusion and then back to me. "Who's Alec? Are you seeing people that aren't here?"

"Don't answer that," Alec said in my ear.

"No, see, Alec is my teammate and he thought I would screw this up-"

"You followed me out here?" she screeched.

"Abort. Abort. Run away!" Alec yelled at me.

I waved my arms rapidly, trying to diffuse the situation. "No, no, no, no. See, I found out your schedule so I could meet up with you out here and talk. And I'm glad I did, because this is a really dangerous place to run alone."

She stood on her tiptoes and looked into my ear, her face morphing into rage when she saw the earpiece. She yanked it from my ear and glared at it angrily. "You have him on the other end of this thing?"

"Yeah, he's down the road in an SUV. He drove me here."

"Unbelievable."

"Which part?"

"All of it! I thought you were going to leave me alone when Sean showed up."

"But...I didn't really get a chance to talk to you. See, I think if-" Something caught my attention out of the corner of my eye and I peered off into the distance. There was a woman running and a man that very clearly was trying to get close enough to try something. I snatched the earpiece back and shoved it in my ear.

"Alec, come in."

"Dude, just walk away. You've lost her."

"There's a suspect on the path. He just entered the woods. He's going after a woman. I'm pursuing."

"I'll call local PD."

"I'm so sorry to have to end our running date, but there's a bad guy over there and I need to stop him before he hurts that woman."

I turned to run, but spun back around when she shouted.

"We're not on a date!"

"Okay, agree to disagree. You know what? Stay right there and we'll talk about this later."

I took off running, sprinting as fast as I could to get to the woman before she was attacked. I cut off the path and ran through the trees to get ahead of them. I heard a scream and put on a burst of speed, barely seeing anything on the ground. My only focus was to get to the woman before she was injured. I burst out of the trees and tackled the man that was straddling the woman just off the path. He rolled with me, trying to pin me to the ground, but I had at least thirty pounds on him and quickly overpowered him and rolled him underneath me. He pulled a knife and tried to shove it in my neck, but I blocked his hand at the last minute, gripping his wrist and shoving it away from my body.

"What the hell was that? See, I was gonna be nice and try not to hurt you before the police arrived, but then you had to go and pull a knife on me."

I slammed my fist into his face for good measure.

"Bullshit, there are no police coming."

"See, that's where you're wrong," I grinned.

"ETA three minutes," Alec told me.

"My buddy says the police will be here in three minutes, which means you have about two minutes and thirty seconds to overpower me and get away."

He tried to kick at me, but he couldn't get the right angle. I didn't dare let go of his hand to get ahold of the knife in the other. It was too risky when help was so close. Besides, he had too much to lose and desperation made men do ugly things.

"You okay?" I asked the woman that was shaking on the ground. She nodded and pulled her legs up in a ball close to her chest. I sighed, upset that another date with Reese had been foiled.

"Bored?" the man sneered.

"No, just pissed. I was on a date with a woman and then I had to cut things short to come kick your ass. And the thing is, this isn't the first time this has happened. I met her at a coffee shop and three guys came in to hold up the place."

"Really? A coffee shop?" the guy asked skeptically.

"I know. That's what I was thinking. I mean, who does that?"

"No shit. There's no money there."

"Right, well, let's not throw stones. You just attacked a woman in a park. You're no saint."

He rolled his eyes. "At least I was going for a better target."

"Yeah, targeting women makes you the winner," I said sarcastically. I heard the sirens in the distance and grinned down at the man. "I'm terribly sorry, but it looks like you're going to jail. I'm sure you probably had a different plan for tonight, but I'm guessing a guy named Butch is going to end the day with you instead."

"Just let me go. I swear I'll never do anything like this again."

"Yeah, I'm gonna say no. I feel like maybe this lady wouldn't be too happy with me if I just got off and took you at your word."

"Screw her. I have money. I can pay you."

"I'm pretty well off. I don't need the money. Besides, I'm kind of already working with the police." I shook my head, grimacing slightly. "It would look bad and then I would probably be out of a job. I'm gonna have to say no."

The police came running up behind me and held the guy down as I climbed off. I was surprised when I looked up to see Reese standing about twenty feet from me. She looked uncomfortable, probably because she didn't know whether to be happy about what I had done or go with her instincts and run. I grinned at her and held out my arms.

"See? I'm a good guy."

Her eyes widened comically and she pointed behind me. "Gun!"

I spun around, drawing my gun from the back of my jeans just as the suspect was fighting the police officer for his gun. I didn't think twice as I fired off three shots, hitting the guy in the chest. He fell to the ground and the police officer was able to secure his gun. The other officer that was checking on the woman started walking toward me.

"Craig, talk to me," Alec shouted. "Tell me what the fuck is happening."

"Fuck," I cursed under my breath.

"What?"

"I'm about to get my gun taken away."

The officer came and thanked me for my quick thinking, but as I suspected, he took my gun from me and now I felt fucking naked. I turned around to talk to Reese, but she was already gone.

"When did she leave?" I asked Alec.

"About the time that you told me you got your gun taken away."

"Shit. I'm gonna have to do a lot of making up."

"I'm guessing there's no making up after this one."

Chapter Four

REESE

He had been knocking on my door for the last half hour. I considered calling the police, but I didn't want him to get in trouble again. And I had a feeling that this time he would actually be put in jail. Sean had warned him. Figuring that he wouldn't go away unless I answered the door and talked to him, I yanked the door open and crossed my arms over my chest.

"Oh, thank God you answered. I was beginning to think I would need to break down your door."

"Why would you need to do that?"

"Because," he said slowly, "you could be hurt, or worse."

I cocked my head to the side and pursed my lips. "And what would make you think that I was hurt?"

"Well...you're here in your house alone."

"And that would lead to me being hurt how?"

"You're tiny and-"

"I'm sorry, did you just say that I could get hurt in my own house because I'm small?"

He backed up a step and shook his head slowly. "No," he choked out. "I would never...ants are small, but mighty."

"Do I look like an ant to you?"

"You...no, just small and....not at all like an ant. More like a spider," he stammered. "Small and deadly."

"So, now I'm a spider?" He shook his head, not knowing what else to do. "Look, I appreciate that you're some kind of warrior and you think that I need you to protect me, but I don't have anyone after me."

"Not yet."

I sighed heavily, trying to find something that would convince him that I didn't want to see him again. "I know some women may be into the whole big muscled, savior, God-like man, but that's not me. I like reliable men. Men that will be there when I need them. Men that will not kill someone in front of me. Twice!"

"Hey, I only killed that man today because he was trying to take the gun from the officer. Plus, he was trying to rape a woman. That had to win me some points."

"I'm not in this for points! I don't know how else to tell you that I'm not interested."

"But...I love you."

I stared at him, completely baffled and unable to respond. I had met this man a handful of times, all unwanted, yet he kept coming back for more. And now he was telling me he loved me? How the hell was I supposed to respond to that?

"This would be when you say that you would love to go out with me and I'll tell you when I'll pick you up for our date."

I slammed the door in his face. The man was unbelievable.

"How about tomorrow at lunch? We'll keep it simple and no pressure," he shouted through the door.

I walked into the kitchen and grabbed a bottle of wine. This day was too much and the man on my porch was even worse. I pulled a wine glass down and was just about to pour myself a glass when I heard voices. I stopped and listened intently, trying to figure out who was at my house. My eyes widened when I heard Brooke's voice and I took off for the front door.

Slipping on the rug, I fell to the floor, smacking my knee into the hardwood, and delaying myself even further. I heard the lock turn and jerked my head up, praying that Brooke wouldn't be stupid enough to let the crazy stalker into my house. The door swung open and Brooke walked in, smiling flirtatiously at Craig, who was right on her heels. He looked up and his face immediately contorted into worry. He rushed over to me and lifted me up like I weighed nothing, plopping me on my feet. His hands started roaming over my body, touching me in places that no one should touch unless they're intimately acquainted with another person.

My face flushed bright red and I swore my panties were filled with a gush of my arousal that he could probably smell since he was down by my vagina. One of his strong hands rested on my hip while the other was brushing over my bruised knee. Shivers raced through me so much that I shoved him away and quickly backed up. My brain seemed to have a seizure or something when he was touching me. Which only confirmed that I needed to stay away from this man. He was no good for me.

"Reese," Brooke snapped. Based on the look on her face, she had been trying to get my attention while I was having an internal freakout.

"What?" I cleared my throat and pushed nothing back from my face. I had short hair. There was nothing to act as a distraction.

"Craig was asking if you're alright." She widened her eyes and jerked her head toward him, like I was supposed to fawn all over the man who had been stalking me. I locked my jaw and gave a minute shake of my head, telling her to back off. She jerked her eyes toward Craig and mouthed *thank him*.

My nostrils flared and I gave another short shake of my head. *Back off*, I mouthed. I was all too aware of Craig staring at my body the whole time and it was impossible to not allow my body to react. The man had me all twisted in knots and I didn't like it. I felt like I was out of control, like he would take charge of me if I allowed it.

I shoved his hands away and moved even further away. "You need to leave," I said firmly.

"But, you're injured."

"I'm not injured. I slipped on the rug, but I'm fine now."

"He's just trying to be nice. That's no way to treat your guest."

I looked at her, completely baffled by what she was doing. "He is *not* my guest. He just followed you into my house uninvited!"

"That's being a little dramatic, don't you think?"

I shook my head and left the room. She may be willing to spend time with him, but that didn't mean I had to. I snatched the bottle of wine, chugging right from the bottle instead of pouring it in the glass. The bottle was snatched from my mouth, spilling wine down my shirt.

"Don't be rude," Brooke glared at me. "Offer your guest some wine."

"Oh, that's okay. I don't drink unless I'm completely off the clock."

"Oh," I said sadly. "Do you have to get back to work? That's too bad."

"No, actually, I'm done for the day, but I want to keep a clear head when I'm with you. You know, in case something happens."

I clenched my teeth tighter, wanting to kick Brooke in the ass for pulling this stunt.

"Like what?" Brooke asked.

"Well, for instance, someone could break into the house. There's no security system in here. If I were going to break in, all I would have to do is pick the lock. And she doesn't lock her windows. I noticed that as soon as I walked in the door. Of course, if I really wanted to come in undetected, I would just crawl in through that basement window that's covered with cardboard. I mean, that's really not a deterrent. And she probably doesn't lock the door from the garage, so I could easily slip under the garage door when she pulls in, hide in the garage, and then enter the house after she's gone to bed. She would never even know that she was in danger."

I stared at him, completely creeped out, and then grabbed Brooke's hand and dragged her into the other room. "Do you see what you've done? You've given a psychopath access to my house and now he's seen all the ways he can come in and murder me!"

She waved me off, like my concerns were no big deal at all. "He's in protection services."

"He's shot two people in front of me!"

"So, you know something about him. He's a good shot and he's willing to do anything to protect you."

I shook my head slowly. "He's. A. Psychopath!"

"Uh, sorry to interrupt, but a psychopath is characterized by persistent antisocial behavior, which I show no signs of. Impaired empathy and remorse, but I'm usually pretty empathetic, well, except to criminals. As far as remorse, I show that when necessary. Also, egotistical traits, which I may be guilty of. So, all in all, I would say that I only show maybe one of the traits. I don't think I could technically be diagnosed as a psychopath."

Brooke nudged me as I stood there staring at the sexy, psychopathic man in front of me. And yes, he was a psychopath. I was sure of that. It didn't matter that I found him attractive or that I was secretly turned on by the way his muscles moved when he fought other men. He was dangerous. Like, way more dangerous than any man I had ever met. Hell, I had never witnessed a fight, but I met this man and suddenly, guns were a regular part of my life. I just couldn't deal with that. I didn't know how to relate my sedentary life with his chaotic one. I was a freaking kindergarten teacher.

"I'm going to start locking the windows and doors. I expect you to be gone by the time I'm done."

"That's good," he nodded. "In fact, I'll check your windows with you. You can never be too careful about security."

I turned and walked away, locking every single possible entry into my house. I had never been worried about it before, but now that he knew all this stuff and had only walked into my house, I worried that this wouldn't be the last time I saw him. I finished with the first floor and moved onto the second floor, taking extra time to make sure that all the windows were shut tight. I had this creepy image in my mind of him crawling through my bedroom window.

When I got downstairs, Craig had his phone out and was typing. I walked to the front door and opened it, waiting for him to turn toward me.

"So, I made some notes and you really need new windows installed. Not only for heating purposes, but these windows are shit. They're probably the ones that came with the house."

He looked up and walked toward me, but he didn't walk out the door, so I stepped out onto the porch, hoping he would follow me. He did, but continued to read from his phone.

"I also looked around the house and checked the basement

windows. You know, you should really put up some blinds in the basement. Someone can get a good feel for how to break into your house if
they can see into the basement. I took some measurements and can
pick some up tomorrow. Also, your driveway shows too much of the
house to people on the streets."

I turned and headed back into the house as he continued to talk.

"I measured for fencing. I can have some put up to give you better
protection. It also wouldn't be a bad idea to put in some trees for
better coverage."

I shut the door and locked it, leaving him standing on the porch,
still talking.

"I'll swing by tomorrow with the guys and we'll get started on basic
security features."

I shut off the lights and headed up the stairs, still hearing him
talking on the front porch. Maybe I should have called Sean, but aside
from being completely oblivious to my wants, he seemed harmless.
Then again, wasn't that what most people said about serial killers?

Chapter Five

CRAIG

"I'm confused," Cap said, rubbing at his jaw. "Is this a paying job?"

I looked at him in confusion. "Cap, this is for my lady. I need to make sure she's protected."

I saw Cap's gaze flick to Alec's. "Right. Um...does she know about this?"

"Yeah," I said slowly. "I told her my plans last night."

"And she didn't say no."

"If she said no, I wouldn't be bringing this to you."

He shook his head and sighed. "Alright."

"You can just bill everything to me. I know this is more than she can afford on her teaching salary."

"Why are you installing security at her house if you plan on marrying this woman?" Alec asked, grinning at me like a fool. He knew damn well why I was installing this at her house.

"Because she's not quite convinced yet that we're supposed to be together. It's going to take a little more finesse, but in the meantime, I need to know that she's safe. Her property is a thief's dream come true."

"I have a job for you at the end of the week," Cap informed me. "You'll need to finish up this job by Thursday."

"No problem, Cap."

We walked out of the conference room and down the hall to load up with supplies.

"Alright, I've been quiet long enough," Florrie said, pulling me to a stop. "You can't just railroad this poor woman into being in a relationship with you. If she doesn't want to date you, you have to accept that and move on."

"Florrie, imagine where you would be right now if Alec had just walked away. Would you be happy knowing that Alec was out there showing some other woman his cannon?"

"No other woman would be interested in his cannon," she retorted.

"You don't know that. There could be some lady out there that's just dying to get her hands on that hard piece of steel. Maybe she wants to feel the power under her fingers as she wraps her hands around the barrel or pulls on that firing shaft and watches his cannon-ball fly through the air."

Alec smirked, but Florrie's face was bright red. A throat cleared behind me. I turned around to see Rob and Becky, our IT techs, standing behind me with shit-eating grins on their faces.

"Who's pulling his firing shaft?" Becky asked.

Rob adjusted the glasses on his face and cleared his throat uncomfortably. "Uh, Cap wanted me to go with you and help set up the computer interfacing."

"Cap never sends you along on these types of jobs," I said curiously.

"Uh..." Rob started fumbling over his words, trying to explain why Cap would suddenly send him on a job when he wasn't needed. "He said, you know...this is a difficult job....with the woman...not total-ly....um..."

"Rob," I snapped. "Spit it out."

"He doesn't trust that you won't put up cameras in private locations and link them to your house."

Becky snickered beside him and I turned a glare on her. "And what are you doing here?"

"Me?" she said innocently. "I'm just here to watch."

"I thought you were leaving us?"

As expected, she got her back up and crossed her arms defensively over her chest. "I decided to stay on until the end of the month. There are still some things that need to be taken care of."

"Then why don't you go take care of them?"

She was furious with me, but she didn't say anything else as she stormed away. Everyone around here was so willing to point out that what I was doing wasn't quite on the level, but they were all just being judgmental. I knew that Reese and I had a connection and I wasn't going to stop until I had her. I headed for the elevator, wanting to get everything ready for the morning. I wanted to get to Reese's house early tomorrow morning.

"You weren't actually planning on hooking her cameras up to your house, were you?" Rob asked.

"Well, I'm not now," I grumbled.

Chapter Six

REESE

The sound of a drill woke me, making me jolt out of bed. I rubbed the sleep from my eyes, sure that I was just hearing things, but then I heard it again. I ran to my bedroom door and snatched my robe off the hook, wrapping it around me tightly. I reached down, wrapping my hand around my Louisville Slugger that I kept next to my dresser. With a pounding heart, I cracked the door open and looked for whatever was making that noise. The hall was clear, so I tiptoed out and peeked into rooms that lined the hallway. Everything seemed to be clear.

When I heard the creaking on the stairs, I shoved myself back against the wall and held on tight to my bat. Taking deep breaths to calm my nerves, I quickly wiped my hands on my robe and got a better grip on the bat. I could tell that whoever it was, they were almost to the top step. I took one last deep breath and screamed as I turned the corner and slammed the bat repeatedly into the tall man that was walking up my stairs. He tried to grip onto the banister, but I slammed the bat down on his fingers and then swung one last time for his head.

He ducked and fell backwards down the stairs, his feet flying up over his head as he tumbled down. His feet were up over his head as he lay smashed up against the front door. Creeping down the stairs, with my bat poised and ready to strike, I stepped slowly up to him and nudged him with the bat. He groaned slightly and then his body flopped down to the side. My eyes flew wide open when I saw my stalker lying on the floor.

"What are you doing here?" I shouted at his lifeless body.

"Installing security," he grumbled as he finally opened his eyes and tried to sit up. "We talked about this last night."

"I never told you to come in my house! How did you even get in here?"

"Brooke gave me your key last night."

"Of course she did. You know, it's my house, not hers. You have to get *my* permission to come in here, which I didn't give!"

"I told you I was coming today. You didn't say no."

"I didn't say yes either!"

"Is everything alright in here?"

I spun around with a shriek and held my bat at the ready. "Who are you?"

"I'm Alec, Craig's teammate."

"Let me guess, you just decided to let yourself in too."

"You didn't get her permission?" he said to Craig accusingly.

"She didn't say no."

A blonde woman walked into the room, wearing some kind of commando gear that made me feel a little lacking. "Oh, good. You're awake. I knew this was how it was gonna go down. Thank you for attacking yours and not mine."

"What are you talking about? Who are you?"

"I'm Florrie. This," she jerked her thumb at Alec, "is mine. That's yours." She waved her hand at Craig, who was starting to sit up and looked to be nursing his ribs. Served him right.

"*That* is not mine. He just keeps showing up!"

"See, I knew this was what was really happening. These men have a way of bulldozing your life."

"He's like that too?" I gestured to Alec and she nodded.

"Unfortunately, they all have this alpha tendency to them that they take to the extreme."

"Craig has already shot two men in front of me. And I've only known him a few days!"

"Yeah," Florrie nodded, "Alec killed a man, just snapped his neck, because he thought that the guy had shot me."

"And you're still with him?" I shrieked.

She lifted one shoulder in a shrug and grinned. "It's kind of sexy, you know?"

"No. I don't know. I've never seen someone get shot other than in a movie and that's not real."

Craig stumbled over to me, wrapping his arm around my shoulders. I shrugged him off and glared at him. "What are you doing?"

"Uh, Reese's Pieces, I think you might want to tie your robe shut. As sexy as those pajamas are, I don't really want Alec seeing your tits hanging out."

I snorted. Like my tits could hang out. I hardly had tits. I was small and that meant that my tits never really grew in. I looked down at my white tank top and blue striped shorts and couldn't see quite what the problem was. Just to piss him off, and because I hadn't had coffee yet and wasn't thinking clearly, I shrugged off my robe and tossed it to him. He caught it and glared at me, rushing over to cover me back up. I swatted at him to get away when Florrie whistled loudly. I glared at Craig when he held out the robe to me one more time. Florrie jerked her head toward my kitchen.

"Come on, Reese. Let me explain to you the anomaly that is the men of Reed Security." She motioned me over and I found myself following, even though I didn't know her. She seemed to have her head on straight, even if she worked with psychotic men.

I stalked over to my coffee pot and stared at the light that was on, signaling that the coffee was made and hot in the carafe. "Just helped himself to my coffee, I see."

"Yeah, your coffee is fantastic, by the way."

Sighing, I pulled down a mug and poured myself a cup. Damnit, it was better than how I made it. And that made me hate him even more.

"So, how do I get him to leave me alone?" I asked when I finally turned around.

"You don't."

"There has to be some way. I mean," I chuckled nervously, getting the feeling that there wasn't actually a way out of this, "if someone doesn't want you to be part of their life, you can't just hang around and wait for them to change their mind."

She just stared at me, waiting for me to get it.

"Okay, normal people don't do that."

"You're right. Normal people don't."

"And Craig's not normal," I surmised.

She set down her coffee cup on the counter and walked closer to me. "I'm gonna let you in on a secret that you may not know yet. Craig is like every other man at Reed Security. He knows what he wants and he goes for it. He doesn't let anything stand in his way, and that includes a woman that doesn't want to admit that she's attracted to him."

"Now, wait a minute. I never said that I was attracted to him." She gave me a pointed look and I rolled my eyes. "Okay, even if I am attracted to him, he's not my type. I don't go for overpowering men. I don't want a man to run my life or shoot up anyone that happens to be in the vicinity."

"Do you want to get married?"

"What?"

"Not right now, but someday, do you want to get married?"

"I guess?"

She rolled her eyes, obviously irritated with my answer. "Look, Craig is as loyal as they come. He would give the shirt off his back to anyone that truly deserved it, no questions asked. So, while he may come off as a psycho stalker, I can tell you that you're the only woman he's turned into a psycho stalker for."

"I'm not sure that makes me feel better."

"It should. It means that you're special."

"Look, I understand that you're loyal to him and you want the best for him. But I'm not the woman for him. I don't know the first thing about guns or fighting. And frankly, his cavalier attitude about the whole thing is just something I can't wrap my head around. I teach kindergarten. You know, little people that don't have anything to do with the crazy world he lives in. I don't see danger around every corner and I would never think that I would need a gun in a coffee shop. So, while I'm sure that he's a great guy, I'm not interested in being stalked or being forced into having a security system installed in my house that I could never afford."

Florrie almost looked sad as she stood in front of me, but I didn't understand why. I was trying to tell her that I would never make her friend happy. Wasn't that a good thing? I glanced at the clock on the wall and realized that I was going to be late for school if I didn't leave soon. I rinsed out my mug and turned back to Florrie.

"Please, tell Craig that I don't want anything installed and I would like him to leave me alone. Maybe he'll listen to you."

I was almost out of the kitchen when she spoke again.

"You know, he was going to charge the whole thing to himself. He just wanted to know that you were safe."

I sighed, not turning back to her, and walked out of the kitchen. I just couldn't deal with this right now. I had to get to work and lead a normal life. One that didn't involve people breaking into my house at the ass-crack of dawn.

Chapter Seven

CRAIG

"You didn't tell us that she wasn't on board with this," Alec spat at me.

I lifted my shirt and checked out the damage to my ribs. Bruises were already forming and I was pretty sure that I had a decent goose egg on my head from smacking it against the door when I fell down the stairs.

"She doesn't realize how much danger she's in."

"What danger? She teaches kindergarten. Do you think a psychotic parent is going to come gun her down when the kid doesn't stay inside the lines when coloring?"

"You never know. Parents are crazy nowadays. Maybe she accidentally calls one of them by the wrong pronoun because the kid decides he's a girl for the day. The parent goes crazy, thinking that Reese isn't compassionate enough, and goes to shoot up her house." He stared at me like I was fucking crazy. "What? It could happen."

"This girl is making you lose your head. This isn't you. You don't go around stalking women, and I know you know how to take a hint. And this woman is waving the red flag right in front of your fucking face."

I didn't know how to describe to him how I felt when she was around. She was normal, a piece of this world that I so rarely got to see. And I wanted to grab it with both hands and never let it go.

"You know how you like Florrie because she gets your life?"

"Yeah."

"Well, I like Reese because she doesn't. She's not part of all the bullshit. She sees the world in a completely innocent way. I only talked to her in the coffee shop for a few minutes and I knew that I wanted her. She's life before all this bullshit. She thought I was joking when I talked about carrying a gun, because that stuff doesn't touch her life. She's fucking normal."

"And that's what you want?" he asked incredulously. "Someone that wants to cuddle up on the couch on a Saturday night? Someone that doesn't want to blow shit up for fun? That sounds fucking boring."

"Really? Because I see what every other normal guy gets out of life. I see a woman that could give me a normal life that I've never fucking had. I went off to war when I turned nineteen and I've never known anything else. I've never had a normal relationship. I've slept with women that only see the man in the uniform. But with Reese, if people would stop interrupting our dates and let me actually fucking talk to her, she would see the side of me that just wants normal."

"But you're never gonna get normal," he stressed. "I hate to break it to you, but you will never see the world the way she does. You'll always be looking for danger when she's totally oblivious to it. You can try to be the normal guy, but you're always going to be the guy that has at least five weapons on him at all times."

"Maybe I'll stop carrying," I snapped.

"Right," he snorted. "I'd like to see you walk around without a gun on you, and then we'll see where you end up."

"I could do it."

"Yeah."

"I could," I insisted. He snorted again and it just pissed me off. "Fine. For the next week, I'll only carry a gun when I'm at work. The rest of the time, you won't find a single weapon on me."

He held out his hand and grinned. "Deal."

I shook it, but dropped his hand quickly when Reese came storming through the room. I rushed over to her, stepping in front of her so she had to listen to me.

"Can you please move?" she asked irritatedly.

"Now, hold on just a minute. I just want to talk to you real quick."

"I don't want to talk to you. Why don't you understand that?"

I chuckled lightly, glancing at Alec who was staring at me like I was the dumbest fuck on the planet. Grabbing Reese's arm, I tried pulling her farther away from curious ears, but she fought me. With no other choice, I picked her up and tossed her over my shoulder.

"What are you doing? Put me down!"

"Sorry, Reese's Pieces, but we need to talk."

"Stop calling me Reese's Pieces! I'm not a piece of candy." She slammed her fist into my back and I laughed. It was so cute that she thought she could hurt me. I smacked her ass and walked up the stairs, all the while she was cursing and screaming at me. I walked down the hall, peeking into rooms until I found hers. Closing the door, I set her down and crossed my arms over my chest.

"Now we can talk without people listening."

"Are you crazy? What am I saying, of course you are! You walked into my house uninvited. You follow me places. You threw me over your shoulder like a caveman! Why won't you listen?"

"Well, to be fair, you're not really giving me a chance to talk."

"I don't-"

"Ah," I tsked her. "See? You're not letting me talk. Now, if you'll just hear me out, I'll let you get on with your day."

She fumed in front of me, her eyes turning molten while her face turned a beautiful tomato red. It was cute to see my little sprite being all worked up and angry.

"Okay, now, I know you have some preconceived notions about who I am, but I want to clear that up. See, I'm just a guy looking for a woman that isn't part of my world. I want someone that isn't tainted by the cruelties of the world I live in. I want someone that's still optimistic and thinks the best of people. I could tell instantly when I started talking to you in that coffee shop that you were that woman. I know you don't see it, but we have something. And if you'd just be open to it, I think we could have something explosive between us."

That was a fucking great speech, if I did say so myself. Women wanted honesty and that's what I gave her. I couldn't help the little grin that split my lips. But when she didn't soften or grin in return, I felt my confidence faltering.

"Are you done?" she snapped.

"Uh...yes?"

"Good. Now that you've so eloquently told me who I am, let me tell you who I actually am. I am a woman that's looking for a man that's just normal. You want a normal woman? I want a normal man. And you think I'm not tainted by the cruelties of the world? I've seen enough to know that there are terrible people out there. I worked in the Pittsburgh school system for years, and let me tell you, you learn a lot about the realities of this world when you see some of those kids show up for school and they're hungry or they're wearing dirty clothes. I know that this world can suck. I don't need you thinking that I'm some clueless bimbo that's just flitting through life without a care."

"That's not what-"

"Don't you dare interrupt me. You've barged into my life and taken over when I didn't want you to. Now, I have to get to work, so kindly remove yourself from my house and my life so that I can go do my job."

I wanted to say something else, but I felt like I had just been slapped back into a different reality. Was she saying that she didn't want to see me anymore? Because that was not cool. I was a good person and I deserved a fucking chance. I would just have to wait for another opportunity to open up. And I knew it would.

Chapter Eight

REESE

"Alright, on your worksheets, there are letters that you need to fill in that are missing. Go ahead and get started and raise your hand if you need help."

My teaching assistant helped me go around the room and help the kids with their work, but about halfway through, I got a call from the office.

"Hello?"

"Ms. Pearson, there's someone in the office to see you."

I clenched my jaw in irritation. The man just wouldn't leave me alone. "I'll be right down." I hung up the phone and tried to collect myself before I left. The last thing I needed was for either of us to cause a scene. Luckily, it was lunch time, so I walked the kids down to the lunch room and headed to the office, trying my best to stay calm. But when I walked into the office, I was shocked to see my grandma there.

"Grandma? What are you doing here?"

"Reese, I just came to talk to you about this man that's been following you around."

I rolled my eyes and let out a long sigh. "Grandma, I can't talk about this now. I have a class to teach."

"I know, I know. But you need to be careful. Men are not to be trusted. Especially those Reed Security men."

"What do you know about those men?"

She glanced around the office and then leaned in to whisper to me. "I've seen them around town. Those boys are dangerous."

"Okay, Grandma. I appreciate you coming by to warn me off, but I have to get back to work." I turned to go, but then thought of something. "How did you find out about Craig following me?"

"Well, Brooke came by for tea this morning and told me all about it. At least one of my grandchildren still comes to visit."

"Brooke isn't your grandchild, and I do come to visit, but I can't during the week when I have school."

She pursed her lips. "Well, she's more likely to give me great-grandchildren than you, so I have to take whoever I can. I'll probably be in the ground for twenty years before you decide to settle down and have a family."

"Don't be so dramatic. It's not like I'm barren and pushing sixty."

"Just remember that I won't be around forever. I want to see my great-grandchild before my cataracts take over."

"You don't have cataracts."

"I could. I could also blow a hip at any time."

I gently pushed her toward the office door. I couldn't stand around and talk about things that didn't amount to a hill of beans right now. I had a class to get back to, and a sexy, stalker man to get away from. The problem was, as I walked down the hallway to my classroom, all I could think about was the man who stalked me. I glanced behind me, sure that I would see him in the hallways, just waiting to make his move. I shook my head and chuckled. I was being ridiculous. I finished out the school day and was pleasantly surprised when Craig didn't meet me in the parking lot. Things were finally looking up.

I ran to the grocery store and picked up a few things without incident. I even went to the bank without encountering any bank robbers. It was like the best day ever! I got home and started whistling happily when my driveway was clear of any black SUVs that could potentially be holding Reed Security employees. However, that joy was cut short when I opened my door and heard beeping. I looked around, thinking I had set a timer somewhere and forgot to turn it off, but the beeping sound grew more distant when I walked away from the front door.

Cursing, I headed back for the door, and sure enough, there was a touch screen on the wall that had a blinking light. I started pressing buttons, trying to make the sound go away, but nothing worked. If anything, it seemed to get worse. I hit another button and a loud, booming voice came from somewhere in the house, like on a megaphone.

Intruder. Intruder. Intruder. Intruder.

Over and over, the stupid thing blared. I continued to press more buttons, but nothing would stop the stupid thing. I ran to the closet and grabbed the toolbox off the floor. After finding the hammer, I raced back to the front door and slammed the hammer against the touchscreen. The sirens and the voice saying *Intruder* continued. I covered my ears and slid to the floor in frustration. On the brink of tears, I was ready to hit that infuriating man with a hammer. He had officially ruined my day.

"Reese!"

I looked up and sprang to my feet when I saw Craig standing in my doorway with his gun drawn. I raced toward him and swung the hammer as hard as I could, but the man was too fast and caught my wrist before I could actually swing the hammer down on him.

"Reese, are you okay? It's me. You're okay now."

"I know I'm okay, you idiot! I'm pissed because I was having a good day and then I walked in my house and alarms started blaring!"

"Didn't you get the note?"

"Do you see a note in my hands?"

He actually looked at my hands like he was expecting to see one and then looked at me all puzzled. "It was under the mat. Didn't you get my text?"

I started shaking and I felt like my whole body was about to explode in rage. "How the hell would I have gotten your text? I never gave you my number!"

"That doesn't mean the text wouldn't have gone through."

I was just about to yell at him again when Sean came bursting through the door, gun drawn and looking at me still holding my hammer above my head and ready to strike.

"I heard the call. What's going on here?" Sean asked. "Who broke in?"

"Nobody broke in," I snapped. "This idiot installed a security system in my house and didn't tell me!"

Sean furrowed his brows in confusion. "How did he install a system without you knowing?"

"My friend gave him a key and permission to come over," I shouted.

Craig released me and walked over to the busted system and pulled what remained off the wall. He did something to the back and the noise stopped. My ears were still ringing as Sean started talking again.

"Who gave him permission to come over?"

"Brooke."

He snorted and then started laughing. "You gave Brooke access to your house?"

"Hey, she's a very reliable friend."

"Yeah, until she hands over the keys to your house to your stalker."

"Hey, I'm not a stalker," Craig said emphatically. "I was just looking out for her."

"I want him arrested, Sean. This has gone on long enough."

"What do you want me to arrest him for?"

"Breaking and entering."

"I had a key," Craig grinned. "That's hardly breaking and entering. As far as I knew, I was allowed on the property."

"Fine, then arrest him for...showing up at my house again!"

"I work for the security company that installed it. I came here because we got a call."

I screamed in frustration and stomped my foot on the ground. I was so angry! "Then arrest him for installing a security system without my permission."

"We talked about it last night. I told you I was coming out here to install it today."

"Would you shut up!" I turned back to Sean and pleaded with him. "Please, Sean, you have to arrest him for something, and make it stick!"

"Reese, I can escort him off the property, but unless you file a restraining order, I'm not sure what you want me to do. He's right about everything you've thrown out so far."

"Then arrest him for...keeping me safe against my will!"

Sean just stared at me with a bored expression. I heard a little snicker and I turned on Craig and swung as hard as I could, punching him in the face. Pain shot through my wrist and I squealed in pain, trying my best not to look like the pathetic wimp that hurt herself punching someone.

"That wasn't bad, little Reese's."

"Don't call me that!"

"Let me see your hand," Sean said, trying his best to hold back a laugh.

"What are you laughing at? I wouldn't be hurt right now if you had taken him away like I told you to."

"You know, Sean, I think I want to have this woman arrested for assault."

"What?" Sean and I said at the same time.

Craig shrugged, giving an innocent as fuck look. "You saw it, Sean. She hit me right here," he said, pointing to his jaw. "That's assault."

"Are you fucking kidding me? You've been stalking me and when I finally lose it and hit you, you want me arrested?"

"Sean?"

Sean shook his head at Craig and then pulled out fucking handcuffs. I shook my head in disbelief and backed up slightly. "Sean, you can't seriously be thinking about arresting me."

"You did assault him right in front of a detective. What do you want me to do?"

"Pretend you didn't see it!"

"I'm sorry, but I have to do it. If he went to my boss and made a complaint, I could get put on probation."

"So, you're arresting me instead?"

He sighed and pulled my good hand behind my back.

"Of course," Craig sighed a little. "I do feel bad about all of this. I could maybe be persuaded to not press charges."

I glared at him, my temper flaring even hotter than it already was.

"What do you want?"

"Just an hour or two of your time where we sit down and talk like civilized adults. You don't yell at me for talking to you or try to assault me again."

I narrowed my eyes at him. I was pissed. There was no way I was going to be blackmailed into sitting with my stalker. This was ridiculous.

"No."

"No?" He snorted and nodded to Sean. "I want to press charges."

"This is not the way to get her to like you," Sean mumbled.

"She'll cave," Craig smirked. "She doesn't want to get thrown in jail."

"Wanna bet?"

Ten minutes later, I was sitting in the back of Sean's car with a grinning Craig. He could suck it. He thought he had won, but there was no way I was going out with him.

"I don't understand why my stalker is sitting in the back with me," I said to Sean.

"He needs to make a statement. It's easier if we all go together."

I glared at Sean and then turned my glare on Craig. He leaned over and brushed his lips against my cheek. I flinched back and kicked out at him, getting him in the leg.

"What the hell are you doing?"

"You need to lighten up. It's just a date."

"I didn't-"

"Children, please!" Sean said from the front seat. "We're here."

Craig's brows furrowed and he sat forward in his seat. "Wait, you said we were going to the police station. Why are we at Reed Security?"

"Because the two of you are acting like rebellious teenagers with out of control hormones. So, I'm sitting you down with your parents for a lecture."

"You called my mom?" Craig asked incredulously.

Sean parked the car and turned around in his seat. "No, fucker, Cap's gonna talk to you."

He got out and opened my door. I stepped out and looked at the new building that was being constructed. It looked like it was almost finished, but Sean led us to another building.

"You know, if you're not taking me to jail, you could at least take off the handcuffs. If you remember, I have a hurt wrist."

"It wouldn't be hurt if you hadn't assaulted me," Craig grumbled.

"Hey, stalker-boy, lay off the assault talk. You really want to walk in there with all your teammates and claim that a woman half your size assaulted you?"

Craig snapped his mouth shut and we headed inside.

Chapter Nine

CRAIG

"Fuck," I swore as I walked into Cap's office with Reese and Sean right behind me. Cap was leaning back in his chair, staring me down, but not saying a word. I knew this was gonna be fucking bad. Cap nodded to the chair, so I sat and waited for him to speak. I wasn't gonna lie, my palms were sweating and I was a little scared at the moment. Cap was fucking scary when he was pissed.

"So..." Cap stood and walked around his desk. He leaned back against the front of the desk and crossed his arms over his chest. "Stalking?"

"I-"

"I didn't tell you to fucking speak." I snapped my mouth shut. "We're supposed to protect people and you're stalking a woman."

"I-"

"Still didn't give you permission to speak."

I felt like a fucking child being reprimanded.

"Look, I get that you like this woman, but if she asks you to leave her alone, you leave her alone."

"Thank you," Reese said with a smug grin on her face.

"Not so fast," Sean said from behind us. He walked around and leaned back against the desk in the same position Cap was in. "Don't think that you're off the hook."

"I didn't-"

"This isn't a discussion," Sean snapped. "You're a fucking teacher. You assaulted a man, even if he is twice your size, right in front of a cop. What the hell were you thinking?"

"I was thinking that the man had been stalking me for weeks and I wanted it to end!"

"He's harmless."

"Hey," I said, a little put off being called harmless.

"Shut up," Cap snapped.

"Whether or not you were being stalked, you assaulted him in front of me and then you purposely refused his offer to get you out of trouble. If you get arrested, you lose your job."

Okay, that I didn't know. Shit, now I felt bad. I hadn't really thought about that at the time, but it made sense. As a teacher, she would need to have a certain reputation. And an arrest record would be very bad for her.

"The two of you need to get your shit together," Sean said. "Reese, you can't afford to get thrown in jail. And Craig, I get that you like the woman, but you're just pissing her off. Back the fuck off."

I turned to Reese, trying to look as sincere as possible. I really felt bad now that I knew what might have happened.

"I'm sorry, Reese. I didn't think about getting you in trouble at work. I'll...leave you alone."

"Thank you." Sean cleared his throat and she wiggled uncomfortably in her chair. "And I'm sorry that I hit you. It won't happen again."

"Good. Now that that's taken care of, I'll send a team over to your house and have your system fixed."

"That's not necessary," Reese said, rising from her chair.

"Yes, it is. And the system is still being charged to this dumbass. I'll have someone walk you through how to use it tonight so you don't have any more issues."

"I can-"

"Don't even think about it," Cap snapped. "You don't go anywhere near her."

I clenched my jaw in anger, but didn't say another word.

"Sean, maybe you could take Reese down to the training center. Hunter's down there and he can take a look at her wrist."

"Sure."

Sean and Reese left, but I knew Cap wasn't done with me yet. I sat there and waited for it. I knew it was coming, but it was just a matter of how long it would take. Cap moved around to the other side of his desk. He sat down and let out a deep breath.

"So, what the hell am I supposed to do with you?"

"Help me get her back."

"You never had her."

"I would have."

He tapped his fingers on his desk as he thought. "What do you want me to do? I can't make her like you."

"I just need a way to get to know her, for her to get to know me."

"You can't go chasing after a woman-"

"Bullshit. You went after Maggie. You put a fucking chip in her."

He cleared his throat and nodded. "Right, but I had her to begin with. You haven't even been on one date with her. How do you expect her to suddenly come around when you just threatened her with jail?"

"Well...okay, so I fucked up there."

"You think?"

"Look, I just said that I was wrong."

"So, again, how do you expect me to help you?"

"Call a meeting."

He snorted and then laughed. "You think they'll help?"

"You owe me," I said pointedly. He nodded, knowing I was referring to his distrust in me when we were attacked. "You didn't trust me when you should have. I was fucking tortured and you turned your back on me. Now, I forgave you for the sake of working together, but that wasn't fucking easy. You know that I would never do anything to hurt anyone I care about. And that goes beyond everyone at Reed Security."

"Fine. I'll get the boys."

"Okay." Cap slapped his hands together and blew out a long breath. "So, I've brought you..." He waved his hand at Hunter, Derek, Knight, and Becky.

"Um...okay. What's Becky doing here?"

"Yeah, what am I doing here? What's this about?"

Cap stepped up in front of everyone and sighed. "As you know, as each of us has fallen to the opposite sex, there have been bumps in the road."

"I'm out," Knight said, heading for the door.

"Stop right there," Cap commanded.

"Fuck this," Knight growled. "I told you, I don't do relationship shit."

"You walk out that door, I'll tell Sean to send over his second pick of candidates for training."

Knight turned around slowly, giving Cap his most menacing glare. "The last ones he sent over were barely qualified."

"So, imagine what the second pick will be like," Cap grinned.

Knight crossed his arms over his chest and looked at Cap like he was just two seconds from pulling his gun and shooting him.

"Okay, I still don't understand what I'm doing here," Becky said. "I have never been in a relationship, as I've pointed out to all of you as one of my reasons for leaving."

"You're here because you offer a woman's perspective," Cap informed her.

"Yeah, but you could have grabbed Florrie or Lola. At least they would have been able to give you a better perspective."

"But you're a regular female," I pointed out.

"What does that mean?"

"I just mean that you're like Reese. This is kind of your life, but you don't shoot people. You're not a killer." While I agreed with Cap's choice of woman, I still thought there was a better man for the job. "What about Ice? He's fucked up a lot," I suggested.

Cap shook his head. "Lindsey had the baby this morning. He's out."

"Damn, he would have been really helpful."

"Wait, is this about the chick you met at the coffee shop?" Hunter asked

"Yes."

"But he fucked up. He's been stalking her," Cap grinned. "Thought you might have some advice, Knight."

I sighed and took a seat. "I haven't been stalking her. I had legitimate reasons for seeing her."

"That's not stalking," Knight agreed with me. "When you're truly stalking someone, you try not to let them see you." He shrugged as if what I was doing was no big deal. "He's just going to see his woman."

"Thank you!"

"Today, he tried to blackmail her into going out with him."

Derek raised his hand. "Okay, I can see why Knight and Hunter are here. They're real psychopathic stalkers."

"Thanks, man," Hunter clapped him on the back.

Derek shrugged. "I just call it like I see it. So, what am I doing here?"

"While we have our friendly, neighborhood stalkers to gain some insight from, we needed you to share your wisdom in getting back in her good graces."

"Hey," Derek said, sounding quite offended. "I didn't-"

"You did," Cap interrupted. "As I recall, your relationship with Claire didn't start off all that great."

"Yeah, but I never blackmailed her." He turned to me with a chin lift. "What exactly did you blackmail her with?"

"I was going to have her arrested if she didn't agree to go out on a date with me."

"You're sick," Hunter retorted.

"Nice," Knight grinned.

Derek shook his head and held up his hands. "I can't help him."

"Why would you do that?" Becky asked. "Why would you think she would want you after that? If a man tried to have me arrested, there would be no love notes in our future."

"Hey, she assaulted me," I said angrily. It was like they weren't listening to a word I was saying. "She attacked me. And all because I was trying to help her out."

"You don't need these other guys," Knight said, stepping forward. "I'll give you some advice, only because I like your style."

Hunter shook his head. "There's nothing you can do to help him out, Hud. Even you never blackmailed Kate."

"No, but I did threaten to kill her."

"What?" Cap barked. "When did this happen?"

"When we were at the safe house that got burned down. Cole asked me to make sure that she knew I wasn't interested in her anymore."

"So, you threatened to kill her?" I asked, curious how this all worked out.

He shrugged. "It worked. She was terrified of me."

"So, how did you end up together?" Derek asked.

He smirked and slapped Hunter on the back. "She overheard this asshole saying that I loved her. It kind of gave away the whole lie."

"See," I shook my finger in Knight's direction as I grinned. "This is the guy I need to talk to. If you can come back from threatening to kill a woman, then I've got this in the bag."

"Not quite. See, I had already been with Kate for some time. We had established a connection. You...have nothing."

I stared in stunned silence. "So, you mean that I don't have a chance?"

Knight sighed. "Everyone out."

"What?" Cap shook his head. "No, there's no fucking way that I'm leaving you alone with him."

"You think I'm gonna shoot him?" Knight chuckled. "I have a plan, but there's no way in hell any of you are gonna be around to hear it."

"Why?" Hunter asked suspiciously.

"Plausible deniability," Knight growled.

Hunter stepped back, almost as if he had been hit. "Hud, this is a bad idea."

"Fuck off."

"He's right," Cap agreed. "You go through with this and get caught, you're fucked."

"Why is he fucked?" I asked.

"Relax, no one's getting caught. Well, except Reese," he smirked.

"What would we get caught doing?" I asked urgently.

"Think of what Kate would say," Hunter said, stepping toward him like a caged lion.

"She's not gonna find out."

"Find out what?" I asked again. Why was everyone ignoring me?

"What are we talking here?" Derek asked. "Code Black or cover your dick?"

Knight thought about it, bouncing his head side to side for a moment. "Depends on which way it goes. Code Black if you don't keep Sean out of it. Cover your dick if any of the women find out."

"My dick is perfectly happy where it is with my woman," Hunter replied. "I'm out. Sorry, Craig, you're on your own."

"On my own for what?"

"I'm out too. I'm trying to have a baby with Claire. I kind of need my dick for that." Irish slugged me in the arm and followed Hunter out of the room.

"My dick is ready for this mission," I pleaded. "Just tell it what to do."

"What about you, Cap?" Knight asked.

He huffed out a breath and nodded. "I'm in. You know if I don't go along, Maggie will be pissed."

"Why would Maggie be pissed?"

Knight chuckled slightly and turned to Becky. "I'll need you on standby."

"Wait, I thought I was here for a woman's perspective, but I don't even know what you guys are talking about."

"Just be ready to do the usual cleanup," Knight instructed.

"See, this is why I'm leaving. I don't have any details, but I'm expected to follow along."

"I don't have any details either, if it makes you feel better," I grumbled.

"That's not why you told me you were leaving." Cap crossed his arms over his chest and glared at Becky.

"Well, I just added it to the list of reasons."

"And when are you leaving again?" Cap asked.

"As soon as I can finish up my projects."

"Right," Cap snorted.

"You know what? Fuck you, Cap." Becky stormed out of the room, leaving me with my boss and a former assassin. I shouldn't be so excited to hear this plan. After all, two of my teammates just walked out of here and refused to be part of it. But it was Knight. Whatever he had up his sleeve, it was bound to be good.

Later that night, we sat outside her house in one of the company SUVs outside her house. Knight had come up with a brilliant plan to get Reese back, but I made one thing very clear. If anything went wrong, they were both to haul ass out of there and have Becky wipe the street cams so that no one could place them at the scene with me. I wasn't about to let anyone else go down for what I was about to do.

"Craig, are you sure you want to do this?" Cap asked. "There's still time to back out."

"Yeah, if you're a pussy," Knight grumbled.

"It's not being a pussy to decide not to break the law."

"Yeah, and you've never broken the law, right?" Knight mumbled.

"Hey, I'm all in. I need to get her back."

"You know that if you don't convince her to listen to you, you're gonna end up in jail," Cap reminded me for the tenth time.

"Yes, I know. Now, can we get on with this?"

"Alright, she called Brooke ten minutes ago and made plans to meet up at a bar in town," Knight said.

"How do you know?" I asked.

"I tapped her phones." He stared at me like I was stupid. This was Knight we were talking about. It wasn't that far fetched that he would do something like this. "Now, when she comes out of the house, you need to snatch her before she comes around to the front of the house. Once she's in view of the street, you're fucked."

"Right. Okay, I'm ready for this."

Chapter Ten

REESE

After having conferences all afternoon and evening, I was exhausted. I kicked off my heels and went straight for the wine in the kitchen. This day sucked. I had parents come in that weren't happy because their child wasn't reading at the level they expected. It was the beginning of the year and they were in kindergarten. Most kids didn't read that well at this age. Then I had another parent that was upset when I sent her child to the office for repeatedly pulling down his pants in class. And that was just in my first hour of conferences. The rest of the night was a little better, but the first hour had really set the tone for me.

My phone rang and I knew who it was without looking. "Please tell me you want drinks at the bar," I pleaded with Brooke.

"I figured you would want some fun. Thank God it's Friday, right?"

"You have no idea. I need this weekend more than I realized. I say we get shitfaced and pick up some hot guys."

"Since when have you ever wanted to do anything to tarnish your good image?"

"Since I've had the Wolf on my mind all day and I need to get laid."

"So, call him and tell him to come over for a hook-up."

I snorted and drank some more wine. "Not a chance. He tried to have me arrested!"

"I know, but he just really wanted to get to know you."

"How is it that you see my stalker as someone that I need in my life? I could be wrapped up in plastic and have duct tape over my mouth by the end of the night."

"Okay, your stalker is a friendly stalker, so that would never happen. He's a wolf."

"Right, and wolves kill people."

"Not true. They hunt their prey, and you my friend are the thing that man wants to devour."

"So, you would have me risk the trunk of a car over a man that could potentially be a good lay."

"Potentially? Oh, honey. Just one look at that man and you know he won't disappoint."

"You know, call me crazy, but I think I'm going to play it safe and just take the average bar hopper home with me tonight."

"Fine," she grumbled. "But I think you're missing out on some potentially nasty sex."

"Right. I'll see you at the bar in thirty."

I hung up and finished my wine, then headed upstairs to get ready for my night out. The hard part about being a teacher was that I had to always have a certain look at school. So, I didn't have a lot of clothes that were just for fun. I threw on my one cute top and some tight jeans and headed downstairs. After spending all day in heels, I opted for flip flops. Not ideal for looking hot, but at this point, I didn't really care.

I snatched my purse off the counter and headed for the side door. I stepped outside and dug in my purse for my keys, but couldn't find them. Opening my purse wider, I practically shoved my head inside my purse to find them.

Something pressed hard to my mouth and jerked my head back. My eyes went wide as I realized what was happening when I started getting dragged backward. Instincts kicked in and I started fighting back, kicking and punching at whatever I could, but whoever had ahold of me was much stronger than me. If I didn't get away from this man, I would end up dead or as someone's sex slave.

Heart hammering in my chest, I knew I had to do whatever I could to get away from this guy. I wouldn't survive if I was taken. I clawed at his face and heard a low curse when I felt his skin tear. I bit down on the hand covering my mouth. I was momentarily released, but when I made a run for it, something hit me hard on the head.

I tilted toward the ground, but was swept up in strong arms before I could hit the ground. The whole world started to grow fuzzy, and somewhere in the back of my mind, I knew this wasn't going to end well for me. I felt myself being tossed somewhere and then it was black. I heard a door slam and then I was jerked around wherever I was lying.

Blinking my eyes rapidly, I forced myself to focus on what was happening. My head was killing me, but other than that, I seemed to be fine. I took a deep breath and felt around me for some sign of where I was. The rocking motion finally clicked in my brain and I realized I was in the trunk of a car.

"Okay, think. Think, think, think."

I slapped at my head, instantly regretting it when it reminded me of how much my head hurt.

"Okay, I'm in the trunk of a car. I need to get away before he drives me too far away. Okay, trunks of cars have...that's right!"

I felt around for the locking mechanism that was installed inside trunks in case someone got locked in, but there wasn't one.

"Shit!" I pounded against the trunk repeatedly until I was tired and slightly less irritated. "I should have stuck by the Wolf. At least he would have found a way to protect me."

As soon as the words were out of my mouth, it hit me that he was probably the one that took me. I rolled into the sidewall as the car turned sharply. Then we were bouncing and my body was collecting bruises like shells at the ocean. My body was flung harshly around the trunk as I felt the car going out of control. I was going to die in this trunk, and it was all because I had a stupid fucking cup of coffee.

Chapter Eleven

CRAIG

"What's happening?" I was just about to go make my move when Knight grabbed onto my arm, stopping me in my tracks.

"I have an alert on the property. Someone else is here."

"Who?"

He flipped through the screens on his tablet as I leaned over his shoulder, and then I saw it. Someone attacked Reese from behind and now they were hauling her over to a car in the alley. I flung the door of the SUV open and sprinted across her property, but I had to make it to the other side, and I doubted I would make it to her in time unless a miracle happened. I saw the man slam the trunk of the car and as he slipped into the driver's seat, he smirked at me and gave me a finger wave.

I pulled my gun to fire at the car, but I couldn't risk that something would happen to Reese if it caused an accident. I ran as fast as I could, but the car was already turning out of the alley and further away from me. Cap screeched to a halt behind me in the SUV. I got in, just barely shutting the door, and he was already tearing down the alley in pursuit.

"What do you have, Knight?"

"There's no signs of her being watched from the camera feed. This looks random."

"How the fuck could it be random? He snatched her right outside her door."

"Maybe if you knew more about her, I might be able to give you something. All I know is that she's a fucking kindergarten teacher that you met at a coffee shop. That tells me jack shit about her life."

"Fuck!" I smashed my fist into the dash and ran my hand over my head, trying to calm myself. I needed to stay calm and think rationally here. I had this. "It's fine. It doesn't matter who the fuck it is. We just have to catch up to him and I'll fucking kill him."

"You're not curious who this is?"

"Doesn't fucking matter right now. I just have to get her back. The rest is just details."

Cap turned the corner and sped up. The tail lights weren't too far away. It would only take another mile to catch up and then I'd make my move.

"What do you need?" Cap asked.

"Nothing. I've got my gun. Anything else is too dangerous. Just get me close enough and I'll jump on the fucking roof of the car."

"Are you sure you want to go that route?"

"Hell yeah."

"That means throwing him out of the car," Cap said, almost like a reminder.

"I'm well aware of what it means."

"He could die before we ever find out why he was after her."

I took a deep breath and calmed myself down. "It's fine. I'll make sure he stays alive for you to interrogate."

Cap drove faster and Knight tapped me on the shoulder. "Here." He handed me a piece of paper with an address. "This is a safe house I have set up. Head there until we give you the all clear."

I nodded and took the scrap of paper, shoving it into my wallet. Cap pulled up on the tail of the car and I lowered my window so that I would be ready when he made his move. He jerked the SUV to the left, speeding up until he was alongside the car. I started climbing out the window, just barely hanging on as he moved into position. With one last nod to Cap, I leapt onto the roof of the car, gripping onto the edges by the doors. My fingertips ached from gripping so tightly.

The guy swerved the car, almost flinging me off the roof. I could see Knight poised in the back, ready to shoot the guy if he made the wrong move. But I wasn't in control of the car, and that meant that Reese could get seriously hurt.

"Fuck this." I pulled my gun and smashed it into the passenger side window. I slipped in feet first and kicked him in the face. He lost his grip on the steering wheel and I grabbed onto it, shoving the gear shift into neutral. The car started to slow, but the man started fighting back.

"Hey there," I said cheerily. "Just dropped in for a quick hello. Beautiful weather we're having, right?"

I punched him in the face, just to get out a little frustration, but he came back with a gun to my face.

"Get the fuck out of my car!"

"That's not a very nice way to greet me after I dropped in," I said, snatching the gun rather easily from his hands. He grasped at the steering wheel, trying to jerk the wheel to throw me across the car. I could use my own gun on him, but guns in close quarters were never a good idea. I slammed my fist twice more into his face and reached across his body and yanked on the door handle.

"I wish we could chat a little longer, but this is your stop." I shoved the door open and just barely caught the terror in his eyes before I shoved him out the door. I pulled the door shut as the car slowed to a crawl and straightened the rearview mirror to suit my needs. There were headlights coming up on us and I had no idea if they were friend or foe. There wasn't time to let Reese out and deal with the hysterics that were sure to ensue as soon as I popped the trunk.

I honked at Cap, waving him down as I pulled away. I motioned behind him and saw his head turn to the oncoming traffic. Knight was out of the SUV and kicking the shit out of the guy. As much as I wanted to go back and give him my own beat down, I needed to get Reese to safety. I watched in the rearview mirror as I took off down the road. Knight had hauled the guy into the back of the SUV and they were heading back to Reed Security. Now the only problem I had was where to let Reese out so that she didn't cause a big scene.

Chapter Twelve

REESE

I had no idea how long I had been in the trunk, but the ride had definitely been easier the last half of it. Now though, it seemed like we were slowing down. I held my breath as the car stopped and the door opened. What would happen now that we stopped? Would I end up dead on the side of the road?

I heard a key in the trunk and then it opened and I was met with darkness and a figure looming over me. My heart thundered in my chest, making me nauseous and dizzy. But I had to hold it together if I had any hope of getting out of here. I saw him move and thought about jumping up and attacking him, but my muscles were sore from laying in such an awkward position for so long.

A bright light shone in my eyes and I squinted, trying not to be blinded by the light. I felt hands on me and then I heard Craig's low rumble.

"Are you alright, Reese?"

I swatted at his hands, fighting to stay free of him. "Stay away from me, you psychopath!"

"I'm not- hey, stop hitting me! I didn't take you!"

I shuffled back further into the trunk, wishing that I could see him. "You're driving the car! How could it not be you?"

"It wasn't me. I swear. I saw you being taken and I came after you."

"Oh, that's a great story! Too bad no one will believe you. Sean knows that you've been stalking me for weeks. He won't believe you!"

"You scratched him."

I stopped for a second and thought back. I had scratched the guy on the face. If I could just see Craig's face, it would prove it was him. "Fine, shine the light on your face."

He turned the flashlight on himself and I immediately saw blood. "It's right there!"

I saw his face scrunch up in confusion and then he started swiping at his face. "Huh. That's weird."

"That's weird?" Taking a chance that he wouldn't attack me or inject me with some deadly poison, I climbed out of the car and backed away from him, realizing that my flip flops were gone when I stepped on something sharp. "You have blood on your face. You fucking kidnapped me!"

"I didn't. I swear!"

"Then explain the blood!"

"It must have happened when I went in through the passenger window."

I couldn't believe this guy. It was just one lie after another with him. First, he lied about why he was in the park and then he lied about the whole assault thing and tried to get me arrested.

"Look, just let me go and I'll forget that any of this happened."

"Let you go? Why would I do that? Someone's trying to kill you."

"Yeah, and I'm looking right at him. You're fucking crazy, you know that?"

He sighed tiredly and took a step toward me. I moved away and he stopped. "Okay, the car died and we have a good ten mile walk into town. Once we're there, I'll get us a motel room. Then, I'll get a new car and we'll head to a safe house."

I shook my head unbelievably. It was like he didn't even hear himself speak. If only he could understand how crazy he sounded.

"I'm not going anywhere with you."

"Where are you gonna go then? Look around you."

He held his arms wide, motioning to the dark countryside. There was nothing around, no one to help. I was either with this guy or wandering around in the dark on my own. And I didn't even have a clue where we were.

"Would it make you feel better if I let you carry my gun?"

"Yes," I answered without thinking twice. At least if I had a gun, I could ward off any potential attacks. Even if I didn't know how to hold a gun.

"Fine." He slowly pulled out his gun and handed it over to me. "But I'm gonna warn you, if we come under fire, I'm ripping that out of your hands."

I nodded, believing that he could take it back anytime he wanted, but I appreciated him letting me think that I had some control. Even if he was a psychotic kidnapper. At least he had a friendly personality.

"Can we get moving? I'd like to get some sleep before we head for the safe house."

I stepped warily in his direction and held the gun at the ready. Or, I thought I did. He sighed and grabbed the gun from my hand.

"Here, let me at least show you how to hold it right." He positioned both my hands around the gun and started pointing out different parts of the gun to me, like I could actually follow along.

"Alright, now, if you're going to shoot me, you want to aim for my chest. It's a big target, and while your shot may or may not be deadly, it should at least slow me down. You could always go for a leg shot too. However, I request that if you do shoot me, try not to hit any major body parts."

"Like what?"

"Well, my head, for one. And try to stay away from my heart and my lungs. That would suck. Also, stay away from my liver and my kidneys. Oh, and if you shoot me in the leg, try not to hit my inner thigh. Aim for the outside. The femoral artery runs along the inner thigh."

I nodded. It was a little strange to get instructions on where to shoot the man that I took the gun from. It was like he was giving me permission. But that couldn't be right. Who would be stupid enough to give all this information? A stalker, that's who.

"The safety is on. That's this button right here. When you carry it, don't point it at anything unless you intend to shoot it."

"So, I can point it at you."

"I would prefer that you didn't. If you shoot me, who's going to protect you from whoever kidnapped you?"

I narrowed my eyes at him, though I was sure that he couldn't see me. "Seeing as it was you that kidnapped me, I think I would be safer if I just shot you and got it over with."

"If you believe that, I guess you would be right. Although, then you're stuck out here with nature."

"Nature is harmless."

"Except for the bats."

"Bats?" I asked, a little creeped out. I had never seen a bat up close, but I had seen them in movies and that was as close as I wanted to get.

"Oh yeah, about eight or nine different species. Most are rare, but there's still a chance you'll see some. And then there are the foxes and coyotes. Now, those are pretty common around here. I wouldn't want to be out when they're hunting. And then there are black bears," he said thoughtfully. "Do you know how to handle a black bear? Because I'll need to give you instructions before I leave you."

"Uh..."

"Now, it's fall, so the bear is trying to bulk up for winter. Which means it's looking for food. You don't have anything on you, right?" Before I could answer, he moved on. "Now, if the bear approaches you, stand tall and spread your arms wide. You want to appear as big as possible. Yell at it, and if it does attack you, fight back. Do not play dead."

The flashlight shook in my hands. His face looked creepy as the light accentuated his features in the dark.

"But..."

"Oh, and if it does approach you, just spray bear spray at it."

"But I don't have bear spray!"

He winced and rubbed the back of his neck. "Well, then just fight back. You'll be fine," he said, slapping me on the arm. "Other than that, the only thing you should have to worry about are skunks. And I hate to tell you, you probably won't see them until you get sprayed. But a little hydrogen peroxide, some baking soda, and liquid detergent- you should be fine."

He turned and started walking away, leaving me alone in the dark with all animals he just told me about. I didn't understand it. How did he go from stalking me to walking away? I spun around when I heard what sounded like howling. My heart raced as I stared into the night for any sign of movement. And Craig, he just walked off. He didn't even have a flashlight or his gun.

Spinning back around, I looked at Craig, growing smaller and smaller in the distance as he walked away from me. I had a choice to make. I could stay here and take my chances or I could go with my stalker and pray that he didn't try to kill me somewhere along the way. Another howl and I took off running for Craig. Better to stay alive now and escape later.

"Craig! Wait!"

The flashlight beam bounced around the darkness as I ran for Craig. I saw that he stopped, a quizzical look on his face. "Is everything okay?"

"I'm going with you."

"Are you sure? Because I want you to feel safe. And if you don't feel safe with me, then I'm not doing my job."

"I'll get away from you at some other point, but I'm not staying out here in the dark by myself."

"If you're sure..."

I nodded.

"Well, in that case, I'd like my gun back."

"Why?"

"Because if a bear or a coyote comes after us, I'd like to be able to kill it before it kills us. Unless you suddenly learned how to use a weapon and you think you can defend us."

He had a point. I handed the gun over and watched as he checked the safety and then slid it into the back of his jeans.

"Ready to go? We should reach town in about two and a half hours if we keep up a brisk pace."

I followed behind him and noticed that he moved closer to me, like he was trying to protect me. I didn't get it. He was just about to walk away from me and now he was guarding me. It didn't make any sense. Why would-

I stopped in my tracks and stared at Craig with a gaping mouth. "You played me."

"What?" He kept walking, not bothering to stop and wait for me. I jogged to catch up to him and grabbed onto his arm.

"You totally played me. You let me think you were going to walk away and leave me in the dark with bats and bears."

"Don't forget the coyotes."

"But you weren't really going to, were you?"

"Does it matter? You needed to decide what you wanted to do and I gave you the space to come to the logical choice."

"But..." He looked at me expectantly. "Fine, we'll do this your way."

"See? Wasn't that an easy decision?"

"I really hate you," I said as I stalked off.

"That won't last forever, my little Reese's Pieces!"

Chapter Thirteen

CRAIG

"Would you just get on my back?"

"No," Reese said forcefully as she limped along the road. She lost her shoes when that guy took her. Her feet were probably all torn up, but she refused to hitch a ride, no matter how much pain she was in.

"Look, I haven't hurt you yet. Can't you see that I'm not trying to kill you?"

"No, I can't see that. Because I ended up in the trunk of a car that you were driving."

"I already told you, I followed you when you were taken and then I leapt on top of the car so that I could get into the car and save you."

"Don't you think I would have heard you jump on top of the car?"

I shrugged. "I bet you were more concerned with how to escape than what was going on outside the car."

She opened her mouth to refute what I said, but then snapped it shut. "Fine. You may have a point."

"Will you please just get on my back? If I do anything you don't like, you can just strangle me."

She bit her lip and thought it over. I prayed to God that she would say yes and get on my back. I wanted to feel her body heat next to mine. I wanted her warm breath blowing across my neck. Anything to be close to this woman. If she said yes, maybe I was breaking through to her. Maybe she would consider what we could have together. It would be like accepting what was between us.

"Fine, but this doesn't mean anything."

I snorted out a laugh. "Of course not." Okay, so I had that all wrong. But it didn't matter, because she was going to be holding onto me.

I bent over and let her climb on, but I instantly realized what a mistake this was. Now that I had the woman I needed more than life itself on my back, I knew I couldn't let her go. Hell, I was about to kidnap her anyway. Would it really matter if I didn't let her go back to her life and just kept her to myself?

I continued walking for the next two miles, trying my best not to let my woody get in my way. It wasn't working so well. And then, to make things worse, she started to doze on my shoulder. I gripped her legs tighter, trying to keep her on my back. Her arms had loosened and were now just hanging loosely by my neck.

After another hour, I was finally at the edge of town. I walked to the closest hotel and checked us in. Reese woke up, but was too comfortable to walk on her own. At least, that's what I told myself. She slid the card into the reader and I opened the door, then set her down on the bed. She laid back and closed her eyes. She looked so damn sexy lying on the bed.

I cleared my throat, trying not to stare at her anymore. There were too many thoughts running through my head. Thoughts of her lying in the bed next to me, or running her hands over my body. Hell, just seeing her like this on the bed had me thinking about what it would be like to be inside her.

"Right, well, I'm gonna go take a shower." I walked over to her and grabbed her hand, pulling her to her feet.

"What are you doing?"

"You're coming with me."

"Uh, no, I'm not."

I chuckled. "It's so cute that you think you have a choice."

"I do have a choice and I'm not going with you," she said forcefully. "There's no way I'm joining you in the shower."

"While I would love to get you in the shower with me, I know that's not going to happen anytime soon. You're just going to sit in the bathroom where I can keep an eye on you."

"Look," she huffed in irritation. "I came with you. I rode on your freaking back. You're the one that pointed out I have nowhere else to go."

"Ah, but see, that was before. Now, we're around people again and you're going to try to run."

"I'm not going to run. I have no money and I have no clue where we are. All I want is to lay down in bed and go to sleep."

I tried to read her face, but it was nearly impossible. She looked nervous, but it could have just been fear. She had been through something terrifying tonight. As much as I didn't want to let her out of my sight, it would work in my favor to show her that I trusted her.

"Fine, you can lay down."

She grinned in satisfaction, but I wasn't through yet. I walked over to the large cabinet that housed the tv and started shoving it across the room to the door.

"What are you doing?"

"Making sure you don't go anywhere."

"But...what if there's a fire?"

"Don't worry, my little pixie. I won't let you burn."

She stomped her foot and then winced. "Don't call me that. I'm not anything to you."

"Sure," I grinned.

"I'm not."

"Oh, I believe you. I know you are your own person. And I respect that."

"What are you talking about?" she asked in frustration.

"I know," I responded. It made no fucking sense, but it seemed to piss her off even more, and I liked it when she got all worked up. It made my dick hard.

"Now," I brushed my hands off after I shoved the cabinet firmly against the door. "I'll be in the shower. Don't worry, I won't be long."

I grinned and headed for the bathroom while she huffed and plopped back on the bed. Turning on the water, I stepped under the spray of warm water and groaned. My body was tired, but my dick was ready for action. I gripped my dick in my hand and imagined my little Reese's Pieces, down on her knees and taking me into her mouth. Damn, I could feel her tongue licking my balls and then taking me in her mouth.

I groaned and pumped a little harder. It didn't take much to push me over the edge. She was just in the other room and I'd carried her on my back for a good hour tonight. I could still feel her breasts pressed against my back. I washed myself quickly and shut off the shower. After drying off quickly, I wrapped a towel around my waist and was pleased to see that she was still sitting on the bed, pissed as hell, but still there.

When her eyes flicked to mine, I could practically see her pulse jump up and take off. Her eyes did a slow perusal of my body, taking in every muscle. She licked her lips and I swore I heard her breath catch when she spotted my erection sticking out from where the towel joined at the front. Yeah, I was hard again. Of course, any guy would be when a beautiful woman was looking at him like a piece of meat.

"Have you changed your mind about me, Reese?"

She snorted, but her eyes lingered on my cock. I released the towel and stood there in all my naked glory, smirking when her eyes widened. She squeezed her legs together and I knew I had her. It wouldn't take much to flip that switch and get her in my bed.

I walked over to the bed and sat down beside her. God, she was so fucking gorgeous. I brushed my thumb over a smudge on her face and ran my thumb along her lip. She didn't try to stop me, instead stared at me like she wondered what it would be like to kiss me. I leaned in slowly, giving her the chance to back away, but she didn't. I pressed my lips lightly to hers, but it was like having my first taste of chocolate. And I needed more of it.

I deepened the kiss, pressing my tongue to the seam of her lips. I almost lost it when she parted her lips slightly and let me in. Hell, this woman was going to be the death of me. I wanted to run my hands over her body and feel every curve. I wanted to know what it was like to feel her tits in my hands. But it wouldn't happen like this. It would be because I knew she wanted me just as much as I wanted her.

Against my better judgement, I pulled back from the kiss and got to my feet. I needed distance so I didn't maul her. Not to mention, my dick was so hard that I needed space to gain control of myself. I stood at the end of the bed and took deep breaths to calm my body down.

But then it was like cold water was splashed on me, because the bottoms of her feet were all torn up and she had to be in pain. Snatching my clothes out of the bathroom, I quickly tugged on my jeans.

"Where are you..." She cleared her throat when her voice cracked. Inside I was grinning. "Where are you going?"

"To get something for your feet. They're all torn up. Why didn't you tell me you were in pain?" But she didn't answer because she was too busy staring at my chest. I yanked on a shirt and snapped my fingers at her. "Hey, focus."

"What?"

"Why didn't you tell me you were in pain?"

"Uh...I guess I didn't really notice."

I rolled my eyes and shoved my feet in my shoes. "Can I trust you to stay here?" She nodded, but it wasn't good enough for me. "Promise me you'll stay here, please. I can't stand the thought of you disappearing on me. Especially not when someone tried to kidnap you tonight."

She flushed bright red and nodded. "I'll stay."

I kissed her again and headed for the door. "I won't be long. Is there anything else you need?"

"Shoes?"

I grinned and tapped the side of my head. "Right."

I moved the cabinet out of the way and headed downstairs. Things were finally coming around. It wouldn't take too much longer to convince Reese that she was mine.

Chapter Fourteen

REESE

I waited for him to shut the door and then I leapt off the bed, wincing slightly at the pain in my feet. I hadn't been lying about not feeling the pain. I was too worried about other things to think about something like pain. I pressed my ear to the door and then ran back to the phone when I didn't hear anything. I quickly dialed Brooke's number and waited for her to pick up. But instead, a man picked up.

"Is this Brooke's phone?" I whispered.

"No."

I hung up and repeated the number in my head over and over until I was sure I had the right one. I dialed again and practically cried when she answered.

"Where were you? You said you would be at the bar, but you didn't show. I spent the whole night warding off some skeevy guy because my best friend couldn't be bothered to show up at the bar."

"Are you done?" I whispered, looking back at the door, sure that at any moment Craig would walk back in.

She sighed dramatically. "I guess."

"I've been kidnapped."

"What? By who?"

"Who do you think?"

"No shit? The wolf finally made his move."

"Why are you saying this like it's a good thing?"

"Well, because he's hot and you need some fun."

My mind was about to explode. "Did you not hear me say 'kidnap'? This isn't fun, Brooke. I'm being held against my will!"

"If you're being held against your will, then how are you able to talk to me on the phone?"

"Because he left to go get something to clean my feet."

"Um...is this like a fetish? Because I was cool with him before he was a foot licker."

"So, him kidnapping me doesn't bother you, but being a foot licker does?" I said exasperatedly.

"Hey, if he kidnaps you out of love, then it's romantic. Foot licking is not."

"Whatever, the point is that I need to get out of here."

"So leave. You said that he's not there."

"He's not going to be gone long. I need a plan."

"Right. Okay, let me think a minute."

I waited impatiently for her to think, but I was irritated with her. "You know, you could at least pretend to be upset that I've been kidnapped."

"Oh, I'm sorry. You're right. I'm terribly upset that you've been kidnapped by a hot guy that wants to take you home and do nasty things to you. It sounds just dreadful."

"You know, sometimes you really suck as a friend."

"Agreed. Okay, you need to make him comfortable with you."

"Already done," I said proudly.

"How?"

"I let him kiss me."

"How was it?"

"Now isn't the time for talking about what a great kisser my stalker is."

"If now's not the time, when is? Because honestly, I'm more interested in that kiss than getting you out of there."

"Would you just help me! He's going to be back soon and I need to get out of here!"

"Okay, okay. What you need to do is fuck him."

"What? That's your plan?"

"Hey, you need him trusting you and distracted. If you want to get out of there, sleep with him. You fall asleep in bed together, snuggle and make him feel good, and then when he's sleeping like the dead, you bolt."

I gnawed on my lip. It was a pretty good idea. And sleeping with him wouldn't be that much of a hardship. He was hot and I would be lying if I said I wasn't attracted to him. In fact, saying I was attracted to him was the understatement of the century. In fact, I probably would have slept with him already if he didn't remind me so much of Jason Bourne.

"Okay, let's say that I do sleep with him. Then I just leave him in the morning?"

"Yeah. Isn't that what you said you were trying to do?"

"I know, but...doesn't it seem a little cruel to sleep with someone and then leave without a goodbye?"

"Reese, the man kidnapped you and you called me to help get you out of there. Either you want to leave or you want to protect his feelings. Which is it?"

"Right. Priorities. Alright, if you don't hear from me by morning, call Reed Security and tell them that Craig kidnapped me and I'm probably dead somewhere."

"Why don't I just call them now?"

"Because I don't want to get him in trouble, okay?"

"Wait. You don't want to get the man that kidnapped you in trouble? Girl, you have bigger problems than I can help you with."

I heard a click. "Brooke? Brooke?" I pressed the receiver button, but all I got was a dial tone. I couldn't believe she hung up on me. Was it really that wrong that I didn't want to get him in trouble? I mean, he was a nice man and despite taking me hostage, he was looking out for me.

I groaned and slapped myself on the forehead. I was losing it. I had a thing for my stalker. This was really too much to take. I needed to get out of here and get back to my life. One that didn't include the man that was as sexy as sin and did terribly wonderful things to my body just by looking at me.

Chapter Fifteen

CAP

"Have you found out anything yet?"

Knight was working over the man that had kidnapped Reese, but he wasn't giving us anything. I walked away to talk to Becky about the footage at the house, but it wasn't giving us any answers. If we didn't know who was behind the kidnapping, how would it ever be safe for Reese? And Craig would be useless if we didn't find out who put her in danger.

"He keeps saying he doesn't know anything. He said he responded to a phone call he got, but when he traced the number, he didn't get anything."

"That's what this guy is hired to do. He can't really think that we'd believe that he doesn't know how to track his contact."

"I swear," the man groaned. He was bent over in the chair and his face looked like it had been rearranged, but he wasn't dead. Yet.

"You can't really expect us to believe that you don't know anything. You-"

"Cap."

I turned around to see Hunter and Derek standing uncomfortably in the doorway. "Put him on ice," I said to Knight. He didn't look too happy about that, but he nodded and got to work.

"What's going on?"

"Uh..." Derek cleared his throat and jerked his head toward the elevator. "We need to talk to you about something."

"Yeah, I figured that when you came down here and interrupted me."

"Well, see, the thing is..." Hunter wiggled uncomfortably. "See, what happened is..."

"Would you fucking spit it out?"

"Remember those women we told you about?"

"Women?"

"The old ladies," Derek corrected. "The ones that ...beat us up."

"Okay, yeah, I remember them."

"See, the thing is..."

"Oh, for fuck's sake. Would one of you just say what the fucking thing is!"

"They're here," Derek spit out.

"Here?"

"Yeah, as in, sitting in the conference room."

"All of them?"

"Uh," Hunter seemed to be doing some weird form of facial conferencing with Derek and then turned back to me. "We're not sure. But there's one woman that we all know."

"Who's that?"

"Elsie Daughtry."

"Elsie. Jessica's grandmother's best friend, Elsie?"

"Yeah," Derek nodded.

"And she's here..."

"Apparently, she's the leader of the group," Hunter grumbled.

I stared at them both for a second and then I burst out laughing. Elsie, an eighty year old woman, was the leader of a group of old grannies that apparently had it out for the men of Reed Security.

"I've gotta see this," I said, sauntering past Derek and Hunter to head up to the conference room.

"I wouldn't be too eager, Cap. You're not gonna like what they have to say."

"Really? Care to enlighten me?"

"One of them is Reese's grandmother."

I stopped in my tracks and slowly turned around. "Shit."

"Yeah, that's what we thought," Hunter replied. "What the fuck are we supposed to say to her?"

"Well, we definitely don't mention that Craig has been stalking her. Or that he threatened to have her arrested. Or that he took the kidnapper's place and whisked her off to an unknown location. You know what, we just won't say anything at all."

"Good call," Derek nodded.

We headed upstairs in the elevator and I prepared to face what could quite possibly be the most frightening thing I had ever encountered. When I entered the conference room, I had to admit, I was a little terrified. All these women sitting around the table reminded me of my own grandmother. All those little, old fingers, just waiting to pinch someone's cheeks.

"Ladies," I croaked out. I straightened my spine and cleared my throat. I would not be intimidated by these grannies. "What can I help you with today?"

Elsie stood and gave a tight smile. "I think it's us that can help you."

I looked at her in confusion. Had I missed something? "Okay..."

"I'm sure by now you've realized that our group looks out for the young ladies in this town."

"We've come to that conclusion," I said evenly, not wanting to cause any trouble.

"Well, one of the ladies in this group is Reese Pearson's grandmother."

I eyed all the ladies, trying to find the resemblance, but they all looked like old ladies to me. However, one lady in particular looked awfully pissed off. It had to be her.

"Ma'am," I nodded.

"Don't 'ma'am' me. If it weren't for that man stalking my granddaughter, she would be at home safe right now."

"Actually, the man that you say is stalking your granddaughter saved her life. She was kidnapped and he witnessed it. I was with him. We went after her and got her back. He took her to a safe location until we can find out who was trying to take her. We captured the man that took her and we're trying to find out right now who was behind it and why they wanted her."

"Mr. Reed, let me save you the trouble," Elsie said. "Mrs. Pearson, Reese's grandmother, hired someone to take Reese away until we could get rid of her stalker."

I stood there in stunned silence for a moment, not sure quite where to start. Who were these women? They put her in more danger by hiring that guy. "Okay, first, who is this guy? Do you know him personally or is he just some thug you hired?"

Elsie looked to Mrs. Pearson. "I found him through an old friend of mine."

"And did you know that this man attacked your granddaughter and threw her in the trunk of a car?"

"He wasn't supposed to hurt her."

"But that's exactly what happened. If you had just come to me and talked to me, I would have been able to reassure you that the man that you say is stalking your granddaughter is actually very much in love with her."

The woman sat there in shock.

"Well, now that you know what is going on, perhaps you could contact your man and have Reese returned."

I nodded to Elsie. "Perhaps I could have a word with you in private?"

She followed me out of the conference room and into my office. "I'm terribly sorry to have to disrupt your day," Elsie said as she took a seat.

"It's no problem. It answers a lot of questions for us and prevents us from having to get rid of a body."

I chuckled, thinking that would get a rise out of her, but she just raised an eyebrow at me, like she wasn't affected at all.

"I'm afraid if you're hoping to frighten me, you're doing a bad job. Remember, my husband worked for the FBI. I heard more stories over the years than you would think."

"Okay. Why don't you tell me why you have a group of ladies that are going around beating up unsuspecting men."

"It's simple. You already know about Ruth."

"But Wallace didn't do anything to her. So why go after all these men?"

"Women are too trusting with men. We're just looking out for young ladies, and making sure that men behave themselves."

"But your ladies attacked two of my men. Both of them married."

"I never said we were perfect. When we see a man disrespecting a woman, we make sure that they're put in their place. And who better to teach these young men that lesson than little, old ladies that can easily shake any kind of police inquiry?"

"You're kind of devious, you know that?"

She grinned at me and stood. "I know. That's what makes us so good. Call your man back and have Reese returned before her grandmother loses it. I hate to say it, but her grandmother is kind of a loose cannon."

"I'll make the call right now."

Chapter Sixteen

CRAIG

I had all the supplies I needed for cleaning Reese's feet. I also stopped and got a change of clothes for her. I had no idea how long it would take to find out why the man tried to kidnap her. It had to have been planned. The man snatched her right after she stepped out of her house.

I was just stepping off the elevator and heading to our room when my phone rang. "Hello?"

"Craig, it's Cap. We found out who's behind everything."

My shoulders sagged in disappointment. I was hoping I would have more time to win Reese over. "What did you find out?"

"It was those old ladies that attacked Hunter and Derek. Apparently, one of them is Reese's grandmother. She hired someone to kidnap Reese to get her away from you."

"What? That's insane. Why would she need protection from me?"

"Because you've been stalking her."

"I was not stalking her. I was just...trying to convince her that we belonged together."

"Craig, I know you're not stupid. You were stalking her. She told you repeatedly to leave her alone. This was never going to work."

"Then why did you help me?" I spat. "I know that if you thought I was going to hurt her, you wouldn't have let me near her."

He sighed heavily into the phone. "I owed you. We both know that I was wrong in assuming you were against us. But we tried. You got some time with her and now it's time to bring her back home and end this."

"What? You want me to bring her back already? Cap, it hasn't even been a day."

"Her grandmother knows that you have her. The threat is gone. You can't just keep her away for no reason."

"Yes, I can."

"Craig-"

"No, I was supposed to have time with her to convince her that we belong together. I'm not just giving up. We agreed that I would return her by Sunday night. I have two full days with her and I'm not returning her a moment sooner."

I heard him shouting at me through the phone, so I ended the call and turned it off. I wasn't going to be tracked. Which meant that I couldn't go to the safe house Knight directed me to. He would most likely give in and tell Cap where we were. I also needed a new car. But since I couldn't use my credit card, that meant I had to steal one. Cap was gonna love that.

I walked down the hall to our room and slid the key in the reader. Opening the door, I released a small breath when I saw that Reese was still here. I had been worried that she would run out on me. Even though we just shared the most electric kiss I had ever experienced, I knew she was still wary about me.

Glancing at the clock, I saw it was near midnight. I needed to get her cleaned up and get some sleep. I had big plans for the rest of our weekend, and I wasn't going to waste that time being tired.

"Hi," I said as I set the stuff on the table.

She smiled, but didn't say anything. Damn, if it was even possible, she looked more gorgeous than the last time I saw her.

"I'm gonna carry you into the bathroom and wash your feet, okay?"

"Sure."

I slid my hands under her and lifted her up against my body. Her arms wrapped around my neck and her breath slid across my cheek. I turned to look at her and our eyes locked. She was so close, close enough that I could just lean forward slightly and feel those gorgeous lips against mine. I could hear her breath turning ragged, and as much as I wanted to kiss her right now, I knew I couldn't. I had to take care of her first, and that meant no fucking around.

I looked away, squeezing my eyes shut to ward off all sexual thoughts. Focus! I carried her into the bathroom and set her down on the edge of the tub. I quickly grabbed the bag from the store and brought it into the bathroom. Running the bathwater, I poured some Epsom Salts into the tub and gently lowered her feet in.

"You're good at this," she said, eyeing me curiously.

I shrugged. "You learn to take care of yourself when you're in the military. Survival skills are what keep you alive. Taking care of your feet is one of the most important things when you're out on missions. If you can't walk for miles on end, you can't keep up with your unit. That makes you a liability."

"Why did you join?" I looked at her, wondering if she actually wanted to know or if it was just a time filler. The look on her face was pure curiosity.

"I was in college and I had planned to follow in my dad's footsteps. I was going to be a lawyer."

"You were going to be a lawyer," she laughed. "I can't see that. I mean, you can be very persuasive, but you just don't seem like a guy that would be happy in a courtroom."

"Probably not," I grinned. "My dad loved the courtroom. He used to tell me about cases he was trying. He would get all fired up and go through his closing arguments. It was always a big thing in our house. Of course, it was always after the trial ended. He couldn't talk about the case while it was going on, but he would get all fired up and come home and tell us about how the trial ended. He really loved being a lawyer."

"Loved?"

I swallowed the lump in my throat and tried not to let my emotions get the better of me. I hadn't let it get to me in years, but I also hadn't talked about my dad in a really long time. He was my hero and everything I had ever wanted to be when I grew up. Which was why it was so hard to walk away from it all.

"He died when I was eighteen. I had just started at NYU School of Law."

"Oh. I'm sorry. So, why didn't you follow in his footsteps?"

"I uh…" I cleared my throat and picked up her foot. I grabbed the washcloth and gently started rubbing some cream I had picked up into the bottom of her foot. "I joined the military instead, because of the way he died."

I heard a sharp intake of breath, but I didn't look up. I couldn't look up.

"How old are you?"

"Thirty-six."

It was dead quiet in the room, but I knew she was doing the calculations. I knew she was putting it all together. I knew she wouldn't be comfortable asking more questions. She was a sweet woman, a little naive, but I knew she cared. Even if I had been stalking her for the past few weeks. She wasn't the type of woman to brush off everything I just said, but I also knew she didn't want to push and ask about something so sensitive.

"When the plane hit the first tower, he called my mom and told her what was happening. He wasn't actually in the building. He was on his way to a meeting and he heard the plane hit the tower. He was just down the street. He knew that people were dying and he was never one to stand on the sidelines. He rushed into that building and tried to save lives. He was a real hero."

I felt her hand on my arm, but I couldn't look at her right now. I was lost in memories of that day.

"I was on my way to school. I lived at home with my parents and I had a late class that morning." I stared at the wall of the tub as I thought back to that morning. "I kept hearing people talk about a plane and it crashing, but I just didn't pay attention. I was too busy thinking about a test I had. And the school wasn't that far from the towers. By the time I got to school, I finally realized what was happening. School was cancelled for the day, but I was too wrapped up in what was happening. I went to a pub and watched the news coverage for most of the day. I didn't even think to call home or worry about my dad. It didn't occur to me that he would be anywhere near there that day. And then I got home that night and my mom was in tears. She told me that my dad had gone in to help save people and she hadn't heard from him since."

"Did she try to call you during the day?"

"This was back when not everyone had a cell phone. He didn't come home that night, but we were still praying that he would. He never did."

I shook off the memories from that day and continued to rub cream into her other foot. When I was finished, I wrapped her feet in gauze to keep the cream from rubbing off. I was about to gather up all the supplies and put them away when she stopped me by squeezing my arm. Part of me didn't want to look up and see that sympathy in her eyes, but the other part of me needed to know if she understood me a little better now.

It wasn't that I was chasing just anything in life. It wasn't just that she was beautiful and I wanted her to be mine. It was that my whole adult life I had been looking for the meaning of life, for something that justified everything that had happened to my family. But when I saw Reese, something just clicked inside me. It was like she was what I had actually been searching for since the day my dad died. I had thought I was looking for justice or redemption. But what I was really looking for was the person that would make my life whole. I was looking for someone that would make me feel like life was worth living. That I hadn't lost everything, but actually gained something I didn't know I even needed. Reese was life after all the bad.

When I looked into her eyes, I saw caring, but I also saw strength and respect. It was what I needed from her. I needed a woman that would stand by me when the chips were down, but I also needed a woman that understood me and could help me through it all, and understand that I needed to do what I did as a way of honoring all those that lost their lives. That had been the turning point in my life, where my life was no longer my own. I lived for all of those that died, and fought for the freedom that they had lost the day they died.

I picked Reese up and carried her back to the bed, lying her down on her back. I pulled back, but she stopped me, placing her hand on my cheek. My breath caught in my chest. This was the first time that she had made any attempt to initiate anything between us. Could it be that she was coming around?

She pressed her lips to mine and I was a fucking goner. I kissed her back, shoving my tongue inside her mouth. Her arms wrapped around my back and she pulled me to her, her fingers digging into my back. I climbed on top of her and pressed her into the mattress. God, I couldn't wait to be inside her. I pressed my cock against her and grinned against her mouth when she groaned. I knew she had been holding out on me.

Chapter Seventeen

REESE

Oh God, what was I doing? I hadn't decided if I was going to sleep with him yet when he walked in the room. But then he told me that story and I was practically melting in a puddle at his feet. Not because his story was sad, but because he showed me a side to him that wasn't just a stalker. I saw how deeply he was hurt when his father died, but I also saw his strength of character. He was a good man, although slightly psychotic.

When he carried me back to the bed, I just couldn't help myself. I wanted to feel his lips on mine again. I wanted to know what it was like to have the weight of his body pressed against mine. And boy, did I find out. When his cock pressed against me, I thought I would explode.

I wanted this man, but it didn't make any sense. He didn't fit into what I wanted in a man. He was cocky and arrogant. He proved that in the coffee shop when he took on those men like it was nothing. And maybe it was nothing to him, but he treated it so casually, like there was no way he could get hurt. It wasn't something I wanted to deal with. I wanted a man who did have fear, because a man that had fear meant that he had something to lose. And I wanted to mean something to someone. I wanted the man I fell in love with to love me enough that he always thought about returning to me. It was one of the reasons I pushed Craig away after the coffee shop. He liked the danger.

But I couldn't think about that with his tongue in my mouth, kissing me like he was passionately in love with me. My hands started moving like they had a mind of their own. I felt his zipper and then I was yanking it down to get at his cock. I already knew it was big. I had felt it pressing against me. But I wanted to feel it in my hands. I wondered if he knew how to use it, how to drive me crazy. None of my previous lovers had been anything special in the sack.

Suddenly, I was flipped on top of him, straddling his body. His hands moved to the hem of my shirt and started pushing the material up. I couldn't take my eyes off his. He stared me down, his eyes drilling into me, daring me to stop him. But I didn't want to. I was done fighting this for tonight. In the morning I would make my decision. I raised my hands over my head and allowed him to push the material up over my breasts. He sat up, kissing my breasts through the cups of my bra, biting at my nipples as he tore the shirt off of me. I threaded my fingers through his short hair, gripping at the strands every time he bit me. God, he was good at this.

My bra came loose in the back and then he was yanking it off me. My heart was pounding out of control. This man dominated me in every way, yet put me in the position of control. I couldn't take the wild sensations flowing through me or control how my body was so willingly handing itself over to him. I rolled back over, needing him to be fully in control. And he took it.

My pants were yanked off me and then he was shoving his hard cock inside me. I wasn't sure when the rest of the clothes had been shed, but they were long gone and he was pounding inside me. I gripped onto his shoulders, hanging on for the ride. I refused to look in his eyes. I knew he would draw me in and never let me go. But then he stopped and his fingers were under my chin, lifting it so that I would meet his eyes.

"Look at me when I make love to you."

"This isn't making love."

He smirked and bent down to kiss me, trailing his lips along my jaw and then nibbling on my ear. "Make no mistake, that is exactly what we are doing. And I'll prove it to you over and over again until you feel exactly what I feel."

I shuddered as his breath fanned across my ear. He nibbled at the lobe and then slowly pulled out of me and thrust back into me. I gasped and then he did it again, pulling out so slowly that I thought my heart would give out at the pace it was racing. He was setting my nerves on fire, lighting my whole body up, just to send me crashing into a massive wreck. And I knew it would end that way.

My panting grew heavy and ragged the more he teased me. I thrust my hips up, needing to have him inside me, harder and faster. "Don't you dare slow down," I panted.

He slid in so hard and fast that my body jerked backwards. I cried out and wrapped my hands around his neck, refusing to let him move away from me anymore.

"Harder," I pleaded. The rest was me trying not to black out from how hard he was fucking me. It was amazing and I never wanted it to end. But when my body started shaking and my legs squeezed together against my will, I knew I wouldn't hold out anymore. I wrapped my legs around his waist and crushed him to me as I fell over the edge.

My whole world went black for several minutes as I tried to recover from the best orgasm I had ever experienced. I was vaguely aware of his body pressed hard against mine, but the weight of him actually seemed to calm me. I found myself running my hand up and down his back as my racing heart started to calm. Who was I and what had I done with the woman that didn't want to get involved with this man?

He lifted his head from my chest and kissed me lightly on the lips. He looked sleepy and satisfied and I couldn't help smiling back at him.

"Tell me you're not going to run."

I didn't want to lie to him, but I didn't know what the truth was either. So, I told him what I was feeling in that moment. "I'm not going anywhere."

He slid off me partially so that all his weight wasn't on me, and then he closed his eyes as he drifted off to sleep. The weight of his arm was still draped across my belly, but it felt good. I couldn't think right now, so I let myself drift off to sleep.

I woke up a few hours later, hot from this big man draping himself across me. It felt suffocating, like I couldn't escape. And that was how I actually felt about him. He was all-consuming. He made me want things that I shouldn't. He made me want him. What was I doing? I needed to get out of here. As much as I wanted this man, as much as I thought deep down he was a good man, he had kidnapped me. Even if I believed that he had rescued me from another kidnapper, which just seemed highly unlikely, he had still followed me around for weeks when I asked him to leave me alone.

And now I had gone and slept with him. I saw the way he was looking at me, like I was the air that he breathed. How was I supposed to walk away now? Would he ever believe that I didn't want him?

I shook my head and gently pried his arm off of me and slid out of the bed. This was why I had decided to sleep with him to begin with, or so I told myself. I knew that he wouldn't let me go no matter what, so I decided to draw him in and make him comfortable, just like Brooke suggested. Well, I'd gotten my way. He was passed out beside me, and if I worked fast, I could get out of here before he ever realized I was gone.

I quickly dressed, doing my best to be quiet, and dug out half the money out of his wallet. I wasn't going to take all his money, but I needed a few hundred dollars to get home. I wanted to go kiss him goodbye for some reason, but I knew that was a risk I couldn't take. I took the shoes and socks that he bought for me and carried them to the door with me. I just wanted to get out before he caught me.

Carefully, I opened the door and closed it quietly behind me. As soon as the door clicked shut, I raced down the hall to the stairwell and quickly pulled on my shoes and socks. I was down the stairs and out on the dark streets in just under a minute. Looking both ways, I tried to figure out which way to go, but nothing stood out to me. I turned left and walked until I disappeared into the night.

Chapter Eighteen

CRAIG

The first thing I noticed when I woke up to the bright sunlight was the fact that the bed was cold beside me. Way too cold for Reese to just have gone to take a shower. I sat up slightly, leaning on my elbow as I looked around the room. She had taken her clothes and the shoes and socks I had picked up for her, but left everything else behind.

I flopped onto my back and stared up at the ceiling. How had I gotten it so wrong? I thought she felt the connection too, but then why did she bolt? Was she just using me all along? Was she just faking it and using our connection to get away?

If it wasn't for Cap calling and telling me that there was no threat, I would be worried sick about her being out there on her own. As it was, she wouldn't get far on foot. We were too far from home. However, there were still plenty of ways that she could get into trouble. I needed to get her back. If she really didn't want to be with me, then I suppose that I could be the bigger person and...I laughed to myself because there was no way I was letting her go. And she could think whatever she wanted. I saw the way she looked at me last night. She wanted me just as much as I wanted her. And it wasn't just so she could lure me into some relaxed state so she could slip away. She wanted me because there was an undeniable connection between us. I just had to make her admit it.

I flung the covers off and hopped out of bed. Turning on the shower, I whistled as I quickly cleaned up and got dressed. This was going to be a great day. I packed up the shit that I had brought with me while I dialed up Becky.

"What do you want?" she snapped.

"I need your help."

"Of course you do. Too bad. I'm busy."

"Yeah, yeah, I've heard that before."

"Hey, I am not just some....computer genius that you can use whenever you need something. I'm busy."

She hung up the phone and I chuckled. Becky could pretend all she wanted that she didn't want to help me, but I knew better. I called her back.

"I already told you that I'm not helping you."

"Technically, you didn't say anything like that. You yelled at me and hung up on me. But I know that deep down you want to help me."

"Yeah? Why would you think that?"

"Because it's your job."

"You're not on a job."

"Then I guess Cap didn't fill you in on my little adventure last night," I grinned, knowing I had the upper hand.

"Actually, he did. He also informed me that there is no threat."

Shit. Well, that didn't help me much.

"Okay, listen, she ran out of here and I need to track her down. We're hours away from Reed Security. Think of all the trouble she could get into."

"She'd probably welcome it if it meant getting away from you," she snapped.

"Wow. That's harsh. I think you just hurt my feelings."

"Oh, please. It's not like any of you guys actually have any. Face it, you're all out for yourselves."

"That's just a very brutal assessment of my feelings. I'll have you know that I love Reese and there's not a damn thing I wouldn't do for her."

"How can you possibly love her? You've known her all of five minutes?"

"Well, hell, I don't know how, but I know what I feel is real. Have you ever walked into a room and talked with someone for just five minutes, but knew that that person was meant for you?"

She was silent on the other end, probably because that was exactly how she felt about Coop, but she was too stubborn to admit it. Hell, I wasn't saying it was love at first sight or anything like that, but that woman had me, balls and all, and there was no way I was letting her go.

"That's the way I feel about Reese and now she's out there, wandering around someplace she doesn't know, and I have to get her back."

"You know I have to tell Cap about this. He called the job off. He told you to come back."

"But you don't have to listen to him. I have a plan and by the end of the weekend, she'll be mine."

"You're not gonna do some kind of blood oath, are you?"

"Just find out where the fuck she went," I growled.

"Fine, but you owe me big time, and believe me, I'll be collecting when you least expect it."

"Okay, she's in the grey Mercedes, just two cars ahead of you."

"Fucking pussy," I grumbled as I put my foot down on the gas. There was no way this asshole was taking her any further than he already had. She was mine, and I was going to make sure that by the end of the weekend she knew it. There were no cars coming, so I pulled up along the asshole and then gently shoved his car off onto the shoulder and pulled in front of him on an angle so that he couldn't drive off.

I got out, gun raised and ready to fire if he tried anything. Looking at his car, yeah, I did just a little more damage than a gentle nudge. Reese was sitting in the passenger seat, wide eyed and fuming. I waved to her with a grin on my face. Knocking on the driver's side window, the man slowly rolled down his window, looking like he was about to shit his pants. I kept my gun trained on him.

"What do you want?"

"The woman."

"I'm not going with you, you psycho!"

I leaned down on the man's window and shoved my sunglasses on top of my head so she could see the seriousness in my eyes. I tapped my gun against the window ledge, watching the man's eyes bug out in fear. "Now, my little Reese's pieces, we had a beautiful night together and then you snuck out on me this morning. Don't tell me you didn't feel it too."

"You told me your car broke down," the man accused.

"I was kidnapped by this psycho and I was trying to get home!"

"That's not the way it went and you know it," I chastised. "You were kidnapped and I saved you. Now, all I ask is that you stick by me before you get someone else killed."

"Killed?" The man visibly gulped and reached across Reese's body to fling the door open. "I didn't ask to get involved in this. You can leave."

"You're leaving me with my stalker?"

"Lady, your stalker just banged up my Mercedes." She got out of the car and crossed her arms over her chest in frustration.

"Yeah," I scratched my jaw, "sorry about that." I took a picture of my insurance card and asked for his phone number. "Had to get my lady back."

"I am not your lady," Reese said, stomping her foot on the gravel.

I stalked toward her, shoving my gun back in my holster. "You are my woman in every way, and there's no fucking way I'm going to let anything happen to you. I swore I would protect you, and I will." I jerked her body to mine and leaned in close like I was going to kiss her, but instead nipped at her ear. "With my life."

I heard her sharp intake of breath and felt her heart racing against my chest. I grinned. Like it or not, she was mine and she was coming with me. I would make things right between us, one way or another. Taking her hand in mine, I led her back to my truck and opened the door for her. Gripping her around the waist, I hoisted her into the truck and walked around to the driver's side.

"Where'd you get the truck?" she sneered. "Did you steal it?"

"No. I used a little thing called my license and I rented the truck." Since there was no one tracking us anymore, I didn't have to worry about whether or not I used my credit card. Well, that wasn't totally true. Cap would be tracking me, but by the time he caught up with me, it would already be too late.

I pulled back onto the road and headed back toward Pittsburgh. We had a flight to catch, and since I already booked it as soon as Becky said she found Reese, we were good to go. It would take us about five hours to get to Sin City, and man were we going to sin when we got there. Well, I definitely was.

Chapter Nineteen

REESE

"What are we doing at the airport?"

"We have to go find out why this guy was after you."

I narrowed my eyes at him. I had a feeling he was lying, but if I was wrong, I could get taken again, and that might not end so well.

"Who are we looking for anyway?"

"An assassin," Craig said, scanning the crowd.

"A what?" I screeched. "Why would an assassin be after me," I practically shouted.

He covered my mouth and smiled at the people next to us. "It's a book we're reading for book club." They looked at us strangely and backed away like we had the plague. "Would you mind keeping those thoughts to yourself in public? The last thing we need is someone innocent getting involved."

"I'm innocent," I hissed. "What did I ever do to get on a hitman's list? I teach fucking kindergarten!"

"We're still looking into it." He wrapped his arm around my waist and I smiled to myself. I didn't want to like the feel of him wrapped around me. I didn't want to feel flutters in my stomach when he talked about me being his. But I did. And it was fucking with my head. I had to remember that this man stalked me for weeks, and now he was here to save me? It all sounded so strange. Besides, what the hell did I do to get targeted by an assassin?

"Do you think I saw something I wasn't supposed to?"

"Could be. Now, just act normal. We're a normal couple, just going on a trip to see your parents."

"My parents live here. It doesn't make any sense that we would be going on a trip to see them," I hissed through a smile.

"Nobody else knows that. Nobody knows you, so just pretend that we're a happy couple and you'll be fine."

"Except for the assassin that's after me."

"You know, the more you say that, the more chance there is that people will hear you and someone will call the cops."

"Good, maybe they'd actually be able to help me," I grumbled.

"The only thing the police will do is get in the way."

I stood in the slow moving line with him for what felt like forever when I felt Craig stiffen beside me. My eyes started darting around the airport, looking for any sign of a threat, but I couldn't see a thing.

"What is it?"

"Just keep looking ahead."

His voice turned to steel and I did as he said. If he was this steely, then it had to be for a reason. Probably an assassin reason. I swallowed down my nerves and did my best to appear calm and collected, but inside I was a mess. In fact, I was pretty sure I was going to puke all over the place in just a few minutes. My stomach was churning with fear and I was sweating so bad that I could feel my hand slipping in Craig's.

"When I say, we're going to get out of this line and walk toward the exit. I don't want you to rush or look nervous. Just follow my lead and we'll be fine."

"What's going on?" My voice quivered and no matter how hard I tried to control it, I was losing it.

"Relax. Everything's going to be fine." He gripped my hand tight and gave a reassuring smile. "Okay, let's go."

I followed him through the crowd, focusing on what was ahead of us, instead of looking around like I wanted to. I didn't want to draw attention to myself in any way. We were almost to the doors when I heard a shout. Glancing behind me, I saw a man with dark hair, built the same as Craig, rushing toward us. Craig swore and grabbed my hand, pulling me quickly out the doors. We rushed through the drop off line and through the parking lot. Craig was on his phone shouting at someone and then we were stopping at an SUV and he was shoving me inside.

I didn't hesitate to buckle up as he peeled out of the lot. I didn't know how he started a vehicle that we didn't have a key to, and I didn't want to ask how he knew where to find this vehicle. All I cared about was the fact that we were on the road and it didn't appear that anyone was following us. Yet.

About five miles down the road, Craig pulled over and yanked the dash panel off the SUV and then ripped out wires. He quickly replaced the dash and took off again.

"What did you just do?"

"I removed the tracking in the vehicle."

I nodded because that totally made sense. What didn't make sense was how he knew it was there in the first place.

"Do all vehicles have tracking?"

"No."

"Then how did you know this one did?"

"Because the IT woman at my work pointed me to the vehicle."

"Right. So...she knew where we were and...I'm sorry, but I'm really confused."

"Don't worry about it. The point is that we're on the road and no one can find us now."

"What about your phone?"

"I tossed it."

"But, that means you can't contact your company," I said in a panic.

He was silent for a minute and then he turned to me with all the confidence in the world. "We'll be fine. I won't let anything happen to you."

Chapter Twenty

CAP

"Goddamnit!" I slammed the door to the SUV that Alec showed up in to drive me back to Reed Security. "What the fuck is he thinking? He kidnapped a woman!"

"Boss, you knew that he was in love with her," Alec shot me a sly grin.

"That does not justify kidnapping! What the fuck am I supposed to say to those old ladies?"

"I think the better question is how did he find your vehicle so fast and get away?"

"No shit. It's not just dumb luck that he came across my SUV in the parking lot. He had help."

"Look, it's not the first time that one of us has gone off the rails over a woman."

"Not like this," I said angrily.

"Okay, I just want to point out that Sinner quit his job over a woman. Cazzo practically got Vanessa killed when he disobeyed protocols. You stuck a tracker in your woman, *and* you keep knocking her up just to keep her out of trouble."

"That's not why I'm knocking her up."

He snorted and headed back for Reed Security. "Keep telling yourself that. And then we have Knight, who was the ultimate stalker. You think Craig's lost it? Knight was way worse and you know it. And then Derek, well, I guess he didn't really do anything. Hunter, well, he took after his buddy, Knight. And then there's Chris. He started a fucking gang war over his woman. And Ice was just a dumb fucker. Lola, she's good. Probably the only sane one of us all. And let's not forget how I got shot in the chest. Not that that was Burg's fault, but he disobeyed protocols also. Chance started a war with human traffickers and got himself and his woman taken. Jackson is pretty normal. Gabe is probably the most disturbed mother fucker of any of us."

"And let's not forget that you broke a man's neck when you thought Florrie was killed."

"See? You get it. So Craig's lost it and kidnapped his woman. Seriously, what's the worst that could happen?"

"See, it's sentences like that that make me fucking hate my job. I could make a whole fucking list of things that could go wrong with kidnapping a woman. One of which is us having the reputation of not protecting our clients."

"But, she was never our client. This can still work in our favor, Cap."

I stared at him for a minute, completely baffled by his line of thinking. "Have you all lost your goddamn minds? What he did is a punishable offense. If she presses charges when, no, if she comes home, we're all fucked."

"It's not gonna happen, Cap. I'm telling you. He loves that woman and by the time they come home, she's gonna be singing his praises."

"You'd better fucking hope so, or we're gonna all be living on the same fucking land with no fucking jobs and our wives running around wild. Take a minute to really think that one through."

His eyebrows furrowed for a minute and then he turned to me with a steely expression. "We have to find that fucker and bring him home."

"No shit."

Chapter Twenty-One

CRAIG

I couldn't believe Cap actually came after me. What a load of bullshit. I always had his back, but this was the second time that he didn't have mine. And I didn't want to hear any of that crap about me going rogue. I was taking my woman, just like every other man that worked at Reed Security. So, my methods were less than conventional. Look at Knight. That guy was more of a stalker than I would ever be.

"Where are we headed?" Reese asked for the tenth time.

"Same destination. Just a different route to get there."

"But, won't they be waiting for us?"

Damn, my woman wasn't just some dumb blonde that sat back and let me do all the work. She was a thinker, which normally I would be grateful for, but it would nice if right now she was the dumb blonde so I could pull off my plan without worrying about her catching on.

"So, if they knew we would be at the airport, they probably know where we're headed. And assassins are smart, right? I mean, they wouldn't just go around killing random people. They need to know which people to shoot and where they'll be. Why aren't you freaking out about this?" she practically screamed.

"Because I'm trained for this type of stuff."

And thank God for that. If I wasn't, there would be no way I would escape Reed Security. I just hoped that Becky didn't rat me out. She was the one that bought the tickets for me. If they knew where we were going, there was no doubt in my mind that they would try to intercept us. I just had to stay one step ahead of them. They didn't know my exact destination.

"So, what's your favorite color?" I asked, trying to get to know my future wife.

"Really? You want to know my favorite color?"

"Of course."

"Blue."

"Favorite animal?" She sighed and stared out the window. "That's okay. I can talk about myself all day. My favorite animal is a Koala. I mean, they're so cute and cuddly, but they can be surprisingly violent." She still didn't say anything. "Not so much koala-on-koala violence. They're usually pretty mild mannered toward each other, but they have been known to go after humans."

Still she didn't say anything, so I just continued talking.

"Favorite food?" Crickets... "Me personally, I like pizza. Any kind of pizza, but I really hate mushrooms. I mean, it's fungus. Who eats that shit? Same goes for fish. I mean, that shit stinks. And when I picture people eating caviar, I picture someone shoving their fingers up a woman's-"

"Stop! I don't need to hear any more of your thoughts on caviar."

"Okay." I drummed my fingers against the steering wheel, trying to come up with something that could snag her attention. "So, how many guys have you fucked?"

Fifteen hours into our drive and Reese still wasn't talking to me. Which kind of sucked for me because I was hoping to take this time to really get to know her. Instead, I was driving down the road with a black eye. Yeah, asking her about how many men she'd fucked wasn't a smart idea. I hadn't even realized she was pissed until she punched me in the face. Of course, she wasn't trained in how to punch people, so I had to stop and get her an ice pack for her hand.

"You know, you hurt yourself because you're holding your hand the wrong way. See, when you go to punch someone-" I looked up and swore that my balls shriveled up into my body. Hell, this woman was giving off all the danger vibes. Danger, meaning that if I didn't shut my fucking mouth, she was going to shut it for me.

That was fourteen hours ago and I was bored out of my skull. I had to find a way to get her to open up to me. Sure, I had kidnapped her after she had been kidnapped, but she didn't know that. As far as she knew, we were on the run from an assassin. She should be grateful right now that I was protecting her from said assassin.

But the problem was how to keep her by my side. So, when I stopped for the ice pack, I called Knight and asked him to do a little favor for me. At first, he wasn't at all into it, but when I told him what I needed, he decided that getting back into his old role could be fun.

I pulled into a motel, rundown and probably reeking of body odor. I hadn't needed to stay off the grid before, but now that Cap was on my tail, I had to pay in cash. Once I got to Vegas, I could withdraw more money. They would already know I was there, but my plan would already be in full swing by then.

"Please tell me that we're not staying here."

"Sorry, my little Reese's Pieces. We have to stay off the grid if we want to stay alive. Stay here while I get us a room."

"Why do I have to stay here?"

"Cameras." I pointed to the office where a camera was mounted outside. It probably didn't work, but she didn't know that. "It's best if your face doesn't show up on any footage."

She shrank back in the seat and I grinned internally. It wasn't that I wanted her to be scared, but my plan was working and I needed it to keep working until I won. I rented the room and then drove to the end of the lot where our room was. I walked around to her side and opened the door for her. She glared at me, but took my hand and hopped down. I opened the door, which was already nudged open, and cleared the room quickly. We didn't have anyone following us, but that didn't mean that there weren't squatters around here. After clearing the room, I shut the door and moved the largest piece of furniture against it so no one could break in.

"Why don't you go ahead and take a shower?"

She bit her lip and looked into the bathroom and then back at me. "Aren't you going to take a shower?"

"Yeah, but I'll take mine when you're done."

She nodded, but didn't move.

"Unless, you wanted to take one with me," I said hesitantly.

"Well, it just seems like it would make the most sense for you to be with me at all times. I mean, if I have an assassin after me, I probably shouldn't be alone."

I bit back a smile and nodded. "You're right. It would be safer."

I slowly took off my shirt, loving the way her eyes trailed over my body. That was good. I just needed to keep her admiring me. As long as she was focused on my body, she wasn't focused on the fact that she was with me when she didn't want to be. When I was stripped completely naked, I cleared my throat to get her attention.

"We should probably go take that shower."

Chapter Twenty-Two

REESE

God, he was so hot. It wasn't fair. Why did all the really hot men have to be either full of themselves or completely insane? Why couldn't I just find a good guy that was hot, but average? Was it really too much to ask that my stalker didn't make me want him more than any man I had ever had before?

Our shower was awkward at best. I stayed on my side while he stayed on his. I could tell that he wanted to do very dirty things to me, but every time he came close, I shuffled away and pretended that washing my body was the most important thing in the world.

I quickly got out of the shower and wrapped a towel around me. I only realized once we were out of the bathroom that neither of us had a change of clothes.

"Crap." I slid into the bed, holding my towel snug to my body while Craig walked out of the bathroom completely naked. I couldn't stop watching him and he didn't seem to care at all that he was walking around showing off his dick. But, of course he wouldn't. That was the point. He wanted me attracted to him. If only Brooke was here right now. She would say or do something to distract and take the pressure off me right now.

"You have a huge dick." I slapped my hand over my mouth and

squeezed my eyes shut. Of all the things to say to my stalker, that was what came out? That was like encouraging him to come closer and let me lick him. Which I very much wanted to do right now, but that was beside the point. I had to remember that this man kidnapped me. It was wrong to want him. I had only slept with him the first time to escape. Okay, that wasn't at all the truth, but I couldn't fall into his web of sexiness again. It was too tempting and I would get lost in him.

But he was dangerous and even just sleeping with this man was so wrong. He would be one of those guys that bragged about being totally awesome and unshootable, and then he would come home with a bullet to the chest. I wasn't one of those women that would be a good military wife. I would cry every time my husband was deployed. I would beg him to call me every night, even though I knew he wouldn't be able to. I wouldn't band together with all the other military wives and talk about how we stood by our husbands no matter what because they were sacrificing for the country. No, I would be the wife bitching because my husband was never home and I felt abandoned. This was why I stayed away from these military types. And retired or not, Craig was still very much a military type. He would break my heart in an instant if I allowed him in.

I wrapped the sheet and blanket tight to my body and tried to ignore the weight of his body as it sank into the bed. Taking a deep breath, I closed my eyes and tried not to smell his sexy scent or imagine what it would feel like to have him just a little closer to me. Then I felt his fingers gliding up my arm and brush my hair out of my face. My eyes flew open and I shot a glare at him.

"Don't tell me you don't want this," he whispered.

My heart pounded in my chest and my vagina was pulsing out of control. The man was right, I did want this. I picked up his hand and flung it off me. There was no way I was giving in. I heard a low chuckle as he moved back to his side of the bed. I growled low in my throat and pretended like I was throwing daggers at him. It made me feel lighter inside to know that I was resisting the sexy man.

It's okay. Just list all the things you hate about him. His sexy muscles, the way he looks at me like I'm everything to him, the way his arms feel around me, the way his cock stretches me and makes me crave him like a grilled cheese sandwich.

Ugh! This is so unfair. I'm supposed to hate him. He's been stalking me. He kidnapped me! I should be trying to call the police right now, not running away with him, all because he says an assassin's after me. Which doesn't even make sense! Who would possibly send an assassin after me? I teach kindergarten for Christ's sake!

"Don't worry, baby. I won't let anyone get you," he whispered to me, his breath fanning across my face.

"What?" I snapped. "What are you talking about?"

"You were grumbling about why an assassin would be after you."

I screamed under my breath and stared him down. "Is there anything that you're not good at?"

"I don't understand the question."

"Well, apparently, you're really good at killing people in coffee shops. You have big, awesome muscles that make me feel like a twig. You walk super fast, which just isn't fair to those of us that have short legs. And you have super hearing! Is there anything you can't do?"

He looked at me quizzically and then sighed. "Well, I always wanted to be able to speak in an English accent." He straightened up and mimicked an English person perfectly. "Hello. This bed is bloody brilliant." His face lit up as he looked at me. "Hey, look at that! I spoke in an English accent!"

I was doing everything I could to not look at Craig right now. I woke up laying on top of him this morning, and the worst part was that he was already awake and grinning at me when I looked up at him. I mean, my leg was draped over his, my arm was on his chest, and I was pretty sure that I was humping his hip. I had been dreaming about the man and I had the feeling that he knew it was about him. Based on how wet his hip was when I extracted myself from him, I was pretty sure that I had been rubbing myself all over him for the better part of an hour.

Now we were back on the road and I was starving, but I didn't want to say anything to him. It would probably come out all wrong and he'd think I wanted to eat him! Which I totally did. Especially when I saw how hard he was this morning. The nice thing would have been to take him in my mouth and suck him down my throat, but that also would have given him the impression that I wanted him. Which I didn't. Sort of.

"Are you ready for breakfast?"

"Hmm?" I said, finally turning to him. He was grinning at me and I flushed bright red. God, it was embarrassing knowing that I had molested his body against my will last night.

"Breakfast?" He quirked an eyebrow at me and I practically melted into puddle. I would not give in to these irrational feelings.

"Sure."

He nodded and pulled off the highway at the next exit. We pulled into a little diner and I quickly let myself out, careful not to walk too close to Craig or even look in his direction. We were led to a table, though I honestly didn't remember too much of walking to the booth or sitting down. I was just too busy distracting myself from looking at the man.

"Reese," he said, snapping me out of my haze. "What do you want to order?"

"Oh, um, eggs over medium, bacon, toast, and a glass of orange juice." There was already coffee on the table, so I poured myself a cup and doctored it up the way I liked.

"Are we ever going to talk about this morning?"

"I don't know what you're talking about." I stirred my coffee and refused to look at him, but I felt his body move across the table and lean in close.

"I'm talking about the fact that you were trying to fuck my leg in your sleep."

I choked on my coffee and wiped the snot from my nose. "That is not what happened," I hissed.

"Really?" He leaned back in the booth with a cocky grin on his face. "So, if that's not what happened, why don't you tell me what that was. Because I wouldn't mind waking up like that every morning."

"Look," I said sternly, "you know what happened, but I can't help what happens in my dreams."

"Dreams about me," he grinned.

"Not about you. I'll have you know that I was dreaming about a gorgeous man that was tall and had a normal body and dark, silky hair. He was a gentleman with a good job and he made love to me like I was his most prized possession."

Craig closed his eyes and dropped his head, making snoring sounds. "What a dud. Seriously, is that the type of guy you want?"

"What's wrong with that?"

"Nothing if you want to be bored to death. Are you telling me that you'd really rather have a gentleman than a man who'll play your body like a fiddle?"

I flushed bright red and ducked my head. "There's nothing wrong with a gentleman."

"Of course not. I would never stand in the way of something you really wanted." My eyes shot up to his, but he just leaned forward and gave a crooked grin. "But that's not what you want and I know it. Remember, I've fucked you and I know exactly what you like in bed. I know how to make you come and I know how to make you feel like your whole body is on fire."

"That's awfully cocky of you."

"It's not cocky if it's the truth. But you know what makes me better than all those gentlemen you think you want?" I just stared at him. "I can do those things to your body, but I also want to keep you for the long haul. I'm not interested in a one night stand or fucking around. I knew I wanted you from the day I met you in that coffee shop. I knew there was something between us and I wanted it more than I've ever wanted anything in my life. You resist me because you think you want something simple and perfect. But let me tell you something, baby, nothing in life is simple and perfect. There's no such thing in a relationship. Relationships are dirty and messy. People get hurt because that's nature. But I would rather have the dirty and messy with a woman that drove me wild and made me feel the way you do than have a boring relationship with a woman that was afraid of getting hurt. I guess I'm just hoping that you're not going to run away because you might get hurt."

I sat there speechless for a moment. I wasn't sure what to say. He was right about pretty much everything he said, but I was afraid of getting hurt. But more than that, I was afraid of losing the man I loved.

"Let's say that you're right and we are meant to be together. What about when you don't come home from a job?"

"Not gonna happen," he grinned.

"How can you be so sure? Are you telling me that what you do isn't dangerous?"

"Not all the time."

"But it can be," I pressed. His face dropped slightly and he nodded. "So, you can't tell me that you will always be safe."

"Look, if this is the reason you don't want to be with me-"

"It's not the only reason. Let's remember that I walked away and you started stalking me."

"I prefer to think of it as refusing to give up when I saw something I wanted."

"Either way, I told you no and you kept coming. Listen, I think you're actually a really nice guy-"

"Ooh," he hissed, sucking in a breath. "That's never a good way to start a sentence."

"I'm just not into the whole bad boy image. I want someone stable and that's not you."

"Well, I hate to break it to you, Reese, but you're stuck with me, for better or for worse."

I got this really crazy feeling in the pit of my stomach and I started to sweat. "What do you mean?"

"I mean that I know the assassin that's after you. Look, I can't get him to just back off because I ask for a favor, but if you're mine, I know that he won't take you from me."

"What do you mean, *if I'm yours?*"

He grinned at me and leaned forward on the table. "Why do you think we're headed to Vegas?"

I shook my head, sure that he was lying to me or something. This was so wrong. How could this be possible? "No, that's not...why would he not kill me just because I'm your wife?"

"Because he's an old friend. Now, he won't turn his head for just anything, but he would never kill my wife."

"So...so, we'll just pretend we're engaged or put a wedding band on my hand. He'll never have to know."

He shook his head sadly. "Look, I've been friends with this guy for a long time. He knows that I'm not already married. And the fact that he's tracking us...I can almost guarantee that he's going to show up in Vegas and he's going to want to witness us getting married. It's the only way he'll do this favor for me."

I was sweating really bad, so bad that I was pretty sure that all the people in the restaurant could smell me. I felt sick to my stomach and spots were dancing in front of my eyes. This couldn't be happening to me. This wasn't my life.

"Reese, Reese!" He grabbed my hand and squeezed, but it was too late. I was passing out in the booth.

Chapter Twenty-Three

CRAIG

I carried Reese to the truck and got our orders to go. The last thing I needed was to stick around and cause a scene. I told the waitress that she was pregnant and I had to get her to the hospital. She looked a little concerned, but didn't say anything when I took off out the door. I had been driving down the road now for about fifteen minutes and she still hadn't woken up.

Okay, I might have gone a little overboard with the whole assassin/marriage thing. It was true, though. Knight was coming to Vegas to play the assassin and he would also be the witness to our marriage. Once we were officially husband and wife, I would suggest that Reese move in with me to help keep her safe and we would really get to know each other. It wouldn't take much for her to see the man I really am.

Reese woke up a little later, but she didn't say a word. Her silence wasn't very good for our impending nuptials, but I wasn't worried. Every woman loved the idea of getting married and having the wedding dress. Sure, it wouldn't be her dream wedding since we would most likely be married by Elvis, but she would be happy when it was all finalized.

It was too late to reach Vegas today. We still had a good four hours to go, and I didn't really want my blushing bride to have bags under her eyes and be worn out. I wanted her to look radiant on our wedding day. I pulled into another motel and helped Reese out of the truck. This time, she didn't suggest we take a shower together or even talk to me. She just laid down in the bed and closed her eyes. When I knew she was out, I went out to the truck and pulled out a burner phone, dialing Alec's number.

"Who is this?" he snapped. Well, it was late at night, so I couldn't be too pissed at his surly attitude.

"Craig."

"What the fuck, man? Cap's pissed that you went MIA."

"He can suck my dick. I'm getting married tomorrow," I said happily.

"Craig, what are you doing? Does she even want to get married?"

"Of course, she does. She might not realize it yet, but once we're married, she's gonna be so happy that this all happened."

I heard him sigh heavily and I knew what he was thinking. Why did everyone always see this type of stuff as a bad thing? Marriages were supposed to be happy.

"Look, you know that I love you like a brother, but you can't force the girl to marry you."

"I'm not forcing her."

"Then why is she agreeing to this?"

"Okay, I may have convinced Knight to come out here and play an assassin that's after her."

"What?" he yelled.

"It's not like it sounds." I rubbed my hand across my face. I was fucking tired. "I needed more time with her and she would have wanted to head home when she found out there wasn't any danger."

"So, you kidnapped her for real?"

"I didn't kidnap her. I told her that an assassin was after her."

"Do you know how fucking ridiculous that sounds? Why would an assassin be after a kindergarten teacher?"

"That's what she wanted to know."

"And what did you tell her?"

"I said...I said I didn't know yet." I hurried on before he could yell at me some more. "But she agreed to come with me. It's not like I forced her."

"Craig, it's the same fucking thing. She thinks that you're the only one that can save her. Of course she's choosing you."

"But I am the only one that can save her."

"From an imaginary assassin," he shouted. "Look, just bring her home before she finds out what's going on and decides to call the police on you."

"She's not gonna find out what's going on. We'll get married-"

"Yeah, and why are you getting married?"

"I told her the assassin was an old friend and he would never kill my wife."

He was silent for a minute. That was a good thing. Maybe he was thinking it over and seeing the logic. "You're such a fucking dumbass." Maybe not. "Why would she want to stay married to a man that was friends with an assassin?"

I opened my mouth to respond with something brilliant, but realized he was right. That would make my life more dangerous, and it was very clear she didn't like danger. "Shit."

"Yeah, no shit, you asshole. You'd have been better off knocking her out and having a fake wedding where you just paid off the minister to wed you."

"I could still-"

"No, you can't. Just bring her home and tell her it was all a lie. At least she won't kill you."

"I can't do that. We were meant to be together."

"Dude, you were meant to end up in a jail cell. This is not going to end well."

"I just have to give her the time to come to the same conclusion," I said, hoping like hell he could just understand. "Listen, I need you to do a favor for me."

"I'm not bringing a tarp out there."

"A tarp- no, I just need you to call the school and tell them that you're her boyfriend and she's really sick and will be out for a few days."

"That's all you're giving her for your honeymoon?"

"You're right. Make it the whole week."

"Wait! I was-"

I hung up and returned to the room whistling. I was feeling really good about this plan. How could it go wrong?

There was no point in hiding where we were anymore. Cap would be on his way out here in no time, I was sure of it. But that didn't mean he was going to interrupt the festivities. By the time he got his ass out here, I would be married and on my honeymoon.

"Reese, let's hit the shops. I want to get you the prettiest dress and we'll get your hair done up and everything."

"What does it matter?" she snapped. "None of this is real."

"It's real to me. I love you and I'm not just doing this to save your life."

"Well, I am. I don't want the whole spa package and everything."

"You have to. If Knight finds out that you don't really want to marry me, you're as good as dead."

She paled and stumbled back a step, but I was there to catch her. I would always be there to catch her. I sort of felt like an ass for scaring her, but not enough to tell her the truth.

"Come on. It's not that bad. I'm a good guy. I have a decent job, and I'll always provide for you."

"It's just...this isn't how I saw it going. I was supposed to fall in love with my husband and my family would be involved. It was supposed to be magical."

"It still can be," I said quietly, lifting her chin with my finger. I brushed my lips against hers, wishing that she would just see how good this was and get on board. "I love you, and I promise, this will be all you ever wanted."

I pulled the ring box from my jacket pocket and opened it for her to see. It was my grandmother's ring. Back when I had planned to just kidnap her for the weekend, I brought it with in the hopes of making her see how right this was. I was planning to propose to her then. This worked just as well.

She looked at my grandmother's ring and shook her head. "This isn't right. You should be giving this to the woman you're going to spend the rest of your life with."

"I am," I said sincerely. She didn't realize how much I loved her. I was going to great lengths to keep her, and I didn't regret it for one minute. This woman was worth ten of any other woman out there.

I took the ring out of the box and slid it on her finger. It was stunning. Simple, but elegant, just like Reese. I smiled at her and kissed her again. She didn't pull away this time, so I deepened the kiss and pulled her against my body. She wrapped her arms around my waist and it felt like fireworks going off inside. Finally, she was mine. I just had to have that little piece of paper to make it legal.

We went out shopping, and I bought anything for Reese that she wanted. She actually smiled when she found the dress she was going to wear. I got myself a tux and then called a chapel for us to get married in. Everything was going perfect.

We pulled up to the chapel, and just as expected, Knight was waiting for us, dressed all in black with visible guns for added effect. Reese stopped in her tracks and gripped onto my hand like she was about to keel over. I smirked slightly and sent Knight a tight nod.

"Knight."

"What are you doing here?" he growled at me.

"I'm getting married."

"To her?"

I looked to Reese and gave her an encouraging smile. I needed her to play her part, or at least, I needed her to think that. God, this was the best plan ever.

"Knight, whatever you're here for, you need to walk away."

"Why?"

"Because she's going to be my wife. You remember what I did for you. Now, I'm asking you, whatever your job is, walk away."

"I can't do that," he said, raising his gun at Reese. I quickly stepped in front of him and raised a hand in front of my body, gesturing for him to take it easy. I didn't want Reese to have a totally fucked up wedding day. But of course, Knight had other plans.

"I can't go back without blood."

"Knight–"

I didn't get another word in before he shot me in the fucking shoulder. I quickly pulled my gun and aimed it at him, ready to fire if necessary. What the fuck was he doing? Reese was trembling behind me and I could feel her fingers digging into my suit coat. The woman was terrified. Not that I liked that, but it did work wonders for my plan.

"Just wanted to be sure you were actually willing to die for this woman," he smirked. "Let's do this then."

He gestured for us to move toward the chapel doors. I took Reese's hand in mine and led her forward.

"Are you okay?" she whispered.

"I'm fine. We just need to do this and then he'll leave."

She nodded and swiped at her face. I grinned at Knight over Reese's head. The man was brilliant. Yeah, I wouldn't be able to fuck her quite as hard as I wanted tonight, but the sympathy vote just went sky high.

I checked in with the woman behind the desk and the wedding music started. Knight walked behind us down the aisle and kept glaring at Reese. Her fingers were wrapped so tightly around mine that I was sure I would lose the circulation. I swallowed hard when it hit me. My moment was finally here. Reese was all mine and it was forever. She would never leave my side now.

I said my vows to Reese and I meant every fucking word. I couldn't say if the same was true for her, but she said it and, well, no take backs and all. When the chaplin declared us husband and wife, I pulled her into my arms and kissed her hard, flinching only when her hands came up to my shoulders and squeezed. She immediately pulled back, flinching in horror.

"I'm so sorry."

"Don't worry about it. It's nothing I can't handle."

We turned to leave and Knight glared at us again. The man was brilliant at being an asshole. I would have to send him a fruit basket or something for helping me out. We walked back down the aisle, signed the papers, and then we were headed out the door. Knight signaled that he needed to talk to me, so I walked Reese to the car and motioned for her to get inside.

"Are you sure this is okay?" She looked to Knight, worry in her eyes. "I don't like you talking with him."

"Don't worry, baby. He won't hurt me."

"He already shot you!"

"Trust me. I'm good."

She nodded, not believing it at all, and sank down into the seat. I closed the door behind her and walked back over to Knight with a grin on my face.

"That was perfect. Great idea, shooting me."

"That was for Cap. He said that you deserved it."

"Well, you can thank him. That's gonna win me major points with the little woman tonight."

"Just don't stay too long. You have a lot of explaining to do when you get back to Pennsylvania. Cap is gonna have your ass."

"Yeah, well, I plan to have Reese wrapped around my finger by then."

He snorted and turned to leave. "You know," he stopped and looked back at me. "I can't blame you for doing things this way. Can't say I would have done it differently, but you know she's gonna find out. You'd better think about how you're gonna keep her when she does."

Chapter Twenty-Four

REESE

I didn't relax until we were back in the hotel room. I was so scared that Knight, my assassin, was going to come back and shoot me, despite his relationship with Craig. Which I still wasn't quite sure how they were friends or why, but that was something to worry about later. As soon as Craig had the door to the suite open, I was dragging him over to the bed and pushing him down none too gently.

"I can't believe he shot you!"

"I'm fine-"

"You are not! You have blood dripping down your shoulder. Your shirt is no longer white. That does *not* signal in any way that you're okay."

"Reese," he said, taking my hand and forcing me to look into his gorgeous eyes. "I'm fine. I promise, this is not the worst I've dealt with."

I sniffled, hating that I was crying over my stalker, or kidnapper. Savior? Whatever, I was crying over him and this was all his fault anyway. I swiped at my nose and nodded.

"I just don't like that you're injured. And I really don't like that this isn't the worst you've had. Promise me this isn't going to be our life."

His eyes practically lit up and then I realized my mistake. I had pretty much just accepted that I would be attached to this crazy man for the rest of my life. I couldn't give him false hope though. This wouldn't last. I would somehow figure out why an assassin was after me, I'd send Craig to take him out, and then I'd go back to living my life. Easy peasy.

Except, a small part of me wondered what it would be like to stay married to Craig. I liked him. A lot more than I wanted to admit. He was sexy and charming in his own stalkerish sort of way. I knew that he would protect me no matter what, which never seemed like something I would even consider as a positive when dating someone. But with Craig, it was nice, even though I was creeped out. I liked the idea of a man worrying about me. And the sex...that was something that I would have a hard time moving on from. How was I supposed to ever sleep with another man again after knowing what it was like to have Craig inside me? Maybe this wouldn't be so bad. Maybe I just needed to accept that Craig was now my husband and I would have phenomenal sex for the rest of my life.

A knock at the door pulled me out of my thoughts. Craig tried to sit up, but one stern look from me and he laid back down. I wasn't an idiot. I looked through the peephole first and was surprised to see a beautiful woman on the other side. Was she here for Craig? Was this some kind of twisted joke on me? He'd better not think that I was into threesomes. There was no way that was happening. Especially on my wedding night.

I picked up the gun that Craig had set on the table just inside the door. I had no clue what I was doing, but the threat of a gun was better than nothing, right? I flung the door open and aimed the gun at the woman. She raised her eyebrows at me and chuckled slightly.

"I'm Kate. I'm here to take care of Craig. Gunshot wound?"

"Oh." I lowered the gun and stepped back. "How did you know?"

"Because my husband shot him."

"Wait–" I grabbed her by the arm and narrowed my eyes at her. "How do I know you're not here to give him a lethal injection or something?"

She smiled at me and walked past me to Craig. "I like her.

Although, I have to say, you and Knight have way more in common than I ever thought possible."

"Yeah, well, you can thank him for me."

"You want her to thank the man that was going to kill me?" I shrieked.

I didn't get an answer though, because Kate was pulling off Craig's shirt and then started cleaning it. I was starting to feel woozy. I wasn't used to all this stuff, blood and bullets. Was that going to be a sign that we hung over our kitchen doorway? It was clever, that was for sure.

"What's going on in that head of yours?" Craig asked me. Kate was already stitching him up and I had to look away. I started pacing around the suite. I was nauseous and feeling lightheaded. I should probably sit down, but I didn't think I could keep from looking at Craig's wound if I didn't distract myself.

"Reese, calm down," Craig said in a stern voice. "I'm fine."

I snorted and bit at my nail, a bad habit I had when I was nervous. "I just can't believe that you got shot. I can't believe that I was there! And I married you! We're *not* a normal couple. You know, I was just thinking about our own little motto. Blood and bullets." I laughed maniacally, throwing my head back as I lost all sense of reason. "That's the sign that'll hang above our door. Not *Welcome to our Mess* or *Doorbell Broken. Yell Ding Dong really loud!*"

I looked over at him, still laughing my ass off as Kate continued to stitch him up. Craig was looking at me like he was really worried. And he should be.

"We're *those* people now!"

"Um..." Craig squinted like he was trying to either figure me out or look for a really tiny bug. I looked down at my shirt, just to be sure there wasn't a bug on me. "Who exactly are *those* people?"

"You know, the crazy neighbors that have more shotguns than toys for their kids."

"You want to have kids?" Craig asked curiously.

"That wasn't the point of my statement."

He nodded. "Well, I wouldn't worry about it. I'm more of a handgun man. I like rifles too, but shotguns really aren't my style."

"This is insane," I muttered to myself as I continued to pace. "I need Brooke." I stopped pacing and turned to him. "Give me your phone."

"What phone?"

"Don't pull that shit with me. I know you have a phone on you."

He sighed and pulled one out of his pocket. I quickly dialed Brook's number and took deep breaths until she answered.

"Brooke! I married my stalker."

"The Wolf? No way, that's so cool!"

"Cool? That is most definitely not cool. I'm sitting in our suite while he gets patched up from a gunshot wound he received from an assassin that was after me! And the assassin's wife is patching him up!"

"Wow. Sounds like you're really living it up."

"I'm not living it up. I'm trying to stay alive with a man that-"

"Yeah, yeah. I got it. You married your stalker, but you like him, right? Did you sleep with him yet?"

I looked over at Craig, who was grinning at me. It was like he could hear our conversation.

"Yes," I whispered.

"Ha! I knew you would! Was it good? Was he worth it? How big is he?"

"Would you stop? I'm not talking about it with you. Don't you understand what's going on here?"

"Yeah, you're finally living your life."

"No," I practically shouted. "I'm on the run for my life. I'm supposed to be back at school, teaching kids and developing their young minds, but instead, I'm in Vegas and I just got married by an Elvis impersonator!"

"That is so cool. I'm so envious of you."

"Are you even listening to me? I married my stalker!"

"Yeah, I totally hear you, babe. But listen, this is a good thing. I mean, he's hot. He has a good job. And if he gets killed, I'm sure his insurance is kickass. You'll be set for life."

I stood there in stunned silence for a moment. "Who are you?" I shouted.

"Listen, I know this is all a little bit of a mind-fuck for you, but look on the bright side, you're on your honeymoon and you can fuck this really hot guy all you want because he's your husband. Just go with the flow and enjoy it. Hell, I would do the same fucking thing if I were you. Besides, I've already heard through the grapevine that you've called off sick for the week. You're good to go."

"How did you hear that? I didn't call off."

"Oh, well, I talked to that guy that works with the Wolf, Alec. He's totally cool and I'm really pissed that he's already taken. Did you know how many hotties your guy works with?"

"Brooke, just stop. Why were you talking to Alec?"

"Well, he needed to know who to call to get you time off work and so he tracked me down. I went out with him and his girlfriend to dinner. They are so cool. They said they would take me shooting, which I am definitely on board with."

"How is this my life? I've been kidnapped and you're making friends with my kidnapper's friends. Do you know how insane that is?"

"Oh, hey, I'm gonna go because Florrie is calling and she said she would teach me how to kill a guy with one hand. So cool, right?"

She hung up before I could answer and I was so baffled that I just sank to the floor and stared at the wall. My life was falling apart. Strangely, it didn't seem like the worst thing in the world.

After freaking out about my freak out, I finally dragged myself off the floor and went to see Craig. Apparently, sometime during my melt-down, Kate had slipped out the door.

"So, is it okay if I sit with you?" I asked.

"Of course. Babe, we're married. You can always sit with me, my little Reese's Pieces."

I sat down on the very edge of the bed and looked over at his hot, naked chest. He had gotten rid of the bloody shirt and Kate had patched him up. He looked pretty normal. In fact, he didn't even look like he was in pain.

"So..."

"Yeah?"

"Um...so I was thinking that...that we're married."

"Yep, I was there."

"So, are we really doing this thing?"

His eyes lit up with amusement and he bit back a grin. The stupid man was laughing at me. "If by being married, then I would say yes. If you're referring to watching the movie that's playing, I'm not really into it."

I turned to see that a movie was playing on the tv. It was a shoot 'em up movie, not really my thing at all. I grimaced and he laughed.

"The marriage thing," I clarified.

"I already told you that I love you. In fact, I've been telling you that for at least a week now."

"So, you want to stay married?"

He leaned forward, grabbing me around the neck and pulling me in so I was just an inch from his face. "Babe, I'm in this for the long haul. I look forward to having you on your back as much as possible. I want little Reese's Pieces running around as soon as you're ready. I want the dog in the backyard and friends coming over for barbecues. I want it all with you."

I melted right there, just a big puddle on the bed. I had never heard such sweet talk in all my life and I didn't want it to stop anytime soon. If this was what he was offering, stalker or not, I was in deep. I sighed and pressed my lips to his. His tongue slid easily into my mouth and I slowly pressed him back into the bed.

"You may have me on my back for the rest of the time, but for tonight, you're staying on your back. You're injured and I'm going to take care of you."

His eyes turned dark and he grasped my hips, dragging me closer to him. My vagina slid over his erection and I gasped. Good Lord, that man was built like a tanker truck. His hands slid up the skirt of my dress. My head dropped back when he slid his finger inside me.

"Oh God."

"Babe, it'll always be this good between us."

"It better be. I didn't marry my stalker just to have mediocre sex."

He rolled me over, hovering over me in such a way that I felt my body just naturally mold to his. It was like my body knew better than my head that this man was all I needed.

"I have you now, Reese. You're mine and I'm never letting you go."

He slammed his lips down on mine and somewhere in the back of my brain, a warning bell went off, telling me that not only was that a promise, it was a threat.

Chapter Twenty-Five

CRAIG

Alec and Florrie were waiting for us at the airport the following Saturday. Reese had her hand tucked into mine and she hadn't quit smiling since the night of our wedding. Sure, there were times that I saw her questioning herself, but it was never for long. She seemed to just accept that we were married now and I wasn't going anywhere. We had gone shopping on the strip when we were in Vegas. I wore simple clothes, but my baby was going to have anything she wanted. Surprisingly, I had to force her to even try clothes on. And the only ones we bought were the ones she needed to make it through the week. That's how I knew it was love.

"Reese, you remember Alec, my team leader, and Florrie, my teammate and Alec's girlfriend."

I grinned as I introduced them and I was happy that Reese seemed pleased to meet them.

"It's nice to see you again," Alec nodded.

"Come on," Florrie said, slipping her arm into Reese's. "You can tell me all about how Craig tricked you into marrying him."

I growled at Florrie, but she just winked and headed to the car with my woman.

"Well, do you think a week was enough to convince her that she's really yours for the long haul?"

"She hasn't stopped smiling since we got married. I'd say we're in the clear."

"You'd better hope so."

"Why?"

"Because Cap called a meeting. The new building is finally ready to be moved into and he wants all hands on deck."

"When's the meeting?"

Alec grinned and slung his arm around my shoulder. "As soon as we pull up to the building."

"What?" I said in panic. "We have to drop Reese off at home first."

He shook his head. "Nope. Cap's orders are that I bring you and the little missus right to Reed Security. I think he has a welcome home present for you."

"Shit. Tell me Knight's not there."

"Sorry, man. I told you this would backfire on you."

The fucker was laughing at me. I punched him in the shoulder and headed for the truck. I had to figure out what to say to Reese before this all blew up in my face.

The problem was, there was nothing I could say to Reese to make this okay in her eyes. I could see that she was happy being married to me. Things were going great. The sex was amazing and our chemistry was off the charts. I had been hoping to have a few weeks at home with her, hide her away before any of this came out. Now, that was all going to blow up in my face and I had no idea how any of this was gonna play out.

"Where are we going?" she asked as we headed down the road for Reed Security.

"We have to stop by my work before we head home."

"Oh. Is everything okay?"

I gave her my most reassuring smile. "Of course. We're opening our new building and Cap wants us all there for a meeting."

"And I have to be there?"

"He probably just wants to meet you and congratulate us."

"Oh. That's nice of him."

We pulled through the gates and Reese's eyes grew wide at the sight of the machine guns that were mounted just inside the gates. Yeah, it was a little intimidating.

"That's the new building?"

"Yeah."

"It's huge. Why does it need to be so big?"

"Well, we have a state of the art training center in there, a gun range, locker rooms, offices, conference rooms...plus a whole bunch of other shit for security purposes."

"What does that mean?"

"Well," I glanced at Florrie and saw the huge grin that split her face. Yeah, this wasn't gonna go over too well with Reese. "We got in a little trouble a little over a year ago with a trafficking ring."

"Oh. What were they trafficking? Drugs?"

I shook my head slightly. "Humans."

Her face paled and she clenched her fists tight. "What kind of trouble?"

"We were trying to find a little girl and got mixed up with them unknowingly. I mean, we knew what we were dealing with, but weren't aware that we were already acquainted with them. They infiltrated our building and we had a bit of a war."

"A war," she said slowly. "Like a shoot out and people injured and dangerous stuff."

"Yeah, it wasn't really a good time for us. But we went on the run and we just came back not too long before we met. Now we're up and running again and it's all good."

She nodded, but I could tell she didn't believe me. Yeah, this was all a little too much for her. Hopefully, the girls would sway her in my direction. We stepped out and went through the very lengthy process of getting into the old training center, where everyone was currently working out of, we made our way to the conference room. My heart was beating out of control. I just couldn't stand the thought of losing Reese after I just got her.

I knocked on Cap's door and glared at him, hoping he got the message to keep his yap shut. He stood and grinned, walking around the desk to shake Reese's hand.

"Hi, I'm Sebastian. The owner of Reed Security."

"It's nice to meet you. I'm Reese."

He grinned and crossed his arms over his chest. "Oh yeah, trust me, we've all heard about you."

She flushed bright red and ducked her head.

"So, I guess you're wondering why you're here." He grinned and motioned for us to follow him over to the table where papers were laid out. "I don't know if Craig has told you yet, but we're expanding our property to better protect ourselves. Which means that a lot of the families are buying up properties around the building. I just so happened to get ahold of one of the properties that I'd been looking at for the past few months."

"Not the asylum," I interjected.

"No. This is a property that an old woman lived on. She wasn't ready to move out of the house because she had recently lost her husband. They had lived there for forty years together. Anyway, I finally convinced her to sell. It's a five acre property. It has a great yard and plenty of room for when you two decide to have kids."

I glanced at Reese, hoping she wasn't freaking out. She wasn't, but she also wasn't looking like this was the best idea in the world.

"So, you want us to take over this property? How much is it?"

"You can afford it," Cap grinned. "Besides, it'll make Reese feel safer to be surrounded by all of us. Especially after an assassin was after her."

I ground my teeth together, but before I could speak, Reese stepped in.

"He took care of that."

"Really?" Cap raised his eyebrows in surprise. "And how did you get an assassin off your back in such a short amount of time?"

"Oh, he knew the guy. Knight? Yeah, his wife even came in and cleaned Craig up after our wedding. You know, because Knight shot him."

Cap nodded, pulling his lips between his teeth to keep from smiling. "Wow, that's some really nice assassin. What was his name again?"

"Knight," I bit out. He was gonna screw me over. I knew it.

"And why did he shoot you?"

"To make sure I was serious about Reese."

I could see Reese looking between the two of us out of the corner of my eye. She was wondering what the hell was going on.

"So, did you find out why you had an assassin after you?" Cap asked Reese.

"Um...I don't know. He never actually said."

"That's kind of strange, don't you think? That he would come after you and then just give up without any reason other than knowing Craig?"

"Um...I guess. Do you think he's still after me?"

"Oh, shoot, I couldn't say," Cap grinned, waving her off. "I'm sure it's fine." He walked back around his desk and pulled out some paperwork. "Here's everything you need for buying out the property. If that's what you want. Oh, and Hud wanted to see you before you leave. Oh, here he is!"

I turned around slowly when I heard Reese gasp. Knight was standing in the doorway, dressed in his typical black and glaring at me in his usual fashion.

"Craig, what's going on? Why is this man here? I thought you took care of all this?"

"Reese, this is Hudson Knight," I sighed. "Knight, you remember Reese."

He nodded and stepped forward slowly. Reese tucked herself into me and Cap chuckled.

"Maybe it's about time you tell Reese what's really going on," Cap said.

Reese spun around and looked at me in confusion. "What's going on?"

"Knight isn't an assassin. Well, not anymore. He was doing me a favor."

"And what was that?" she asked warily.

"I needed to convince you that you had to stay with me. Okay, here's what happened, and I swear to God, I'm not lying. I was going to kidnap you so that we could spend some quality time together, but when I got to your house, someone had already snatched you. Cap and Knight were with me-"

"You were going to let him kidnap me?" she accused Cap. "You're his boss and you thought this was okay?"

"Well, see, I owed him..." he said dumbly.

"Yeah, not such a good idea to tell her, was it, dumbass?" I spat at Cap.

"So, what happened? Who really kidnapped me?"

"Your grandmother hired someone to do it to keep you away from me."

She threw her hands up in the air in frustration. "Is there anyone that isn't trying to run my life?"

"Listen, I really did protect you and get you back from that kidnapper. I got you to the hotel and it wasn't until I went out to get that shit for your feet that I found out what was really happening."

"That was a week ago!"

I winced at her fury. "Yeah, but see, I love you, and I needed to show you how good it could be. And look! This last week has been great. I love you. I know you're starting to love me. We're married now, so it's all good!"

Her mouth opened and shut as she tried to come up with something to say in response. I just grinned at her, thinking my adorable charm would be enough. But then she turned around like she was going to leave. I grabbed her arm to stop her and she swung around, slugging me right in the nose. I gushed blood, jumping back in surprise.

"Holy shit. You just punched me."

"You manipulated me! You made me think that I needed to marry you to stay safe!"

Chapter Twenty-Six

REESE

I couldn't believe this. I was such an idiot. How had I not seen that my stalker was manipulating me? And here he was, pretending like everything he did was perfectly logical.

"I just don't understand why you thought that this would work. You had to know that I would find out!"

"Well, I was kind of hoping it would take you longer to figure it out."

I shook my head in shock. "So, you were hoping I was stupid enough to fall for it and let you keep manipulating me."

"Well, I don't want to say yes because you'd probably be pissed at me. Am I right?"

I screamed in frustration and turned to go, but then I saw my would be assassin just hanging out and smirking at my situation. "What are you laughing at? Do you get your kicks out of making an ass out of other people?" He didn't say anything, but his eyes turned cold and hard. "Are you a mute now? Got nothing to say?"

"Uh, Reese, I wouldn't poke the bear," Craig said from behind me.

"Why?" I asked, spinning around. "He's a coward. He shot you for some unknown reason and you seem perfectly fine with it. He let me marry you even though he knew that it was under duress. Hell, he was the reason I felt I had to marry you. And now he just stands here like an idiot, laughing at the fact that you pulled one over on me!"

I heard a growl from behind me, but I was too worked up to care. I glared at Knight, crossing my arms over my chest. "Oh, now you have something to say? I feel bad for your wife. She's seems like such a nice person and instead she married a wannabe assassin!"

"Uh..." Craig snatched me by the arm and pulled me behind him. "Obviously, she doesn't know what she's talking about."

"You don't speak for me. Especially not after the crap you pulled."

"You're stupid if you walk away," Knight grumbled.

"Excuse me?"

"You think you want some pussy that respects you and doesn't lay a hand on you until you've been on so many dates? You want a man that acts like a gentleman all the time and fumbled over himself for you?"

"Yeah, that would be nice."

Knight smirked and shook his head at me. "I'm not one to get involved in other people's relationships, but Craig chased you because he wants you more than anything in this world. He tricked you to make you his because he knows something you're too stupid to figure out."

"Watch it," Craig growled from behind me. He wrapped his arm around my waist, his palm resting on my stomach possessively. I felt him tug me just a little closer to him, like he was worried for my safety. I had to admit, I did like that Craig was so possessive of me. It gave me tingles deep inside in places that I didn't want to admit were turning red hot. I couldn't want him still, not after he tricked me into marrying him.

I stepped away from Craig as Knight walked out of the room. This was all insane. I just needed space, and Brooke. Surely she would see logic now that all the facts were out. And just like that, Brooke stepped off the elevator and came skipping over to the conference room.

"Hey, it's Wolf! I hear you're my brother-in-law now!"

"Wolf?" Cap asked.

"You know, because he chased her down, sniffing her scent until he captured her and took her back to his lair."

I rolled my eyes as Brooke waggled her eyebrows and started jumping around excitedly. "So, you must be the bossman. I'm Brooke, Reese's twin."

"I thought you were her friend?" Craig asked in confusion.

"Well, yeah, but we're soul sisters. I encouraged her to give in to her animal instincts and take a chance on you. I knew you were the one that could loosen this girl up."

"I don't have animal instincts," I muttered. "And I didn't take a chance on Craig. I was tricked into marrying him."

"Nice," Brooke grinned. "I like your style."

"You know, it would be nice if for once you were on my side," I grumbled.

"I am. Totally. It just so happens that Craig is the man for you. I mean, he installed that security system for you. He saved you from being kidnapped-"

"And then he kidnapped me!"

"And he married you. Girl, you should be down on your knees, thanking the Lord for bringing this man into your life."

I threw up my hands in annoyance, pissed when I saw Craig's smirk. "I don't believe this. For just once, I thought you would hear 'liar and manipulation', and you would be on my side. But you're taking his!"

"That's because he's your shoelace."

"What?" I turned to Craig, thinking he might understand, and apparently, he did. He was nodding along, like she was the most sane person in the world.

"Yeah, I ran into this really hot guy on the way up. Sinner. And let me tell you, he was definitely sinful. Anyway, we had this really intense conversation about you. That's when he informed me that you were Craig's shoelace. Something about a shoe needing a lace to stay on your foot. I don't know, but it totally made sense when he said it."

I looked to Cap, thinking that he might help me out, but he just shrugged. "It's true."

I glared at him and turned back to Craig. "Don't call me."

I stormed out of Reed Security, or I would have if there weren't so many damn security measures. Some guy named Tony Tacos had to help me get out of the damn building. I swear, these guys were worse than my grandmother.

The sunlight poured into my bedroom, reminding me that I only had one day before I got back to work. I didn't know what I was going to tell people, but I would definitely take my rings off so no one saw the evidence of my stupidity. I yawned and stretched, screaming when I touched a hard body next to me. Leaping from the bed and screaming my head off, I shoved myself back against the wall, my heart hammering out of control.

"Hey, babe." Craig grinned and stretched, his muscles pulling and rippling in front of me. God, he was so sexy. "What are you doing over there? Come back to bed. We don't have to do anything today. It's Sunday."

"What are you doing here?"

"Uh," he chuckled and motioned me over. "I'm your husband. I came home to sleep with my wife. Though, I was hoping you wouldn't be passed out in bed and I could get another taste of that sweet pussy."

My body clenched in desire, but I shoved it aside so I could be angry. "We're only married because you tricked me. You need to leave. I didn't invite you into my home."

He leaned on his elbow, his face crinkling in confusion in his still sleepy state. He rubbed at his eyes and smiled. "Honey, this is my home now. I even brought a suitcase with me. I'll need at least one drawer and a little closet space, but don't worry, I'm very tidy."

"That's great. Go to your own home and be tidy!"

"Well, that'll be hard to do since I put my house on the market this morning. I have an agent...did you meet Isa? Well, anyway, she's Gabe's wife and she's a realtor. She went over to the house this morning with some of the ladies to get it ready to be put on the market. She's great at staging homes. I'm pretty excited."

"Why would you do that? I already told you that I don't want to be married to you."

"Did you? I'm not sure you actually said the words. I think you told me that I had lied to you and manipulated you, which is all true, but it all worked out in the end."

I squeezed my head in frustration. I could literally pull my brains out right now and be happier than having to continue with this ludicrous conversation for one more minute.

"Look, we're heading back to Vegas today. We're getting this marriage annulled immediately before you find some other way to get your way."

"Hmmm. I don't think that's really a great idea. I mean, we wouldn't be able to get a flight out there and be back for school tomorrow. And since you called off for a whole week, I don't think the principal would be too happy with you taking another sick day."

"*I* didn't call off work! Someone else did it for me!"

"Yeah, but you didn't exactly use every last resource to get back home."

"I can't believe this. You have an answer for everything, don't you?"

He grinned and climbed out of the bed. Completely naked. Holy hell. I swallowed hard and pretended to cover my eyes as I ogled the man's huge sausage dangling between his thighs. It just wasn't fair.

"Don't worry, my little Reese's Pieces, if you really don't like being married to me, I'll let you have your divorce. Of course, it wouldn't look very good as a kindergarten teacher to run off to Vegas and get married one weekend, then get a divorce. Let's give it a year."

"Are you nuts?" I shouted as I stood and marched over to him. "I'm not waiting a year for a divorce. I want one now!"

"Reese, I'm looking out for your best interests here. I don't want you to lose a job you love over something that can easily be put off for a more appropriate time. And that's if you even decide that you don't want me."

"I don't care if I lose my job right now. I'll march down to the school and tell them exactly what you did to me. Whose side do you think they'll be on then?"

He thought about it for a moment. "You know what? If you really think that's necessary, go ahead. I'm gonna hop in the shower," he said, gesturing to the bathroom. "Anything I need to know about the shower?"

"Yeah, you have to turn on the cold water to get hot water," I sniped.

He grinned and waggled his finger at me. "I see what you're doing, but it won't work, pixie."

"Stop calling me nicknames! My name is just Reese."

He stalked over to me and tugged me to him, pressing his lips to mine. I melted a little, but refused to let him see it. "You're anything but *just Reese.*"

He smacked my ass as he walked into the bathroom and shut the door. I'd find a way to get rid of him if it killed me.

Chapter Twenty-Seven

CRAIG

I had a towel slung around my hips and I was just brushing my teeth when Reese called for me. Thinking she had made me breakfast or some really great coffee and I would need a way to thank her, I went downstairs in just my towel. When I got to the bottom of the stairs, Sean was waiting for me.

"What can I do for you?"

"Hey, Craig. Sorry to interrupt your morning, but Reese called me and said that she woke up with you in her house."

"Our house," I grinned.

Sean looked to Reese and then back to me. "Uh, sorry, what?"

"We got married last week."

Sean's eyebrows shot up and he looked to Reese for an explanation. "You want to tell me what's going on?"

"He tricked me into marrying him."

"That's a pretty serious allegation. Did he force you in some way," he said sternly, obviously in cop mode now.

"Not exactly."

"Well, then I'm confused."

"He kidnapped me!"

"No, I saved you from a kidnapper," I corrected.

"You admitted that you were going to kidnap me. Your boss even confirmed it!" Reese yelled at me. She was obviously not taking this whole living together thing very well.

"Sebastian was going to kidnap you?" Sean said in bafflement. "Reese, I've known him a long time and I just don't see him taking part in kidnapping."

"He did it as some kind of payback for Craig. Just ask him!"

"I will, but you're saying they didn't actually kidnap you?"

She pursed her lips, crossing her arms over her chest angrily. "I didn't see who took me."

"And you didn't do it," Sean confirmed.

"I was just outside her house when I saw her getting snatched. Cap and Knight were with me, but they weren't going to do anything. We were just sitting in an SUV."

"Just sitting there," Sean nodded. "Right, and what were you doing?"

"Just watching the house, and it's a good thing I was or she might not be here today."

"Sean, you can't tell me you believe this," Reese spat. "He just admitted he was at my house when I was kidnapped."

"He did, but I'm guessing that if I ask Sebastian, he's going to confirm what happened. Sitting outside your house is not illegal. If he wasn't on your property, legally, he has every right to be there. Now, if you had filed a restraining order and called the police, I would have been able to do something."

"How would I have called the police? I was too busy being kidnapped!"

Sean sighed and I laughed.

"What?" Reese said angrily. "Why are you laughing?"

"Because you just admitted that you were being kidnapped while he was sitting in his SUV."

"Well...he found out that I wasn't in danger when he got me back and then he told me that an assassin was after me. He even had one of his friends play an assassin and he shot Craig!"

"Knight?" Sean asked. I nodded.

"Did you at any time try to leave, but were restrained?" Sean asked.

"No, but when you're told that an assassin wants you dead, you go with the safest option."

"And how did you end up married?" Sean asked.

"Craig told me that the assassin would back off if we were married."

"And you believed him?" Sean laughed. "Reese, that's the most ridiculous thing I've ever heard."

"I was scared," I shouted.

"But you married him willingly. I'm not sure why you called me here. What exactly do you want me to do?"

"Remove him from my property!"

"It's technically my property too," I interjected. "I paid off the mortgage yesterday."

Her eyes went unbelievably large right in front of me. I wasn't sure if I should get her a bag to breathe in or just back up in case she decided to punch me again. I didn't see what the big deal was. I made life easier for her. She didn't have that huge debt hanging over her head anymore.

"How did you even do that? Don't you have to be on the loan agreement or something?"

I grinned, pretty proud of myself for my accomplishments. "Becky helped me out with that. You are now looking at a partial owner of this home." I winked at her and Sean groaned.

"This may not be the best time to play the charm card," Sean whispered. "I think you're very close to her actually committing murder. And then I would get dragged into this whole thing, and honestly, I'm not sure whose side I would be on."

"Reese," I said with a touch of swagger, "come on, you have to admit that we were meant to be. This past week has been unbelievable, and I'm not just talking about the sex. Who knew you'd be such a hellcat in bed?"

She looked to Sean, her lips spread thin. "Sean, remove him from this house before you have a domestic disturbance to deal with."

"Can you prove that you own half the house?" Sean asked me. I nodded and ran upstairs, grabbing the paperwork that confirmed what I told them. When I showed it to Sean, he just sighed and handed it over to Reese to look at. "I'm sorry, Reese, but this is something you're going to have to deal with in the courts. Craig, I would suggest you remove yourself from the house so that your wife doesn't become a widow a week after you were married."

He turned and walked out the door, leaving me with my beautifully enraged wife. "So, what should we do today?"

She took a deep breath and tried not to look like she wanted to murder me. I appreciated her effort. After all, if we were going to make this marriage work, there had to be some give and take. Mostly on her part.

"Craig, I would really appreciate it if you would leave for the day and give me a chance to get used to all this."

"I appreciate you asking." I stepped toward her and ran my hand down her cheek. "But I'm not going anywhere." I bent over and threw her over my shoulder. She yelled and started punching me in the back, but I just chuckled and walked upstairs. She just needed a good fucking. She was always calmer after I was inside her and she worked out that burning rage inside her. I stepped into our bedroom and threw her down on the bed.

"Craig! Let me go. Get out of here now!"

"Sorry, my little pixie. There's just so much to do before you go back to school tomorrow." I kissed her hard and ripped her shirt from her body. She gasped, but her nipples perked up. "Most importantly, I have to fuck you." Next were her shorts. I flung the towel off me and pushed inside her. She moaned and clenched around me. It was so fucking good. I started fucking her hard, not giving her a chance to deny me what I wanted.

"Craig," she panted. "We shouldn't...this is wrong. We're getting a divorce."

"Not if I can help it." I threw her legs over my shoulders and grinned. "In case you haven't noticed, we haven't used a condom once."

She opened her mouth to yell at me, but I didn't let her get a word out. My mouth was on hers, taking all the pleasure that I craved. The sting of a harsh slap had me pulling back.

"You asshole! Why would you do that to me?"

My eyes practically rolled back in my head when she started thrusting her body against mine. Her head was saying no, but her body was saying yes. "I know that you're not on birth control, and if I know, then you know. The real question is, why didn't you tell me to stop?"

She didn't say anything, but then again, she probably couldn't since I started flicking her clit and an orgasm was rolling through her body. I came inside her again and then laid down beside her, draping my arm over her chest.

"You're an asshole," she panted.

"Yet you still keep fucking me. I think you like being married to me."

"About as much as I love spiders," she huffed.

I nipped at her shoulder, laughing under my breath. I loved that she kept pushing me away. It made the chase so much more fun.

Chapter Twenty-Eight

REESE

I snuck out of the house before Craig woke up the next morning. I had fucked him all day yesterday, despite protesting every time he took me. It was my own fault. If I really didn't want to sleep with him, he would have listened and backed off, but he knew me better than I thought. It was only six o'clock in the morning and nowhere near time for me to be at school, but there was no way I could stay in the house with him for one more minute. I had to figure out a way to get him away from me. The man was insane.

With no other choice, I went to Reed Security and practically did a happy dance when someone answered. I didn't know who it was and I didn't care. I just needed all this to stop. I drove to the training center where I had been last time and smiled when I saw Sebastian waiting at the front door.

"Reese, what can I help you with?"

"I need you to change all the locks on my house and make sure that Craig can't get in ever again."

His eyebrows raised in surprise. "I thought that he owned half the house now. Becky said she helped him with the paperwork. I assumed that you were on board with it."

"I didn't know a thing about it. Sebastian, that house is mine. I bought it with my own hard earned money and I won't let him come in and take over. We're not even supposed to be married. And then he snuck into my house last night and slept with me. He doesn't even use condoms! I'm probably pregnant right now. I can't take any more of this."

He blew out a breath and nodded. "Okay, I'll take care of it, but Reese, I hope you know that no matter what, you're part of the Reed Security family. You may not like that you're married to him, but you have a huge family now. I hope you'll take the time to get to know us before you decide to jump ship."

"I appreciate that, but I never asked for this. For whatever insane reason, Craig has fixated on me and he's like a bad date that just keeps going and going."

"I'm sorry to hear that," he said sadly. "You know, Craig's one of the most loyal people I know. And I had that blow up in my face recently. I didn't trust him when I should have, but he stuck around and managed to forgive me. There aren't many people that would do that when their trust is broken. Anyway, I think you're making a big mistake, but I'll do as you ask."

"Thank you."

I got back in my car and pulled out of the driveway. Sebastian made me feel like a terrible person. I knew that Craig was a good man. That was never in question for me. I could see it the same as everyone else. But that didn't mean that I had to deal with him for the rest of my life, did it? I drove to my grandmother's house. The two of us had some things to discuss.

"Reese?" She looked at me in confusion. Her hair was still in rollers and she was in her ratty, old robe. I shoved past her and headed for the kitchen for some of her famous tea. When I sat down at the table, she sighed and put the kettle on. "Is this about last Friday?"

"Why would you have me kidnapped?"

"I was just trying to protect you. That man that's stalking you needs to be stopped."

"That man that is stalking me is now married to me."

"What?"

"Yeah, see, he rescued me from your kidnapper and then he tricked me into thinking I was still in danger and that marrying him would keep me safe. So, we got married in Vegas and I only found out two days ago that it was all a farce. But none of that would have happened if you hadn't interfered."

"Oh dear. Well, I can't say that I'm sorry. I thought I was keeping you safe and that's all I care about. You can just go get the marriage annulled."

"Yeah, I would, but I was gone for an entire week from school. It's not like I have a buttload of sick days that I can use. In fact, I'm pretty sure if I took any more sick days, the school would fire me, considering that I wasn't really sick and ran off and got married!"

She pursed her lips and stood as the kettle went off. She poured us some tea and sat down, not saying a word. It was like she wasn't the least bit sorry. I was just about to tell her that when she spoke.

"Well, I say you take advantage of the match you've made."

"What? You just said you had me kidnapped to get me away from him. Now you think I should stick around?"

"Well, that company has a lot of power in this community. This could be a good thing. I'll have to talk to Elsie about it, but now that two of us have a connection to them, I'm sure this could benefit our little group greatly."

"Are you serious right now? Does everyone want to use my marriage as some sort of bargaining tool?"

"I didn't tell you to run off and get married. In fact, I tried to get you away from him. Now you'll just have to live with the consequences."

"Do you think it's possible," I said slowly, "that anyone in this town is going to be on my side in all this?"

"I'd like to say yes, dear, but I'm afraid that's just not true."

It was a rough day at school. As soon as I got there, the principal caught me and dragged me into his office. Not literally, but it sure felt like it. Explaining to him what happened didn't really do me any favors. I had the feeling that now he thought me to be an idiot, which wasn't really helpful since I was hoping to look like a competent teacher. Of course, I got a subdued congratulations and I was sent on my way with a firm warning not to ever call off like that again to do something so frivolous. I had to agree. I shouldn't have assumed that Craig was right about the assassin thing.

I got home and was pleasantly surprised to see that the locks had been changed and Sebastian had left me a spare set of keys hidden in the backyard. The text he sent was kind, but I could tell from the tone that he wasn't happy about any of this. For the first time since I got home from Vegas, I felt like my house was officially mine again.

A loud bang on the front door had me cringing. It was most likely Craig, wondering why his key didn't work. But relief washed over me when I saw Brooke standing at my door.

"What's going on? My key doesn't work?"

I stepped aside for her to enter and shut the door after her. "I had the locks changed. I woke up yesterday morning to Craig in my bed. It freaked me the fuck out."

"Why? A sexy man in your bed and you're scared? Girl, you need your head examined."

"So, you'd be totally fine with your stalker showing up in your house, in your bed?"

"If I had a stalker like the Wolf? Hell yeah. I'd be climbing on top of him and riding him until his dick was broken."

I rolled my eyes and went into the kitchen for wine. "You know what your problem is? You don't have any sense of danger. A man could literally drug you at a club and take you home to have his way with you, and you would thank him for the fuck at then end of the night."

She shrugged. "What can I say, I like sex and I'm not going to apologize for it. By the way, I think it's really shitty that you're married to someone at Reed Security and you've done nothing to introduce me to the sexy single men."

"Right, because this is about you."

"Hey, it should be. I'm the single one here, in need of a good fucking before my vagina shrivels up and decides to die of boredom."

"I thought you met someone a few weeks ago. What ever happened with him?"

"Eh. He was okay. I mean, he's stable and he's not terrible looking."

"Are you kidding? His facebook photo looked great."

"Yeah, but it was photoshopped. See, that's what's wrong with dating nowadays. Nobody can be themselves until way further into the relationship than is normal. I don't want to date someone for three months before I find out that he likes missionary in bed."

"Is there something wrong with missionary?"

"Only if you don't want to be totally boring. I want a man that's gonna take me from behind and ram his cock into me. Or throw me up against the wall and fuck me so hard that the pictures rattle off the walls."

"Maybe the problem is that you're not vocal enough."

"How's that?"

"Well, you said the guy you met is okay. Maybe you just need to be this version of yourself. Tell him what you want and make him give it to you, or you walk away."

"You may be onto something there." She slapped her hands down on the counter and hopped off the stool. "Okay, I'm off to go wrangle a man to fuck hard."

"What, now?"

"Why wait? Hey, I need to get laid before my pussy turns to sand."

"And how would that happen exactly?"

"It would dry up," she said slowly, even though I was just teasing her. "Geez, I think you need the Wolf in your life. You really need to loosen up. Hey, maybe he can take you out on a job with him."

I walked with her to the front door, rolling my eyes at her crazy ideas. "Sure, I'll just be the person that hands him the guns and reloads his weapons."

"It could work. Hey, it might be a really good bonding experience for you. You know, kind of like those couples that do really stupid shit like go paint together. You could be them, except cooler."

"I'll keep that in mind."

"Alright, let me know how it goes."

I shut the door and not more than two minutes later had my stalker banging on the door.

"Hey! Reese, I think there's something wrong with the lock. I can't get in!"

"That's because I had the locks changed," I shouted back.

"Why would you do that?"

"So you couldn't get back in."

It was silent and I grinned to myself. That should teach him to come into my house uninvited.

"I'll just wait out here."

"For what?"

"For you to open the door."

"I'm not opening the door, so you can just leave."

"Can't do that."

"Why not?" I screamed in frustration. "Don't you know when you're not wanted?"

Okay, that might have been a little mean, but since when did I need to be nice to my stalker?

"You may not want me, but I'm your husband and I'm not leaving. I won't leave you unprotected."

I unlocked the door and opened it. Craig was standing on the porch with a big grin on his face that just pissed me off. He had to learn that he couldn't just barge into my life and take over.

"I don't need any protection, but if you don't feel you can leave, then you'll just have to sleep on the porch."

I slammed and locked the door and went upstairs to get ready for bed.

Chapter Twenty-Nine

CRAIG

I walked into Reed Security, a little sore from my night of sleeping on the porch. I couldn't believe that she locked me out of our house, but worse than that, she actually thought I would leave her unprotected.

"What's wrong with you?" Alec asked.

I plopped down in the chair in the conference room with a sigh. Florrie was smirking at me, like she already knew what had happened.

"Reese locked me out of the house."

Florrie snorted, but covered it with a sad face. "What'd you do?"

"I don't know. I went home last night and she had the locks changed. I don't know what I have to do to get through to that woman. It's like she doesn't believe that I really love her."

"You know, it could be that she's pissed that you manipulated her," Florrie suggested.

"I didn't manipulate her. I did what I knew was right so that we could end up together."

"So, what's your plan now that she's kicked you out of the house?"

"I don't know. But you know what bothers me?" Alec shook his head. "How did she get the locks changed? I mean, we have sensors that we set up with the door. And I added in a few...extra features. Not just anyone could have changed the locks."

Florrie sighed and kicked her feet up on the table. "Cap did it."

"What? How do you know?"

"Because I was walking by his office when he was telling Cazzo's team to change the locks."

I stared at her in complete shock. I didn't understand it. I thought Cap was on my side. "But...that doesn't make any sense. Why wouldn't he at least talk to me about it?" She shrugged, like it was no big fucking deal. "Why didn't you tell me?"

"Because you're psychotic and you're stalking the poor woman."

"Hey, I helped you out big time when you were fucking it all up with Alec. You should be on my side."

"I'm trying to be. I really am, but what do you want me to do when you practically forced the girl to marry you?"

"I expect you to help me plan out how to get her to stay. I went to fucking therapy for the two of you. I had a counselor suggest that we have a threesome!"

"That was totally on you," Florrie shot back. "Alec and I were completely aware of what she was suggesting and why. You were just too dense to catch on."

"Well, that's besides the point. I was there for the two of you, supporting you through all your fights and fucking up against the wall when I was right in the other fucking room. The least you could do is stand up for me to my wife. Tell her that I'm not a psycho. Convince her that she really does love me. Help her to see reason, that me kidnapping her was necessary, and that tricking her into marrying me was completely logical when she couldn't see what we had."

"Is that all?"

"That should do it," I said with a nod. "Now, if you'll excuse me, I'm going to find someone that can give me some actual advice on how to win my woman back."

"Who would that be?" Alec asked.

"Who else? The ladies."

I headed to the common areas of the panic room where most of the women worked from during the day for their sex shop. It was weird. They had a store that they were setting up, but most of their orders were online or sex parties. I wasn't quite sure how any of these men allowed their women to do this shit. It was fucking dangerous if you asked me. Especially since their first sale had turned out to be with drug dealers.

I was pleased to see that I had a good crowd today. "Good morning, ladies!"

"Hey," they responded, but went back to their work. I could see that I needed to give them a little more. Claire was my most obvious choice. She was the romantic at heart. And then there was Kate. She had been seduced by Knight, my hero at the moment for his mad stalking skills. Maggie was hit or miss. Either she would freak Reese out with her ability to turn any situation into something violent, or it would show her how awesome it could be. Raegan was maybe my best bet since she was more like Reese than the others.

"I'm telling you," Kate said to Maggie, "that diagram isn't medically accurate."

"I'm not asking for it to be medically accurate. I want it to appeal to my target audience. I just need it to be close enough."

"Sure," Kate mocked. "It's close enough, as in, the dildo will go into the woman's vagina, but her spleen might get in the way."

"Uh, not to interrupt, but I have a problem, and I think you ladies can help me."

"I wouldn't be so sure about that," Maggie snorted. "The last man that came here looking for help ended up saying he wanted to eat his woman's pussy like a starving, mangy dog. Does that sound like advice that you want?"

"Look, you all know about Reese, and I'm sure you've heard about my latest predicament."

"You got her to marry you," Raegan nodded. "I suppose it wasn't the stupidest thing you could have done. Though, I probably would have gone for knocking her up. That's more binding."

"I'm already on it," I grinned. "But I need someway to keep her now. See, she locked me out of our house last night."

"You already have a house with her?" Kate asked.

"I bought her house. See, she originally bought it, but the mortgage was ridiculous and I didn't want her paying that much. So I had Becky help me out and I paid it off."

"And you thought that was a good idea?" Maggie said slowly.

"Well, it made her life easier."

"You need something romantic," Claire sighed dreamily.

"Yeah, romance hasn't worked out so well for me."

"Hmmm, well, then you should save her," Claire said with a nod.

"Already did that. I saved her from the kidnappers that interfered with my kidnapping. She didn't seem to appreciate it too much, well, not when she found out what really happened."

"That's because it wasn't dangerous enough." Claire's eyes lit up as she jumped up and started pacing the room. "You need something so dangerous that she can feel it in her bones. Am I right, ladies?"

"Personally, I like Jackson more now that we're not running for our lives, but I will admit that it was a lot of fun to be on the run together. I mean, besides the really terrifying parts. However, I did get to shoot a gun and that was pretty cool, now that I look back on it."

"Right!" Maggie exclaimed. "You need some kind of Bonnie and Clyde situation. Something that she can get involved in. Make it fun for her too. If you save her, but don't let her have any fun, then of course she's not going to love it."

"Good, right. So, what are we talking here?"

"Well, Knight and I were in a building that blew up. Maybe you could do something interactive like that. It was scary as hell, but then he came back from the dead. I'd have to say, that made me want him all the more. Maybe you should fake your death. Nothing makes a woman realize her true feelings like the man she loves coming back from the dead."

"Good. Good. What else? How do I get to me being killed off and then rising from the dead to stay with her for all eternity?"

"Well, you definitely don't want her to be the one to kill you, so watch what you say," Maggie said thoughtfully. "And I wouldn't recommend knocking her up. Some may like that aspect of how two lovers come together, but personally, I find it to be too cliché. And since you already used Knight as an assassin, I think you need a real life situation. Something that's a bit more believable."

"Okay, so we should probably rule out human trafficking. I'm guessing that would be going overboard for her."

"Right, and we've already done that here. I'm pretty sure Morgan would not suggest that."

I nodded in agreement. Man, this evil planning was hard.

"Okay," Claire said excitedly, "you guys are gonna think that I'm totally crazy, but have you ever seen the movie *Megamind?*"

"No."

"Okay, so Megamind is evil and he needs a good guy to fight. So, he creates a hero. Only, the hero that he chooses is terrible. So, Titan, the hero, flies with Roxanne Richie to the top of the Metro City tower and drops her from the sky and then flies down to save her." Claire's eyes were so big and she was so excited, jumping around and clapping her hands. "Perfect, right?"

"Right." I cleared my throat uncomfortably as I had to break a few minor hard truths to her. "Well, first of all, while I think that idea has great potential, there are a few minor problems. First, I can't fly, so catching her would be a problem. Second, I think dropping her off a tower would probably make me seem like the villain. So, saving her would kind of make me look like an ass."

"Sure," Claire nodded. "I suppose that makes sense."

"But she has a point," Kate said thoughtfully. "You need that level of danger. So, what you really need is to be like Megamind, but instead create a villain. Maybe get her kidnapped again, only this time, the stakes have to be higher. You have to prove how far you're willing to go to save her."

"But I've already done that. I mean, Knight shot me already."

Kate raised an eyebrow, pursing her lips like I was an idiot. "Knight was stabbed in the chest, fighting off a man that would kill me just to get back at Knight. I highly doubt that your tiny, insignificant gunshot wound ranks as high as Knight's wound. Besides, Knight technically died in that fire. I was without him for a whole year. See, you haven't made her miss you yet."

I nodded. "Right, well, I have a job I'm going out on. Maybe I'll get shot or maimed on the job. That should gain me some sympathy while I work out a plan."

"And hey," Maggie said as I turned to go. "You know, I'm always available with guns and grenades if you need me."

"Thanks. I appreciate that, but I don't think blowing me up will help with getting her back."

"It's an option," she grinned.

Yeah, Maggie definitely wasn't the one to go to. With my luck, Maggie would teach Reese how to kill me.

Chapter Thirty

REESE

I slid my key into the door, but it wouldn't turn. I tried again, but still nothing. What the fuck? I went around to the side door and tried that, but nothing happened. Going around to the back door, I got the same results. I peered in through the window and my jaw dropped. Holy shit. I'd been burglarized. Pulling out my phone, I called Sean. I felt kind of bad. He had to deal with me more than he probably wanted, and he didn't even know me that well.

"Reese," he said, almost as if he expected trouble.

"Sean, I'm so sorry to call, but my house has been broken into. All my stuff is gone," I rambled.

"Whoa, slow down, Reese. What do you mean? Did you get a call from Reed Security?"

"Why?"

"Because the alarm would have gone off if you were burglarized."

"No, I didn't. But I'm standing outside my house and there is nothing inside. It's all gone."

"Hold on, I'll be right there. Don't go inside."

"I couldn't if I wanted to. My key doesn't work."

He was silent for a moment. "I'll be right there."

I paced around my house, trying to find out how they broke in and managed to steal all my stuff. And why did they change the locks? This was crazy. But then I stopped in my tracks. Sean was right. Reed Security would have notified me of a break-in. And who would have been able to replace my locks like that? It had to be someone at Reed Security. But then, why was all my stuff missing?

Sean pulled into my driveway and winced as he talked to someone on the phone. "Yeah...uh-huh...okay, I'll let her know."

He hung up and sighed.

"What? Just tell me, did Reed Security change the locks again?"

"Uh...I think you need to talk to your husband."

"Why?"

"Well, see, the thing is that...well, you don't live here anymore."

"What?" I screeched. "What do you mean *I don't live here anymore?* Sean, this is my house. I bought it with my own fucking money!"

"Look, I really don't want to be involved in this."

"Too bad! You know something and you're going to tell me right now!"

"It appears that your house was sold earlier today."

"By who? I didn't authorize that or even put it up on the market. And how did it sell so quickly?"

"Look, you really need to call your husband. I don't know how or why he did it. All I know is that as of this morning, this house belongs to someone else."

I was fuming. I knew my face was red and my whole body was shaking with rage. Who did he think he was? This was my property and I wasn't giving it up without a fight. Besides, how did he even do it?

I stormed down the steps and got in my car, heading for the one place where I was sure to get the answers I needed. On my way, I called Craig. That bastard was going to get my foot up his ass if he kept this shit up.

"Hello, my little pixie-"

"Don't you fucking dare call me cutsy little names right now, Craig. How the fuck did you sell my house without my permission?"

"Now, darling-"

"Don't. I'm not in the mood for your games right now. This goes beyond stalking and kidnapping, or manipulating me into marrying you. You sold my house! The house that I saved up for and worked my ass off to be able to afford. That meant something to me and you just snatched it out from under me!"

"Well, you locked me out of our house."

"So, your solution was to sell mine? Where am I supposed to live now?"

"At our house."

"You just sold it!"

"No, our house on the Reed Security property, the one Sebastian suggested we buy. I purchased it from Reed Security and all your things have been moved over there."

"How did you even do that? I was at school for eight hours!"

"I hired the best movers there were. I mean, it cost me an arm and a leg, but I wanted it to be a surprise for you. Now, you're all moved in and you didn't even have to do anything."

"And you thought I'd be happy about that?" I shouted.

"Well, yeah. I mean, I thought it over and I think the fastest way for us to move on with our lives is to live together in someplace that is both of ours. Hey, and Maggie said that she would teach you how to shoot. Of course, I would prefer to teach you myself, but I'm out of town."

"Wait, you moved me into a new house and you're not even here?"

"Well, I got sent out on a job. Cap thought it would be best if I wasn't in town when you got the news of your new digs."

"So, you just left me to deal with all this mess?"

"Yeah, but don't worry. I know that you're busy, so I left you Storm's girlfriend's information. Her name is Jessica and she does interior design. Have her do whatever you want. I left my credit card on the kitchen counter for you. Get whatever you need."

"Whatever I need. Just like that."

"Yeah."

I grinned as I pulled into Reed Security. Do whatever I want? I would do that and more. This man would regret fucking with me by the time I was through with him.

Chapter Thirty-One

CRAIG

"I don't understand this job. I mean, this sounds more like a domestic matter than anything," I said, studying the file from the backseat of the SUV.

"It's fucking ridiculous, if you ask me," Alec grumbled. "Who hires someone else to watch out for their teenage daughters?"

"Maybe the man just wants to make sure his daughters are fully protected," Florrie said.

I leaned forward, resting my elbows on her seat. "Since when are you so touchy feely?"

"I'm not. I just think that the man is obviously worried about this neighbor and wants the best protection he can get."

Alec snorted, "Are you kidding? All he needs is a gun and good aim. Hell, even bad aim would work. He just needs to scare away those punk kids."

"I would have to agree with you. A man that can't protect his own home doesn't deserve a family."

"That is such a sexist thing to say." Florrie spun around in her seat and shot a glare at me. "I suppose a woman would be just fine hiring a security company to protect her family."

"Of course," I said indignantly. "Not you, but any normal woman can and should. See, women are fragile creatures that need strong men, like us, to watch over them and keep them safe."

"Not all women are fragile. In fact, if you bothered to look close enough, you would see that we are all pretty much capable of taking care of ourselves. Take Reese, for example. She was doing just fine in her life until you came along and fucked it all up for her."

"Hey, I saved her from a kidnapper."

"Yeah, and that kidnapper was hired by her grandmother to get her away from you."

"Okay, but what about those guys in the coffee shop? She could have seriously been injured."

"Sean showed up right after you disarmed them," Alec pointed out.

"Yeah, but they still had to be disarmed," I grumbled. "Tell me, what would have happened to her if I hadn't been there?"

"I imagine that she would have done what every other person in a hostage situation does," Florrie said. "She would have kept her head down until the police came and got her out."

"You just don't get it," I said, sitting back in my seat. "You couldn't possibly understand what us men go through when our women are in danger."

"Right," she snorted. "I have no idea what it's like to see someone I love about to die."

"And you felt helpless," I added, "like any normal woman would."

"Craig, I would suggest that you shut your mouth before she shuts it for you."

I sat back in my seat for the rest of the drive and ignored the two of them talking. It was pissing me off, hearing their romantic bullshit when I was currently separated from my wife. Not that you could really consider the shit they were saying romantic.

We pulled down the driveway of an old farm, about thirty minutes from Reed Security. The farm was rundown with a tractor broken down in tall weeds. There was a wagon that only had two tires left on it and was covered in what looked like bird shit. There were old appliances all over the yard and a few broken down cars sitting in the yard.

"This place is a dump," Alec said. "I'm surprised they even called us. Hell, just walking through this place is likely to severely injure someone."

"Maybe Cap understood them wrong. Maybe they just want sensors installed," I said hopefully.

"This place is creepier than the asylum," Florrie said with a shudder. "Let's get this job done and get the fuck out of here."

We pulled up to the house that barely looked like it was still standing and got out of the SUV.

"This place looks like something out of *Deliverance*," I muttered.

A loud barking had me spinning around with my gun drawn. There was a dog behind a chain link fence that looked like it would eat anyone that came close. I jumped when a hand clamped down on my shoulder.

"What's the matter? Scared of a dog?" Alec grinned.

"That thing's not a dog. It's a fucking beast."

"Come on." Florrie walked up the steps to the house and knocked on the door. When no one answered, she knocked harder and the door creaked open. Alec and I walked up behind her, ready to check out whatever was going on. She shoved the door open the rest of the way and drew her gun.

"Why are you pulling your gun? Someone just left the door open," I said quietly.

"When doors are left open, that usually means that something's happened," she said, stepping further into the house. I didn't believe her, but I cleared the first floor along with both of them. It was silent.

"I told you nothing was going on. They probably went to town and now we're trespassing."

"We had an appointment," Alec pointed out.

"And you've never been late for an appointment?"

"It is weird though," Florrie said, looking to the stairs. "Why would they ask to meet with us and say it's urgent, but then not be home?"

"This assignment blows," I grumbled. "I was talking with the ladies, and they all said that I needed something bad to happen. You know, to make Reese realize how much she loves me. Now I've got nothing. Nobody's here and there's no fucking danger in sight."

Alec pointed his weapon at my leg.

"What are you doing?"

He fired his gun, lodging a bullet in the muscle of my leg. "Son of a bitch! What the fuck did you do that for?"

"Well, you were fucking bitching about needing something bad to happen so you could get your woman back. Now something bad has happened," he shrugged. "You can go home and tell her that you were shot. Problem solved."

"I was already fucking shot. I needed something more serious than a shot to the fucking leg!"

He pulled the trigger again, hitting me in the foot that belonged to the same fucking leg he shot.

"Ow! Would you stop fucking shooting me?" I bent over, clamping one hand over my leg and the other over my foot, which did absolutely nothing to help me.

"What? You said you needed something more serious. You have two bullet wounds now. Tell me how that's not more serious?"

"Who's there?"

We all spun, pointing our guns at the stairs where the male voice came from.

Alec took one step forward, his gun drawn toward the stairs. "It's Reed Security. We've come to install the security sensors, sir."

"What security sensors? Get the hell off my property before I pump you full of lead!"

"Sir, we're here because of a call we received from Mrs. Allan."

"You're a liar!"

A gunshot sounded, hitting the wall behind us. I scrambled to find a hiding place so I didn't get shot for a third time in the span of five minutes. Florrie and Alec were across the room from me, hiding behind furniture.

"Sir, put your weapon down or we'll be forced to take you down," Alec threatened.

"You could try," the old man shouted.

More gunshots sounded, but now bullets were flying above us like we were in the middle of a fucking war. I looked around the room in confusion. The bullets were flying from all different directions.

"What the fuck! Stop shooting!" This was getting fucking old, and my leg was throbbing from Alec shooting me.

"You're with them Carter boys, ain't ya?"

"Sir, we're here to help," Alec shouted. "Now put down your fucking gun down before I'm forced to take it from you!"

"You mother fuckin' hicks think you can come in here and take my property? I'll see every last one of you dead!"

"Can we get the fuck out of here?" I shouted to Alec. "This guy obviously doesn't want our help."

"Sir, we're leaving–"

"Damn right you are!"

He fired again, tearing up his own house with bullets, but he wasn't the only one firing, which was going to make getting out difficult.

"Head for the front door," Alec shouted.

"Sure, I'll just hobble along and catch up with you," I shouted back as I started making my way over to them, ducking behind furniture as I went.

"You wouldn't have to fucking hobble if you hadn't decided that you needed to be fucking shot."

"I didn't tell you to shoot me," I shot back. "I was hoping to get injured on the job. You know, maybe a leap off a tall building that broke my leg or taking a bullet for one of my teammates in a hail of gunfire."

"Just fucking stand up. I'm sure Mr. Allan would be happy to shoot you to get you to shut the fuck up."

"Are you two gonna keep arguing or can we leave before one of us is shot again?"

"One of us?" I asked Florrie. "I'm the only one with fucking bullet holes in my body!"

"Stop your whining," Florrie spat at me. "If Reese heard you right now, she'd dump your ass. Now move!"

I shot out from behind the chair I was hiding behind and ran as best I could for the door. I was just running through it when another bullet hit me in the ass.

"What the fuck? Stop fucking shooting me!"

"That wasn't me, asshole."

Alec hauled me up, stretching the wound in my ass as he started half running, half carrying me across the yard.

"Whose fucking brilliant idea was it for us to come out here?" Florrie yelled.

"Talk to Cap," Alec said.

"Can't we just shoot him?" Florrie asked as she put her shoulder under my other arm to help support me.

"Hey, I'm your teammate. How about a little fucking sympathy before you decide to take me out behind the barn and shoot me?"

"Not you, the old man."

"Thank God," I grimaced. "I thought you'd finally had enough of me."

"Don't be ridiculous," she said. "If I really didn't want to see you anymore, I'd just send you back to that therapist."

My leg was really starting to fucking hurt, but we were almost to the SUV. That is, until someone started shooting it up and we had to duck behind some bushes.

"What the fuck are we gonna do?" Florrie asked. "He shot up the SUV!"

"It's not just him. There are too many bullets flying. He's got help," Alec said, pulling out a second gun.

"Alec, we need to take them out before they take us out!" Florrie shouted.

"They're civilians."

"Yeah, but so are the drug dealers and gang members that we've shot up," I added.

"But we had a reason. This guy is just defending his property. We were in his fucking house and he didn't want us there," Alec reminded us. "Okay, we need to head to the neighbor's property over there." He pointed off in the distance where I could just barely see light shining from someone's house. It was getting dark now, so at least it would be harder to see us. "Florrie, wrap up his leg, and well, all his wounds the best you can. I'm gonna see if I can tell how many people are shooting at us."

He took off across the yard to get a better angle of sight on the house. Florrie tore at her shirt, wrapping the torn piece around my thigh. I hissed in pain when she yanked it tight.

"What? Does it hurt?"

"Of course it fucking hurts."

"Then maybe you shouldn't have wished to get injured on the job," she snapped.

"It's not my fault. I would never have thought up that stupid shit. It's those damn wives. They were telling me all this shit about glory and making Reese see that she loves me. They used fucking Knight as an example. It's not like I can back down from that challenge. All those women are obsessed with Knight because he's dark and scary. A guy has to be able to compete, you know."

She took my boot off and wrapped another scrap of her shirt around my foot. "You know, having a contest to see who can get hurt the worst is so juvenile. You'd have been better off just leaving her alone. Then she would have come to you."

"What do you mean?"

She sighed and shoved me onto my stomach, then yanked my pants down to look at my ass.

"Hey!"

"Oh, stop being a baby. I'm just seeing how bad it is."

"Just pull my fucking pants back up before your man friend comes back and puts a bullet in my head."

She yanked my pants back up and rolled me back over. I winced at the sting of the bullet.

"You've chased that woman for weeks and then you convinced her to marry you. She wanted out and you kept chasing her. Your best bet is to fucking walk away and leave her alone. Then she'll start to wonder if she shouldn't have pushed you away, because she'll start to realize what you had was really fucking good. Didn't you pay attention at all to my relationship with Alec?"

"What about our relationship?" Alec said as he sat down beside me.

"I was just telling him how you won me back."

"Excuse me? I didn't win you back. I had you fucking crawling back to me."

"Really? You want to do this now?" Florrie snapped.

"Hey, if we die here, I will not go down in the books as the man that had to *win you back*. I have too much fucking pride for that."

"Oh, well I'm so sorry that I almost damaged your sensitive male pride. I thought our relationship had evolved into something, oh, I don't know...mature? I thought we were past the bickering over useless crap."

"We never bickered over useless crap. It was always over your inability to commit. Now that that's out of the way, I'm sure there's a bunch of other shit we can argue about."

"Well, at least I-"

"Hey!" I looked at the two of them, wondering if Cap was going to send us back to therapy. I didn't think I could handle any more sessions with Dr. Sunshine. Or any more dreams that might come out of them. "Can we please focus on the task at hand? We can pick this shit up when we get somewhere that bullets aren't flying and I'm not about to fucking bleed out!"

They both glared at each other and nodded in agreement.

"And when we get back to Reed Security, neither of you better say a fucking word about Alec shooting me. If anyone asks, I was shot by a pack of wild hillbillies."

Alec snorted, but stopped when I shot him a death glare.

"There are four from what I can see."

"Four what?" I asked Alec.

He rolled his eyes. "Shooters. In the house. You know, the reason we're here? Anyway, I think it's dark enough that if we crawl to the edge of the bushes, we should be able to make a break for the barn and get there before they see us."

"What about this dipshit?" Florrie asked.

"Hey-"

"I'll have to carry him. There's no way he'll make the distance without giving us away."

"I think I can-"

"I'll cover you," Florrie nodded. "Don't wait for me. I'll make sure you have enough cover to haul his sorry ass out of here."

"You know-"

"Don't get shot," Alec said sternly, but Florrie growled at him.

"What? Just because we're officially together and I said that I would ease up doesn't mean I won't fucking remind you to be careful. I expect your ass at home tonight in my bed."

"Trust me, after saving your ass and this idiot's ass, I'll still be able to make it home in one piece," she snarked.

"Hey! Can you please stop talking like I'm not here?"

Alec grinned. "We meant you to hear every word of that."

He hauled me up and threw me over his shoulder in one swift move. My stomach lurched from the impact with his shoulder.

"Hey, I thought we were crawling out of here?" I whispered.

"It's just faster this way. Besides, you're covering half my backside. You're more likely to get shot than me."

"Gee, thanks."

"Hey, anything I can do to help."

Alec took off running, me bouncing painfully on his shoulder. I could feel the blood seeping from the wound in my ass, but there was nothing I could do about it. Right now, we just had to get the fuck out of here. We weren't more than fifty yards away when the shooting started again. I couldn't reach my gun, so I pulled the one from Alec's back and started returning fire.

"Don't get any ideas," he shouted over his shoulder.

"I'm just using your gun, fuckhead. Unless you *wanted* to get shot."

"Just keep your hands to yourself," he bit out.

"Hey, you're the one that has your hands on my ass."

"I'm holding you in place, asshole."

I pushed off his back so I could talk to him better. My stomach was killing me. "I'm just saying, you were the one that initiated things."

"What are you talking about?"

"In my dream! You shoved your cock...well, it was someplace it shouldn't have been."

He stopped suddenly and threw me to the ground. "What the fuck? You're sick!"

"You were the one that made me go to a fucking counselor with you. You fucked with my head!"

"It was your fucking dream!"

"And I wouldn't have had it if you hadn't dragged me into all your bullshit!"

"Boys!" Florrie yelled as she ran up. "You're both pretty. Now, can we get the fuck out of here or would you like to go tell your story to the man with the gun?"

"Fine, but if he brings up his fucking dream again, I'll shoot him myself."

"You already shot me, asshole."

"Yeah, well, next time I'll make sure that I hit a major organ."

Florrie came over to me and lifted me up. "Hey, what are you doing?" She hoisted me over her shoulder and took off running. "What the fuck? Put me down!"

"I'm getting your ass out of here."

"I can't be carried by a woman."

"Why the fuck not?" she panted. "I'm your teammate."

"Because. What would the guys say? I'll be the laughing stock at work."

"No more than when I tell everyone that Alec shot you because you wanted to win back a woman," she grumbled.

We were just about to the other house when more gunshots sounded, this time from the house we were approaching.

"Why the fuck are they shooting at us?"

"Fuck if I know." Alec shouted. "Over to those trees!"

Alec and Florrie took off toward a large clump of trees that would provide us cover. As for me, I just bumped along for the ride and tried not to lose my lunch. Florrie practically threw me down on the ground when we got into the thick of the trees.

"Geez, I'm fucking wounded over here. You could be a little more gentle!"

"Stop being such a baby," Florrie spat back.

I grumbled and moved back toward a tree to sit more comfortably. Using my good leg, I pushed myself back when suddenly, I was flung into the air and dangling from my good leg.

"This day fucking sucks."

I hobbled into Reed Security, Alec and Florrie propping me up on either side. I was in so much fucking pain, but I refused to show it. As far as Cap and Chance's team knew, I was shot in the line of duty. I had been very unlucky. *Extremely* unlucky.

"You really need to go see Kate," Cap said for the fifteenth time since we headed home.

"No, I don't. Just let Hunter check me out."

"He's not here. You'll have to see Rocco."

"Whatever."

Cap sighed and led the way down to the med room. For some reason, everyone followed, which meant they thought there was a story to dig up. I looked to Alec and hoped he read my eyes, telling him to keep his fucking mouth shut.

"I still don't understand why you didn't just fucking shoot them," Chance said. "They deserved it."

Alec sighed next to me. He was tired of trying to explain his decisions. "Because we were on private property. There were three of us showing up armed, and he was claiming that we weren't supposed to be there. Tell me how the fuck I would explain that to Sean."

"Cap would have gotten you out of it," Jackson said.

"No, I wouldn't have," Cap retorted. "I can't just make shit up so that you guys don't get in trouble. We do have to obey the law, you know."

"Since when?" Gabe asked. "It seems like the last few years, we've been playing pretty fast and loose with the law."

"Yeah, well, that stops now. Alec was right. There was no way to handle that on private property without huge blowback. The company would have been ruined and we're just getting back on our feet."

Cap swung the door open and walked inside where Rocco was waiting. Alec and Florrie flung me on the table not so gently. I gasped in pain, but they fucking laughed at me.

"How the fuck did you get shot three times and Florrie and Alec are okay?" Rocco asked, stepping over to examine my wounds.

"Bad luck."

He took scissors to my pants, shredding them to get to my leg wound. Then he pulled my boot off and the wrap that Florrie had made. He examined both closely and then looked up at me suspiciously. I glanced at Alec, nervous now that he was examining me up close.

"This wound is close range. Very close range. How did he get the drop on you?"

"Uh...it was dark?"

He raised an eyebrow and stood tall, crossing his arms over his chest. I started sweating bullets. I was usually pretty good at lying, but there was something about being surrounded by your teammates and trying to lie to all of them that made me nervous as fuck. I didn't know what to say, how to explain that I had been shot up close without making myself sound like a jackass. So, I blurted out the first thing that came to mind.

"It was Alec."

"What?" Cap said, stepping forward, staring me down. "How the hell did Alec shoot you?" I looked to Alec, but Cap snapped his fingers in my face. "Don't look at him. If your teammate is hurting you in some way, then you need to tell me."

Well, shit. Now that just made me sound like a fucking cry baby. *Oh, my teammate hurt me. Please, Cap. Come and save the day!*

"Uh, it wasn't like that." Crap, I had to talk my way out of this fast. "Uh...see, the thing is...." Think. Think. Think! "It was a..."

Alec was making some motion behind Cap's back, but I was never very good at charades. I squinted to try and make out what he was doing, but then Cap turned around and I blurted out the first thing that came to mine.

"It was a goat!"

Cap turned back to me and stared at me like I was an idiot. Of course, I was. Alec shot me because of a goat?

"See, those hillbilly neighbors were always letting their animals out."

"And?" Cap asked.

"And...one of the goats ran over to us and...it was attacking me."

"Attacking you where?" Rocco asked. "Did it bite you?"

"Uh....yeah."

"Where? I need to see. Animal bites can be dangerous if they're not looked at."

I choked, unable to say anything. How the fuck was I gonna get out of this one. Florrie stepped forward quickly, coming to save the day.

"It bit his dick."

Okay, that was not helpful.

Rocco grimaced, but motioned for me to remove my underwear.

"No. I'm good."

"If a goat bit your dick, you're not good."

"Of course not," I laughed slightly. "Only, Alec scared it off before it could do any real damage."

"I still need to see," Rocco insisted.

"I'll make an appointment with my doctor." I motioned Rocco in closer. "Please, I don't need everyone seeing this."

He nodded and backed off.

"I still don't understand," Cap said. "How did you manage to shoot him three times?"

"I only shot him twice," Alec corrected. "And I couldn't help it. The goat kept moving around."

"You were right the fuck in front of it," Rocco said. "By the look of these gunshot wounds, you were standing right in front of Craig. How the fuck did you miss the goat?"

"Bad shot?" Alec said hesitantly.

"Bad shot. That's all you have to say after you shot your teammate?" Cap growled.

"I couldn't help it. I freaked out," Alec shouted. "The goat was attacking him, biting off his junk. And the whole time, Craig was crying out for his mom, begging me to end his pain. I swear, I could feel the goat biting my own dick." Alec came over to me and gripped my hand in his, winking at me just before he contorted his face in pain. "I swear, Craig. I just wanted it to end. I never meant to hurt you. You have to believe me," he pleaded.

I internally rolled my eyes. There was no way that everyone was believing his little show. It was so out of character for him. He never pleaded to anyone but Florrie, and there's no fucking way he would ever be down on his knees for me.

"It's alright," I croaked out, trying not to swallow my own tongue.

"Well, because of Alec's horrible aim, you're gonna need surgery on that foot," Rocco said.

"Rocco can handle transport with Alec and Florrie." Cap turned to Alec with a menacing glare. "You get to stay with your teammate until he's out of surgery since you had the brilliant idea to shoot him instead of the goat." He waved everyone else toward the door. "Everyone else out."

Cap shooed everyone out of the room, leaving me with my team-mates and Rocco. When the door shut, Rocco turned back to me with a raised eyebrow.

"A goat, huh?"

I looked Rocco dead in the eye and lied. "Scary motherfucker."

I was dead asleep when a noise woke me up. I sat up and listened, but it was silent. It was probably Craig coming back from his job. I laid back down, but a loud bang had me jolting out of bed and grabbing my trusty bat. The same bat that I hit Craig with. I tightened my grip and took a step toward the door. This was ridiculous. I was on Reed Security property. I was supposed to be safe.

A light flicked on in the other room and my breath stalled in my chest. Not knowing what else to do, I called out to the other person.

"Hello? Who's there?"

"It's Alec!"

I sighed and dropped the bat. These guys were going to kill me. I walked into the other room where Alec was loading up a bag.

"What are you doing here? And how did you get in?"

"Uh..." He set down the bag and eyed me warily.

"What's wrong? Did something happen with Craig?"

"Sort of."

"Sort of, as in something bad?"

"Well, it's not too bad. I mean, he was shot three times–" I gasped and took a step back.

"No, no," he rushed on. "He's fine. He's just in surgery right now."

"Surgery?" I squeaked. "Oh my God! How can that not be bad?"

"It's on his foot. I swear, he's fine."

"But you said he was shot three times. How can that be fine?" I said hysterically. I was losing it. How could I be losing it? I should be glad. My stalker was in the hospital. Maybe he would die and I would never be stalked again. I would never see that sexy body or feel his big dick inside me. Oh God, I was so messed up. Was I really wishing my stalker dead? Was I really worried that I wasn't going to have sex with him again?

"I was just going to put a bag together for him. I don't...I don't suppose you want to go with me."

"Where?"

"To the hospital. It would mean a lot to him."

"It would make him more delusional than he already is."

He sighed and stuffed some more things in a bag. "Do you know where his clothes are?"

"Um...yeah. I think they're in the bedroom. I haven't really seen where everything is."

I led him back to the bedroom and went straight for the closet. Sure enough, there were some boxes of clothes that hadn't been unpacked.

"Thanks. I'll just grab his stuff and I'll be out of your hair."

He quickly packed while I went back and forth in my head about going with Alec to the hospital. On the one hand, it was completely ludicrous to even consider going. He was my stalker and it would only add to the idea that we were staying together. On the other hand, I was his wife, whether I liked it or not. I should be there when he needed me. Even if it was only to make sure that he got the treatment that he needed.

Alec walked out of the closet and headed for the front door. I walked behind him, still trying to decide what to do. He opened the door and walked outside. Shit.

"Wait!" He turned and looked at me questioningly. "I'll go with you."

"I'll be waiting in the truck."

"Crap," I grumbled to myself, racing back to my bedroom to throw on some clothes. This was completely idiotic of me. I could end it all now. He could die in the hospital and I would finally be rid of him, but I just couldn't allow myself not to see him one last time. This was my opportunity to show him that his life just wasn't for me.

I ran out to the truck after getting dressed and slammed the door behind me. Alec stared at me for a minute.

"What?"

"Are you sure you want to do this?"

"I don't get it. You were just trying to convince me to come and now you don't want me to?"

"I just don't want him getting hurt. And I have a feeling that you're going to use this to end things."

I buckled my belt and sat back. I wasn't going to answer anything right now.

"So, how did he get shot, anyway?"

Alec cleared his throat and threw the truck in reverse. "Um...goat."

"He got shot by a goat?"

"No, there was a goat and...never mind."

We arrived at the hospital twenty minutes later. Surprisingly, I was actually nervous. Not about seeing Craig, but because he was injured and I was scared to see how he was.

"He's not out of surgery yet." Florrie stood from her seat in the waiting room and was staring at me in shock.

"What? I'm his wife. It would be weird if I wasn't here."

"It's weird anyway you look at it," Florrie mumbled.

We all took our seats and waited. It was irritating. Alec and Florrie were sitting there like they didn't have a care in the world. Like this was all perfectly normal. But the longer I sat there, the more I felt concern and worry. I stood and started to pace the waiting area. How long did surgery take, anyway?

"Reese," Alec said as he stood. "Just sit down. You're wearing a hole in the floor."

I snorted. "Yeah, like that's actually possible. How can you just sit there? I mean, I've known him all of five minutes and I'm going out of my mind here. Aren't you worried?"

"No," Alec said bluntly.

"What do you mean? That's your teammate."

"Yeah, and I also know where I shot him."

"You what?" I screeched.

"I mean, where he was shot. It was an accident. The goat and...it was dark."

"The goat? What are you talking about?"

"Look, the point is, he's not seriously injured. You'll see when he gets out of surgery."

"Right. Sure. I'll just wait calmly and pretend like my husband isn't in there, possibly fighting for his life! Surgery is dangerous. Anything can happen!"

"Careful," Florrie said. "You're starting to sound like you care."

I sat down and didn't say anything the rest of the wait.

"Oh my God!"

I rushed over to the bed and stared down at my husband. God, it was weird saying that. It was strange because he looked perfectly normal. Maybe Alec was right. Maybe it hadn't been serious.

He opened his eyes and a drugged up smile filled his face. "Reese! My beautiful peanut butter cup, how are you?"

"Better than you. How the hell did you get shot?"

I gripped his hand, chastising myself internally. Holding his hand wouldn't lessen his attachment to me. But I'd think about that later.

"I ain't too bad." He motioned me forward and then cupped his hand like he was going to whisper in my ear. "Only one of these bullets is from the bad guy."

"Where are the other ones from?"

He grinned real big. "It's a secret. I can't tell you or you'd know that Alec shot me so that you would want to take care of me and realize how much you love me."

I gasped and shoved Alec. "Tell me you didn't actually do that!"

"Hey, he was going on about getting injured on the job so that he could win you back. But there was no danger, so I provided it for him."

I stared in stunned silence at my injured spouse, then stepped back from him in disbelief. "Why would you do that? Why would he think that would work?"

"Because that's what the ladies told him to do." Alec turned for the door and walked out. I sat on the edge of the bed and wondered what the hell I was going to do.

"Craig, you are the stupidest man I have ever met. Why would you think that getting shot would make me want you?"

"Knight came back from the dead and Kate took him back. Sounded like a good idea to me." He laid back and smiled dazedly at me. "You're so pretty, my little pixie. I'm the luckiest man in the whole fucking world."

Alec walked back in and tossed a donut on the table. "He needs to sit on that."

"Why?"

"Because he was shot in the ass." I glared at him and he held up his hands. "I didn't do it. I just shot him in the leg and the foot. All easily recoverable."

"That's besides the point. Who goes around shooting their friends? You know, the whole lot of you are insane!"

"Not insane, just one hundred percent in love with you," Craig said, then promptly passed out.

"What the hell am I supposed to do? I'm a teacher. I can't be taking care of him."

"He's fine. It's not like you have to watch him. I mean, help him out around the house, but he should be fine during the day. You can swing by on your lunch break, right?"

"No. I don't have enough time to drive home and take care of him. Besides, you're his teammate. You take care of him."

"But, you're his wife."

"Only because he tricked me! I don't actually want to be married to him."

Alec stepped closer and looked down at Craig. "You know, he's a good guy and he's only so protective of you because he loves you. I know he's being a bit insane, but he's a good guy."

"So everyone keeps telling me. But why does that mean that I have to just drop my life and suddenly be with him. I didn't ask to be stalked and I don't want to be married. I have a very set idea of what I want in a husband and he's not it."

"What *do* you want?"

"What?"

"You want a guy that'll walk away when you're in trouble? Or maybe you want someone that only cares about himself. Maybe you need someone that would be afraid to tell you he loves you. Or a guy that can't afford to take care of you. If that's what you want, then you're right. Craig definitely isn't the guy for you, because he's the type of guy that would walk through hell to get to you and make you happy."

He turned and walked to the door, but stopped before leaving. "I'll come get him tomorrow and bring him home."

I stared down at Craig and wondered what the hell I was going to do. I didn't know anything about taking care of someone. Why weren't his teammates taking care of him? Why wasn't Sebastian here? I dropped my head in my hands and sighed. I didn't ask for any of this, but I was stuck right in the middle of it.

I stayed for another hour before I left. I had to call Brooke to come get me since Alec left me at the hospital. I didn't even bother to talk on the way home, and when I walked in the door, I slumped down on the couch and didn't move the rest of the night. I was just too tired to move.

I woke with the feeling of being on fire. I was so fucking hot and I could feel sweat slipping between my breasts. My mouth was dry and my whole body ached. What the hell was wrong with me? I opened my eyes and groaned. I wished that I had my nice, warm bed.

"Shhh. It's okay," Craig murmured. I felt something cool touch my forehead. It felt like heaven. "I'm here and I'll take care of you."

"Hmm?"

"You're burning up. We need to get you to bed."

I groaned and shoved his hand away. It was too bright here and as uncomfortable as I was, it was better than getting up and moving. He shoved his hands under me and that's when my brain came online. He couldn't carry me in the other room. He was shot up. How did he even get here?

"Stop. I can do it," I mumbled. I shoved myself into a sitting position, but that's as far as I made it. My body just didn't want to go any further. "I'll just stay here."

"No, you don't," he said, catching me as I started to lay back down. "Come on. You need to be in bed and you need sleep."

"No, I have school," I said, suddenly remembering that I had no choice but to go to school. The principal would be pissed if I took off more time.

"You're not going anywhere. I'll send the principal a picture if I have to. He's not gonna want you around students like this. Now, stand up or I'm going to carry you."

With his help, I barely got to my feet, but I was leaning on him heavily. I could hear his sharp intake of breath and straightened. He didn't need me leaning on him. But when I tried to push away from him, he pulled me closer. I made it to my room and laid down just as my legs were about to collapse. I shoved my feet under the covers, but Craig only pulled the sheet up over me.

"I want the covers. I'm cold."

"Just a blanket."

I felt the warmth cover me and relaxed back into the bed. "You should lay down," I mumbled.

"I'm fine. Besides, Hunter's coming here this morning to check me out and he can look at you."

"I don't need a doctor."

"I say you do, so you're being seen by one."

"Whatever," I grumbled, rolling over on my side.

Sometime later, I heard Craig talking with someone. I felt so terrible. My head was pounding and the light coming in was way too bright.

"You should be laying down. You're the one that's recovering from surgery."

"She's my wife," Craig said.

"Only because you tricked her. What the hell are you doing, man? She's made it really fucking clear that she doesn't want you, and you're in here taking care of her when you should be taking care of yourself."

"I love her," Craig said fiercely, making me feel it hard in my chest. "I don't care what any of you think. She's sick and I'm going to take care of her."

"She has the flu. It's not like it's serious."

"I don't give a fuck. When you're sick, you want someone around to take care of you. I'm here and I can do that for her."

"Whatever, but she's gonna break your heart. She's only going to tell you so many times before she's gonna get pissed. And then she's gonna do something that will make you want to fall in a river and drown."

"You don't know her. She's not like that. Look, thanks for coming by, but we're fine and I can take care of her and myself."

"Just stay off your leg and don't put pressure on that foot. And don't forget to schedule a checkup with Kate."

I heard the other man walking away and then I felt the bed dip. I didn't open my eyes. I didn't want him to know that I had been listening to his conversation. He had been so open and honest and he probably wouldn't appreciate me listening in. I drifted off again and when I woke up next, Craig was sleeping next to me. I slid from the bed and walked on shaky legs to the bathroom. After peeing and exhausting what little energy I had, I headed for the kitchen to get a glass of water. The nice thing about the movers was that someone put most of the stuff away. Not that it was all where I wanted it, but it would do for now. I sank back in bed and placed the glass on the night-stand. The sun was starting to set outside.

"You feeling better?"

I startled. I hadn't realized that Craig was awake, let alone watching me.

"Um..tired, but not quite so hot anymore."

He placed his hand on my forehead. It was so strange. I'd never met a man that actually stuck around when a woman was sick. Weren't they supposed to go running in the other direction?

"You feel much better. Are you hungry?"

"Not really."

"I'll make you something when you're up to it."

I chewed on my lip as I stared at him. God, he was beautiful. Way more beautiful than any man I had ever seen. If he hadn't been so weird in the coffee shop, I would have gone out with him.

"So, why did you really get shot? Was it on the job or something else?"

He looked at me funny and shook his head. "This old guy shot me in the ass on the job."

"Right, I know that, but the other wounds...are they also from the job?"

He snorted and scoffed at the same time. "Of course they are. I mean, where else would they be from?"

"So, you didn't get yourself shot on purpose so that I would feel obligated to take care of you?"

"What?" He laughed nervously. "Of course not. I'm not that desperate." I raised an eyebrow and he shrugged. "Fine, I may have suggested that it would be the right way to go about getting you back, but I never told him to shoot me. Alec decided to take matters into his own hands."

I laughed lightly, shaking my head. "I can't believe that you thought this would work."

"It's not working? Not even a little?"

"Well, since you ended up taking care of me, I think it backfired on you a little."

"I suppose it did."

"So, you weren't gone very long. How did you manage to get yourself shot?"

"Well, we got called out to install security and protect this man's daughters. But when we got there, the man pulled a gun on us and started firing."

"Was this before or after Alec shot you?"

"After. It wouldn't have made any sense for him to shoot me if I had already been shot."

"Right, because shooting you at all made sense."

He shrugged. "Anyway, we booked it out of there, but then he shot up our SUV. We ran for the neighbors, but then they started shooting at us too. Then I got caught in a booby trap and ended up hanging from a tree."

"No way."

"I'm serious. We had to call in backup."

"You couldn't handle it on your own? I find that hard to believe."

"Well, we tried to find another way out, but we were sort of boxed in. There was a river running behind us, and then the two neighbors' properties were on either side of us. Hell, by the time Cap showed up, there were landmines going off and at least five cows were dead."

"No people?"

"Luckily, no."

"Do you normally get cases that are so odd?"

"Not me personally, but a few of the other guys have had some really weird shit happen to them."

I nodded and sank down into the bed further. I was tired, but oddly enough, I really liked laying here talking with him. He didn't seem quite so strange when we were just talking like friends.

"So, now that we're married and all, maybe you should tell me a few things about yourself. You know, where you're from and that sort of thing."

He grinned and sat up a little in bed. "Well, I already told you that I'm from New York."

"Does your mom still live there?"

"No, she moved to Connecticut to live with her sister."

"Do you get to see her often?"

"I usually see her at Christmas. What about you? I already know you have a crazy grandmother. What about your parents?"

"They live in town. I'm not as close with them as I am my grandmother. I spent a lot of time with her as a kid. My parents weren't really that into parenting. Don't get me wrong, they're good people, but I spent more time with Grandma than them."

"Why did you choose to become a teacher?"

"I don't know," I said with a shrug. "I guess I was always that little girl that dreamed of having a desk and getting to write on the chalkboard. Of course, we don't use chalkboards anymore, so I can't even send students out to bang erasers when they've been bad."

"I banged a lot of erasers as a kid. I was always in trouble."

"No," I said in mock shock. "You? I can't picture it."

His grin sent tingles through my body. Why did I have to be so attracted to this man? "I was always pulling some girls hair or giving wedgies on the playground. My parents got called a lot."

"So, did having a dad as a lawyer help?"

"No, half the time I felt like he was negotiating for me to have a harsher punishment." He shifted to his elbow and stared at me curiously. "So, what's with you and Brooke? You don't really seem like you have that much in common."

"She lived next door to me as a kid. If you can imagine it, she was always picking on me and telling me what to do."

"Actually, I can. She still does that."

"Yeah, she just kind of bulldozes over people, but she has good intentions."

I yawned and Craig pulled the cover up over my chest, tucking me in. "You should get some more sleep. We can't have you missing any more school."

"I don't think I'm going in tomorrow."

"We could just spend the day in bed," he said softly.

My eyes were getting heavier, but for some reason, I fought to stay awake and look at him. "I might like that."

I let my eyes slide shut and then I felt his fingers running through my hair. I loved it when he did that. It struck me right before I fell asleep that I was getting way too comfortable with my stalker.

Chapter Thirty-Three

CRAIG

"Hey! Where's the Wolf?"

I looked up from where I was working in the conference room, filling out papers from the last job, to see Brooke wandering around. I stood with my crutches and hobbled over to her. I had no clue what she was doing here, but she was always causing trouble.

"Brooke?"

She held up her hands and then dropped them in a huff. "Well, you screwed that up, didn't you?"

"What?"

She pointed at my leg. "That! You couldn't have done better than that?"

"I'm confused. What are you talking about?"

She sighed and tossed her giant bag/suitcase on the conference room table. "I'm talking about the fact that you planned to get yourself fucked up on the job and you did a piss poor job of it. I mean, come on. Do I have to do all the work for you?"

"I'm sorry, but you're not doing any of the work for me."

"Oh, puh-lease! I let you into the house the first night. I gave you the keys to her house. If you had informed me that you were going to kidnap her and make her marry you, I would have made sure that she was going along with it willingly."

"Wait, so you really want to help me?"

Her eyes went wide and she held her arms out wide like she was completely baffled by my stupidity. "Yes! Geez, you should see the boring dates she calls men. It's pathetic. You know, one guy actually slobbered on her when he kissed her? He didn't even realize that you don't kiss like that!"

"Okay, so what's your plan?"

"My plan?" She sighed and plopped down in the chair. "Well, I guess we're going to have to come up with one, and not one where you try to kill yourself to get her attention. Honestly, I'm not sure what was running through your head."

"I knew I shouldn't have done that," I grumbled. "It's those damn ladies."

"Yeah, well, I know Reese. You should really take advice from me. Those ladies don't know her like I do. Okay, first thing you need to realize about Reese is that as soon as she sits down and really thinks about the fact that she's married, she's going to decide that she needs to get as far away from you as possible."

"Okay, and when might that happen?"

"Well, since she's feeling better, I would imagine that's happening right now."

"Then I need to get to the house and convince her to be with me."

"No, you need to sit your ass down and listen."

I sat down, and for the first time since I met Reese, I really listened.

"Now, the problem is that she doesn't want to want you. You're not on her prescribed list of acceptable men. You have a dangerous job, you follow her around like a lost puppy, and you don't listen at all to what she wants."

"So, she wants an accountant that doesn't give a shit what she's doing, but hangs on her every word?"

"No, that's just what she thinks she wants. You just have to wait out the storm."

"What storm?"

"Jesus, it's like I'm talking to a man that's never dated a woman before."

"Well, if you want to get technical–"

She held up her hand to stop me. "It doesn't matter. She's going to do everything she can to push you away and hope that you'll end this for her. Then, when that doesn't work, she's going to start finding other men that she thinks are better than you."

"So...what do I do? Do I let her?"

"No! You have to keep stalking her! That's what's going to help you win in the end."

"But you said she doesn't like that."

"Well, no, but when she goes out with all those other idiots, she's going to realize that she actually likes that you stalk her. As a matter of fact, I'm sure she already realizes it, but thinks it's wrong. You just have to give her time to come to her senses."

I nodded and tried to come to grips with the fact that she might try to date someone else, and I was going to have to witness that and even let it happen so that she could realize that I was the one for her.

"There's just one problem."

"What's that?"

"I think I might kill anyone that tries to kiss her."

"Well," she stood and slung her handbag over her shoulder, just barely missing my head, "you're going to have to do something about that. When you know she's going out on a date, you'll just have to have someone with you so that you don't end up in prison. I'm pretty sure that's a line you can't cross."

I slumped back in my chair as she walked out of the room. This was going to be harder than I thought. I was going to have to really steel myself so that I could make it through this. I had no clue what I would be in for when I went home tonight.

"Hey, was that Brooke?" Alec asked as he came into the room.

"Yeah."

"What did she want? Was she trying to give you tips on stalking?" There was something about the way he was grinning that set me on edge. But then Hunter walked into the room and howled.

"What the fuck are you howling for?"

Hunter smirked, "I heard about your new nickname. The Wolf. Sounds scary," he chuckled. "Only problem is, you're more of a puppy dog, following your woman around all the time. Ahooo," he howled again.

"Shut it," I growled.

"No, it's good. I mean, we didn't really have a nickname for you before, but now we have something. Although, I think we should come up with something more fitting. Maybe Oscar or Buddy."

I stood from the table and shoved my crutches under my armpits, heading for the door.

"What? You don't like those?" Hunter asked. "How about Scout... Charlie...Max. Cooper!" I headed down the hall, but he kept hounding me.

"We already have a Cooper," Alec chuckled.

"Right, no Cooper. Uh...Bear...Duke...No! I've got it! Benji!"

I spun around, losing my balance slightly and glared at him. He was still laughing his fucking ass off.

"You can call me Craig."

"Nope," Hunter grinned. "Sorry, but your new nickname is Benji, just like the dog in that movie."

I couldn't pull out my gun and shoot him. Unfortunately. Cap would be pissed if I shot one of our medics. But I could beat the shit out of him, even if it wasn't with my fists. Lighting fast, I swung my crutch, hitting him in the ribs. He bent over in pain.

"What the fuck? I was just teasing."

I swung again, this time hitting him in the back. "Are you gonna call me Benji?"

"Fuck, is it really that big of a deal?"

I swung again, this time hard enough to drop him to the ground.

"Alright, alright. I won't fucking call you Benji."

"Good." I turned and headed for the elevator, punching in my code and doing the scanner. I stepped in and followed the same procedure and smirked as the doors started to close. Hunter was just getting up and he smirked at me.

"See ya later, Benji!"

Fuck. I was never gonna get rid of that nickname.

Chapter Thirty-Four

REESE

I was pacing around the house. I just couldn't shake the feeling that I had made a huge mistake by letting my guard down around Craig the last few days. He had been so sweet though. I mean, I'd never heard of a man that actually took care of a woman when she was sick, and there he was, ready to carry me to bed despite his wounded leg.

I just didn't get it. What did he even see in me? It wasn't that I was a bad catch or anything. But we had completely different lives. He was some crazy security guy and I was a teacher. And no matter how many times I said it in my head, it just didn't make sense. *We* didn't make sense. Somehow, I had to make him see that.

As if on cue, the door opened and he hobbled in, grinning like he did every time he looked at me. It was pathetic really. No man should ever look at a woman the way he looked at me. It was like he could envision me naked whenever he saw me and he was ready to fuck me instantly. And on top of that, it didn't matter what I looked like. Something was seriously wrong with him.

"What?" I snapped.

His smile faltered and he set a bag down on the ground, coming over to me and cupping my cheeks.

"What's wrong, my little Reese's Pieces?"

"You know," I shoved his hands off my face, "I'm not little. I mean, technically, yes, I am. But that doesn't mean you need to point it out all the time. Besides, it sounds perverted."

"How does it sound perverted?"

"Because....it's like calling me a little girl or something. Is that what you want? Some little girl in your bed?"

"What?" He stepped back and shuddered. "That's disgusting."

"Well, that's what it feels like to me. And stop being so damn sweet all the time. I know you're a killer. You don't have to put on an act for me."

"It's not an act. And trust me, I've never been like this for any other woman. It's just you. You're special."

Crap. Why couldn't this man just shut up? I wouldn't be able to walk away if he kept up with this shit. Men were supposed to be rude, disgusting pigs. I was supposed to love the man I married, but secretly want to kill him in his sleep. I just couldn't see me ever wanting to kill Craig. He was too sweet, too pretty. And even his stalking wasn't enough to make me want to take shooting lessons.

"Well....then just pretend that I'm someone else."

He took another step back, leaning heavily on his crutch as he bent over and picked up the bag. "So, does this mean that I should get rid of this?"

"What is it?"

"Soup. I told Jackson's mom that you were sick and she made a pot of chicken noodle soup for you. But hey, if you don't want it, I'll just throw it in the trash."

He made for the kitchen and had the trash can open before I came to my senses.

"Just stop! I'll eat the soup."

"Are you sure? Because, I don't want to force you to eat something that will make you feel better."

I walked over and snatched the bag out of his hand. I opened it on the counter and pulled out a warm tupperware bowl of soup. God, I could already smell just a little bit of it and my mouth was watering. I poured myself a bowl and sat down at the table, taking my first taste. It was heaven. Craig sat down at the table with me and watched me eat, almost like he was afraid I was going to run away.

"Are you feeling better?"

I shrugged, but nodded when I realized what a bitch I was being.

"That's good. I was hoping it wouldn't last long."

"What about you? How's your leg?"

"It's good. Cap bitched at me for being at work today, but I had to fill out paperwork from the job."

"I'm sure he would have let someone bring it to you."

"Yeah, but two days of lying around were enough. I can't stand to just sit around all day. And I'm pretty sure that you would have killed me if I had stayed home with you again."

"Look," I set my spoon down and leaned back in my chair. It was better to get this out now instead of dragging it on. "This has been... interesting, but we weren't supposed to be married. That never should have happened. And then you went and sold my house without my permission....I think we need to be smart here and admit what this really is."

He smiled at me and slid his hand across the table, resting it on top of mine. "I think you're right. We need to admit that this was fate throwing us together and telling us that we shouldn't fight this."

I blinked and then shook my head in disbelief. "Fate? This...this had nothing to do with fate. This is you trying to force me into having a relationship with you. And it's not going to work. I want an annulment."

"Remember, we can't do that. You can't take the time off. Especially after just being sick."

"Then I want a divorce. I don't care if it looks bad or not. I want out of this marriage!"

"Baby, you're just saying that because this is all a bit overwhelming. You'll come around. You'll see."

"You're delusional."

"I'm right. Trust me on this."

"Trust me on this point, if you don't give me my divorce, I will make your life a living hell. I don't want to be married to you and I don't want you being sweet to try and win me over. It's not going to work no matter how many times you try."

"Alright, I respect your decision."

"So, you'll give me my divorce?"

"Not a chance in hell, my little pixie."

I was completely irritated when I got out of bed the next morning. Despite trying my best to make Craig not want to sleep with me, nothing worked. I shoved my cold feet against his legs and he wrapped my feet between his legs to keep them warm. When he started snoring in the middle of the night and I couldn't get back to sleep, I smothered him with a pillow. Of course, he's stronger than me, so he gently pushed me back to my side of the bed and rolled over to his side. And he didn't even snore the rest of the night. And then when he snuggled up to me in the morning and I slammed my fist back into his erection that was prodding me in the ass, he just chuckled and told me he liked a feisty woman.

So, here I was, showering in a new house, and I didn't even have all my stuff in the shower that I needed. But then I saw Craig's razor and I got an idea. Lathering up, I shaved every single inch of hair from my legs, armpits, and even my nether regions. I whistled cheerily as I got out of the shower and dried off quickly. Craig knocked and walked into the bathroom on his crutches, kissing me hard before setting his crutches aside and stepping into the shower. I was temporarily shocked into complete submission before I pulled it together and got the hell out of there.

I dressed quickly and then walked back into the bathroom. Peeking into the shower, I saw Craig was shaving his face. "Oh, sweetie? I'm sorry, but I couldn't find my razor, so I used yours. Everywhere."

He slid the door open and grinned at me. "So, what you're saying is that it's like your pussy is on my face right now. I like it."

I screamed in frustration as he laughed at me. Eyeing the toilet, I walked over to it and slammed the handle down, laughing as I imagined the water going cold.

"Just so you know, my little pixie, when you flush the toilet, the water in the shower gets warmer."

I stomped my feet as I left the bathroom. "Can't something go my way!"

Chapter Thirty-Five

CRAIG

The new building was open now and I was excited to check it out and see where I would be working from now on. It was impressive. We had the same security measures as before, but there were a few more added. There were cameras mounted everywhere, and from what I understood, there was facial recognition that was immediately sent through a system check. If you weren't on the approved list to get in, the elevator shut down immediately and you were stuck until someone got you out.

There were also three other elevators that had been put in at each side of the building that were only used as escape elevators. With the right code and hand print, any of us could get on the elevator and it would take us immediately underground to our old escape route. We had SUVs loaded down there and ready to go at a moment's notice. And that was only the beginning of our new security measures.

"Hey!" Sinner said, jogging around the corner and into the lobby. "It's the WolfMan. Ahooo!"

"Shut it," I grumbled as I made my way further into the office.

"What crawled up your ass? Things not working out with the little missus?"

"I'm working on it."

"Ooh, working on it? That's like saying you're trying to save a sinking ship."

I made it into the conference room and plopped down in a chair.

"What are you doing here anyway? Aren't you off until your 'gunshot wounds' heal?"

He grinned at me. Fuck, he knew. What was the point in putting on that big act if everyone was going to find out anyway?

"There was nothing to do at home, and unfortunately, the school won't let me sit in with Reese's class."

"You asked?"

"What? I love my wife and I wanted to spend time with her."

He shook his head at me. "That's not the way to do it."

"Well, I need to do something. She's trying to get rid of me. Last night, she actually tried to smother me with a pillow."

"No shit?"

"Yeah, if I hadn't been so in tune with her body, I might not have woken up and you would have never seen me again."

"Can't say that's a big loss."

"You're an asshole."

"You know, what you really need is to get focused. Right now, you're just trying to do anything you can to win her back, but you're not centered with yourself."

"What does that mean?"

"You need to be in tune with your own body so that you can make the right decisions. You need yoga."

"Stretching. Your answer to getting my woman to love me is that I need to stretch more?"

He chuckled, "No, yoga is about being in a better state of mind for you and your body. Listen, Cara does yoga all the time now. She started it a few years back to help her deal with her anxiety. It's done amazing things for her."

"Really?"

"Yeah, it really heals your soul."

I grimaced. "Can we not talk about shit like 'healing your soul'? It makes me wiggly."

"What makes you wiggly?" Alec asked as he walked into the room with Chris.

"Sinner wants me to do yoga to get in touch with myself and heal my soul."

"So?" Chris said, shrugging his shoulders. "Ali works with a yoga instructor for some of the patients at the clinic."

"For what?"

"What do you mean 'for what'? To work shit out."

"But it works?"

"Yeah. I can get the number. Hell, I wouldn't mind trying it myself."

I looked to Alec, who was shaking his head furiously.

"I'm in," Sinner grinned. "I've seen Cara do it, and she's always such a nicer person after she's done yoga."

"I guess..." I cleared my throat and sat up straighter. "Yeah, I guess I could do that."

"That's the spirit," Sinner grinned.

"But, if I'm doing it, so are you," I said to Alec.

He shook his head again. "No. There's no way in hell I'm getting down on some mat and doing all that stretchy shit."

"You owe me," I said fiercely.

"For what?"

"For telling everyone about my gunshot wound."

He laughed uncomfortably. "What are you talking about?"

"I'm talking about you telling everyone that there was no goat. You just couldn't leave it alone, could you? You just had to tell everyone that you shot me so I could win my woman back."

It was deadly quiet. I turned back to Sinner who was trying to hold in his laughter. "You had Alec shoot you?"

"Fuck."

"Yeah," Alec cleared his throat. "I didn't tell them, but I'm sure everyone will know in about an hour."

I tossed my crutches on the ground in the training center. Chris had gotten on the phone right away with Ali and got the number for the yoga instructor. As I looked at her, preparing for our class, I had to wonder why I hadn't done yoga when I was younger. The woman was sexy as hell, not that I cared. I only had eyes for Reese, but when I was younger, it would have been great.

"You ready to do this?"

I turned and choked on my own spit. Sinner was standing in front of me in a wife beater and running shorts, with leg warmers and a sweat band.

"What the fuck are you wearing?"

"Yoga's tough. I wanted to be prepared."

"For what? You look like you belong in the 80's."

"Hey, this outfit is amazing, and I brought some for you too."

"I'm not wearing that."

"Come on," he whined. "Get in the spirit of it all. If you're not going to do it right, then you shouldn't even be here."

"Fine." I snatched the bag out of his hand and pulled out a sweatband of my own and some leg warmers. "Don't chicks usually wear this?"

"I suppose you're too good for leg warmers now," he grumbled.

"No, I just don't want to look like a woman. Besides, I'm wearing sweatpants."

"Then take those off."

"What? No. I only have on my boxers."

"Just take them off," he said, reaching for my waistband.

I slapped his hand away. "Knock it off. Stop trying to pull my clothes off."

"Just take off your pants!"

"No!"

"Then get the fuck out of here. You're ruining it for everyone else."

"There's no one else here!"

"Take them off," he said sternly, reaching for my waistband again. I shuffled backwards, but my foot gave out and I fell to the ground with him on top of me. He started yanking my pants off and I struggled to get them back up.

"Stop it! Leave my pants alone!"

"No! You're doing this the right way."

He had my pants down around my ankles, yanking at the material. "Stop!"

"No!" He yanked hard, his fist slamming into my foot. I yelled out in pain and punched him in the face. "Get the fuck off me!"

He fell backwards, ripping my pants the rest of the way off as he fell backwards. I struggled to my feet and glared down at him.

"What's going on here? Why are you in your underwear?" Chris asked.

"He was pulling my pants off, telling me I had to do yoga in my underwear."

He looked down at Sinner in question. "Really?"

"You're supposed to be in a relaxed state."

"I'm pretty sure he was relaxed in his sweatpants."

"Whatever, when Cara does yoga, she's in as little clothes as possible. Something about feeling at peace with her natural self."

"Why the fuck are you in your boxers?" Ice asked as he walked in with Jules.

"Hey," Jules pointed a finger at Chris. "You didn't say anything about doing this shit in our underwear."

"He pulled them off me."

"Alright," Sinner stood, holding up my pants. "Let's just all calm down. I was just explaining that when you do yoga, you should feel as close to nature as possible."

"Aw, shit. Not this crap again." Burg walked in with Cazzo, shaking his head in disbelief. "Seriously, I didn't come here to get naked with a bunch of guys. You said yoga."

"I also said not to bring Cazzo," Sinner grumbled.

"Why? What's wrong with me being here?"

"Let's just say that you don't exactly have an open mind."

"Can we just get on with this?" I asked. "It's already six o'clock and I was hoping to be home for dinner tonight."

"Is everyone ready?" a perky blonde asked. We all walked closer to her. Her smile faltered when she saw all of us. She probably wasn't used to dealing with men. "Okay, well, this is an interesting group. Alright, so let me start by telling you a little about what we're doing here today. First of all, yoga, when practiced properly, helps you to thrive, prosper, and to bring the spiritual world and the material world into one. I'll show you techniques that will help you attain spiritual and material prosperity."

I couldn't really say that any of us were particularly gleeful at the thought of doing yoga. Well, except for Sinner. He was bouncing around like he was about to get in the ring with Evander Holyfield.

"Okay, the first thing I want you to do is shed those clothes. Let's just be one with nature."

"See?" Sinner shouted. "I told you."

"Whatever."

"Is that really necessary?" Cazzo asked. "I mean, I'm wearing workout gear."

"Yes," the woman smiled, "but we're not working out. We're digging deep down to find out what is blocking us, both mentally and physically."

"I told you not to bring Cazzo," Sinner snapped at Burg. "He's messing up our aura or some shit."

"I am not," Cazzo growled. "You want my pants off, fine." He shoved his pants down, but he wasn't wearing underwear like me. "Hey, you wanted to be one with nature. Doesn't get more natural than this." He yanked off his shirt for good measure and crossed his arms over his chest.

"Right," the woman cleared her throat. "Mr. Cazzo has the right idea. And this is a perfectly natural way to do yoga. Now, I'm Chastity. Why don't we go around the room and introduce ourselves? Get to know each other a little better."

"How about we just get to it," Cazzo snapped. "I'm kind of blowing in the wind here."

"Perfect," Chastity said a bit too cheerily. "Okay, I want you all to spread out, leaving enough room for you and your partner to move, and we'll get started."

I raised my hand. "Partners?"

She nodded and motioned for me to do as she said. I sighed and turned to Alec. "Hey, you want to partner up?"

"That just sounds wrong."

"Well, I didn't make up the rules. And if I have to be in my boxers, so do you."

"Bullshit."

"Bullshit, everyone else is doing it. Hell, Cazzo's buck ass naked."

"Fine." He shoved his pants down and took off his shirt, standing in front of me in his underwear. "Happy?"

"Are you asking me if I'm happy standing in front of my teammate in my boxers as we're about to get in touch with nature?"

"Point taken."

Sinner was paired up with Cazzo. Jules was with Chris, and Ice was with Burg. It was a little weird, but if it got my girl back, I would do anything.

"Alright, now, we're going to do the boat pose. This will help strengthen and stretch, and when done with your partner, will help you connect."

"What?" I asked Alec, but he just shrugged.

"Now, sit on the floor facing each other, and with your arms outside your legs, reach for your partner's hands. Starting with your knees bent, lift your legs to place the soles of your feet against your partner's feet. Work towards straightening your legs as you lift your feet towards the sky."

I sat with my knees bent like she said and held out my hands for Alec. He glowered at me, but did the same. "Alright, can you put your feet against mine?" I was barely able to reach his arms as it was, let alone trying to position my feet against his. I was a big guy and I just wasn't that flexible. He gripped my hands and together, we worked to get the soles of our feet touching.

"We did it!" I said excitedly.

"You want a fucking medal?"

"Lighten up. Geez, this isn't doing crap for your attitude."

"That's because I'm practically naked and stretching with another dude."

"Quit your bitching. Now, we're supposed to raise our feet in the air and I guess we hold each other so that we can stretch backwards."

"This is so wrong," Alec grumbled.

"Just do it."

Slowly, we started raising our legs, but it fucking hurt.

"Ow, ow, ow, ow!" I cringed as my legs stretched in the air, my feet pressing against Alec's. "Why does this hurt so much?"

"Because it's not natural. I fucking told you!"

"I think my ass is giving out. I need my donut."

"Just hold still," he shouted.

"I can't. I'm falling." I tilted to the right and Alec gripped my hand harder, trying to hold me up, but my ass hurt too much. "I'm going!"

We fell to the side, our legs tangled together, my foot way too close to his dick. Luckily, when I looked up, we weren't the only ones that were having trouble staying in position. Sinner and Cazzo had also fallen over and Cazzo was shoving Sinner off his naked body. Chris and Jules were struggling to get in position, but Burg and Ice had it down perfectly.

"Alright," Chastity smiled. "That was good for the first time, but maybe we should try something a little easier. Sit cross-legged facing each other. Place your right hand on your partner's heart and your partner does the same. Then each of you places your left hand over your partner's right hand. As you tune in — both to the physical beating of your heart and the energy around it, the heart chakra. The feeling becomes increasingly powerful and you bring your breath into harmony."

"What the fuck does that mean?" I asked Alec.

"Hell if I know. What's a chakra?"

"I thought there would be more stretching and shit? Why are we having to...you know...touch each other? Isn't that a little weird?"

"Craig, two guys are sitting in their underwear, touching each other's hearts. There's nothing about this that isn't weird."

I nodded. "That's what I thought."

I glanced around the room. Ice was slapping Burg's hand away from his chest. "Dude, stop feeling me up. I know you had your shot once, but it ain't gonna happen with me."

"I'm not fucking gay! When are you guys gonna let that go?"

"When it stops being funny," Ice shot back.

I snorted in amusement, but schooled my features when Alec glared at me.

"Right, now align your breathing with your partner's and breathe in harmony. In and out. That's right."

"Sorry, but why are we with partners?" Chris asked.

"Yeah, my wife doesn't do this shit," Sinner added. "I thought there was like downward dog and stuff like that."

"What's downward dog?" Cazzo asked.

"It's when you lay on your belly and howl like your downwind from a dog," Sinner said, mimicking the pose.

"That's not it," Jules said, standing and walking over to Sinner. "Get up on all fours." Sinner did as he said. "Now, you want to stand and bend so your ass is in the air and your arms and legs are straight." He stepped behind Sinner and ran his hand over his back. "That's right. Nice and straight." He kept running his hand up and down Sinner's back. "Good. That's just how Ivy does it."

Chris cleared his throat loudly. "Should we leave you two alone?"

Jules snatched his hand back and quickly backed away. "Anyway, that's how it's done."

"That's correct," Chastity smiled. "You know, I think the two of you should be partners. You have great chemistry."

"I'm good," Sinner said.

"Yeah," Jules agreed. "I'm just gonna-" He pointed over to Chris and walked back to him. Chris shoved him away when he stood too close.

"Don't get any ideas," Alec said when I turned back to him.

I held up my hands in defense. "Hey, you're not gonna see me rubbing your back."

"Now that we've all had a chance to become one with our breathing, let's move on to our final pose of the night. Now, I would like one of you, the larger one, to sit cross-legged on the ground. The other one of you will sit on your partner's thighs with your ankles crossed behind your partner's back."

"Hell no," Alec said, stepping away from me. "I was okay with the yoga, but there's no fucking way that you're sitting on my lap."

"Why wouldn't you sit on my lap? I'm bigger than you."

"Are you fucking serious?" Alec spat. "You want me to sit on *your* lap?"

"Well, it's what the teacher said to do."

"No."

"Hey, I went to therapy for you."

"And?"

"And you know what. Don't give me that shit."

"No."

"Fine. I'm sure all the guys would like to know what happened after our last therapy session."

"What happened?" Burg asked.

"Oh, I'm sure Burg of all people would be very interested in this information."

"Why me? What happened?" Burg asked excitedly.

I grinned and turned to Burg. "At our last session–"

"Fine!" Alec shouted. "I'll do it. Sit down and shut your fucking mouth."

I punched Alec in the arm and took my seat. Everyone else gathered around to watch, which was a little weird, but if I had to be the guinea pig, I guess that's what I had to do. Alec came over and sat down on my thighs.

"Cross your legs behind me," I ordered.

"No."

"How is this going to help me if you don't do it the way it's supposed to be done?"

"Yeah, Alec," Sinner grinned. "Show us all how it's done."

Alec clenched his jaw and crossed his legs behind me. Yeah, it was fucking weird, but there had to be an end result that would make this all right for me.

"Alright, now that you're in position, allow your foreheads to touch, while keeping your back as straight as possible, and breathe deeply and slowly."

"I'm gonna kill you," Alec said, right before he allowed his forehead to meet mine.

I took a deep breath, even allowed my eyes to drift closed as I felt myself relax.

"Isn't this a little gay?" Cazzo asked. And that snapped me out of it. I was just about to shove Alec off me when I heard Cap's voice.

"What the fuck are you two doing?"

My head shot up and my mouth dropped open as I tried to figure out something smart to say. Alec jumped out of my lap, his face bright red. Chance's team and Coop's team were standing behind Cap, staring at us like we were insane. Well, all except Gabe.

"Seriously, enough of this shit! First, waxing, and now you're climbing into each other's laps? This is a workplace!" His eyes went big when he saw Cazzo. "I expected better from you."

"Hey, I work here too."

"And you're fucking naked," Cap shouted. Cazzo looked down and covered his junk, looking up sheepishly at Cap.

"What *are* you guys doing?" Chance asked.

"Uh..." I looked to Alec, but he refused to meet my eyes.

"It's Tantra Yoga," Chastity said as she walked forward.

"What?" all of us shouted.

"Wait," Alec shook his head slightly, "this was supposed to be yoga. Just yoga."

"No, I'm a Tantra Yoga teacher."

"Wait..." Oh, this was not good. Not good at all. "Tantra as in..."

"Well, I was a little confused myself. I mean, I don't have any male partners in my tantra class, but I'm open to helping all understand the role of dominance in sex."

"Whoa," Sinner yelled. "We're not gay! We were using yoga to clear our minds. Not...seduce one another."

"Well, actually, it has very little to do with seduction. Tantra is actually about a man worshiping a woman's breasts and vagina by writing mantras on them. Then, the man pulls the woman towards him by the hair and has sex with her. It's very domineering."

"So, why didn't you tell us that?" I shouted. "He was sitting on my fucking lap!"

"Wait," Ice interrupted. "So, is this something you give lessons on?"

"Alright," Cap shouted. "That's enough. I can take waxing and I can take the spa days, but this is taking it too far. Next time, do your fucking research before you hire someone to come here and..." He shook his head and stalked out of the room. Coop's team followed him out, but Gabe walked over to us and grinned.

"So, where can I learn more about this stuff? And why was I left out of the fun?"

Chapter Thirty-Six

REESE

I ran around the house, checking every last decoration, making sure everything was exactly as I wanted it. I called Jessica, Storm's girl-friend, first thing this morning and told her what I needed, expenses didn't matter. I had a deadline, which was today, and she got to work. People showed up just an hour later. In fact, there were so many people here that there was really nothing I had to do. And the point of it? To freak Craig out so much that he would up and leave.

I hated that I had been moved here, but the fact was, this house was really nice. And being on Reed Security property, I felt very safe. Still, that didn't mean that I liked the fact that the house I had bought for myself, loved with all my heart, had just been snatched out from under me. And when I finally got my divorce from Craig, what was I supposed to do then? I had put everything I had into that house. Would Craig give me the money back or would he hold it so that I would have to stay with him?

I grinned as I took in the living room. I had the entire place painted the color of Pepto Bismol. The paint was still drying, so the windows were open, letting in the cool fall breeze to help air out the house. There were deer heads all over the walls and the bedroom was decorated with several bear heads. It was creepy as hell. I couldn't imagine actually staying here because if I woke up in the middle of the night, I would probably get scared and run screaming from the house. But this would work.

I walked over to the coffee table and adjusted the book with the giant vagina on it. Perfect. Next to it sat a plastic vagina that could be opened and closed for demonstration. I had a stack of books on the other end about feminism and the power of women. A book titled *What Do Women Need Men For* sat on top. I didn't actually read any of that crap, but I figured it would irritate Craig, and that was what this was all about.

I heard his truck pull in and I quickly ran to the bathroom to check my appearance. I was happy to see that I looked quite disheveled. I checked my armpits, grimacing at the smell. I had run around the house several times to work up a sweat so that I smelled gross and I hadn't bothered to take a shower. The door opened and I stepped back into the living room to greet him. He looked stunned or shocked, but it wasn't because of the decorations. He wasn't even looking at that.

"Craig? Is everything alright?"

"Yeah," he said, just staring at the ground.

"Work was okay?"

"Uh...sure."

"You're not acting right. Did something happen with one of the guys? With Alec?"

"What are you talking about? Of course nothing happened with the guys. Especially Alec. Nothing would ever happen with him. I don't know why you would even say something like that." He chuckled nervously and was fidgeting with his jacket.

"Okay. Um...I wasn't implying that...well, I don't even know what you thought I was implying."

"Never mind. Just...nothing happened."

I nodded and he finally looked me in the eyes. "So? What do you think?"

"About what?"

"The decorations, silly."

He looked at the walls finally and practically jumped back. "What the fuck? Why are there heads on the wall?"

"You don't like it?"

I could see his throat bob as he swallowed hard. "Uh...it's great. Really...creative."

"I thought you might like it. And I know how much you like sex, so I got something special for you!"

I led him over to the coffee table and showed him the vagina. He grimaced, but tried to hide it. "That's...so...cool."

"Isn't it? I also picked up a book for you about the anatomy of the vagina."

He swallowed hard again and looked around the room in misery. Yeah, just as I thought it would go. I stepped up to him and ran my hand up his chest. "Now, why don't we go to the bedroom and you can examine my vagina?"

He nodded, but didn't look at all enthused about it. He dropped his bag and used his crutches to get over to the stairs. I watched his ass as he climbed the stairs. Damn, he was so good looking. I reached forward and grabbed his ass just for the fun of it. He jolted and laughed a little, but he looked so uncomfortable. We made it to the bedroom and I managed to restrain myself for the rest of the walk to the bed. I shoved him backward and climbed on top of him, straddling his body and wrapping my legs around his waist.

"What are you doing?" he asked nervously.

"I'm getting comfortable."

"But...why are you sitting like that?"

"Because, I want to be close to you. I want our bodies to be one."

He shoved me off him and stood, running his hand nervously over his head. He started limping and pacing the floor, but I had no clue why. It must have been something I said.

"I thought you wanted the same thing. I thought you wanted us to be close."

"I do. I just...we can't...I can't..." He gestured to the bed and shuttered violently. "Not that."

"Okay."

I stood and walked over to him. I wasn't sure why because I had what I wanted. He was freaked out just like I wanted, but this didn't have anything to do with the decorations, and for some reason that bothered me. Because if it wasn't the decorations, it was me.

"Did I do something wrong? Is this not what you want?"

He looked around the room, taking it in for the first time and then looked back at me. "This is really fucking weird."

"You said to do whatever I wanted."

"Yeah, but I thought you would paint the room a girly color or hang pictures of babies dressed like sunflowers. This is...brutal."

"Well, I did paint it pink."

"It's so pink that I want to throw up."

Then I did my job. I grinned internally, but put a frown on my face. "You don't like it?"

He sighed and walked over to me, wrapping his arms around my shoulders and pulling me into him. "If this is what you like, then I'll learn to love it."

Shit. Well, that backfired. I should have known that Craig was the man that would go along with anything to make his woman happy. I gave him a wary smile and pecked him on the cheek.

He grinned wolfishly at me. "Glad I could get you to come around."

And then the asshole took me to bed and gave me some of the best orgasms of my life. What an ass.

"Oh my God. What did you do to this place?"

Brooke walked into the house and looked around in disgust.

"I redecorated."

"I can see that, but why? This is terrible."

"I did it so that Craig would back off."

She sat down on the sofa and picked up the vagina on the table. "Did he?"

"At first. Well, I don't think it really had anything to do with the house. He was off from the minute he walked in."

"What happened?" She opened the vagina and squealed when it all fell apart all over the floor. "Please tell me he doesn't play with that."

"That's the thing. He barely paid attention to any of it. He came home and he was all...weird."

"Weirder than he normally is?"

"Definitely. He was saying something about how nothing happened between him and his teammates."

"Nothing happened? Like...sexual?"

"You don't think..."

"Uh yeah. What else would you think?"

"I don't know! But I definitely wasn't thinking about him and another guy having sex! Ew! He had his mouth on me after that."

She sighed and set the vagina back on the table. "Well, you know, everyone's all about being different now. There's all these different sexualities that you can be. Maybe he wants to experiment."

"Or maybe he already experimented and he's regretting it. I mean, based on the way he looked when he walked in, he was tormented by something."

"Maybe he had to do something for a job. Something that would make him appear... you know...gay?"

"No."

"Well, then it was with one of the guys. Which one do you think it was?"

I thought about it for a minute, but there were so many of them, and I hadn't even met them all yet. "I barely know them. I mean, Alec is his teammate, but he seems pretty protective of Florrie. I just don't see him going off and becoming...bisexual."

"Okay, what about his boss?"

"Sebastian? No, he has like five kids."

"And I bet he's feeling pretty lonely," Brooke pointed out. "His wife is probably busy with the kids and he has no one to see to his needs. Is it really that unlikely that a boss would demand one of his employees gives him a little nookie in exchange for a pay raise?"

"No," I said, somewhat baffled at how easily she had put that all together. It couldn't be. But then again, she had a point. "Do you really think..."

"I think anything's possible nowadays."

"But...no. He was so nice to me. He got the locks changed on the house for me when I told him I wasn't comfortable with Craig being there."

"Exactly. He did whatever he had to in order to make sure that Craig didn't find someone else."

My eyes widened in shock. "Oh my God. You're right. You're so right. Why didn't I see it before? He told me that he owed Craig and that's why he was helping him, but if he really felt he owed him, he would have done whatever he needed to make sure that I stayed with Craig."

We sat there in silence for a moment. I was still trying to wrap my head around everything I just found out. It all made sense now. It was so clear.

"What are you going to do?"

"I don't know."

"Well, it stands to reason that if you approach Sebastian and tell him you know, he might just do whatever you ask."

"What do you mean?"

"Well, you have a choice. You can ask him to step aside or you can ask him to finally make his move and take Craig off your hands."

"But, isn't that weird? I mean, he probably doesn't want attention drawn to the fact that he's...you know...gay."

"Not gay. Bisexual. And plenty of people are doing it. Maybe he just needs to feel comfortable to step out of the closet."

"So, you think I should do it?"

"It's the fastest way to make this end. Or to help you move on with Craig."

I could do that. I could approach Cap and tell him that I was totally cool with it, and if he would just open up and tell Craig what he wanted, we could both get our way.

"But Reese, are you sure?"

"Sure about what?"

She sighed and grabbed onto my hand. "You know I'm not about all the sentimental shit, but this guy is perfect for you. I know that you're only pushing him away because you're scared."

"I'm not scared."

"Yes, you are. You are the biggest scaredy cat in the world. And if you don't work it out soon, someone like Sebastian is going to swoop in and scoop up all that male hotness. I'm just saying, don't fuck this up."

"I didn't know you cared," I said sarcastically.

"I don't. I just don't want you to fuck this up for me. There's a whole building of hot men and there's bound to be one that's just waiting to be scooped up."

"Sorry, I thought we were talking about my problems."

"Yeah, see, that's where you're wrong. We may be talking about you, but in the end, it's all about me."

I shook off my nerves and stepped onto the elevator at Reed Security. Sebastian had come down himself to take me up. But this wasn't the right place to talk about this. I needed privacy with him. We got off the elevator and he led me to his office. It was nice. Very big and had an excellent view of...well, the other building. I guess these guys didn't care very much about views.

I sat down in the chair across from him at his desk. I cleared my throat, going over in my head one last time what I wanted to say. It was a touchy subject, after all.

"Reese, whatever it is, just say it."

I nodded. "Okay, um...I want you to know that if you feel that you're ready to...move on, I'm fine with it."

"If I want to move on from what?" Sebastian was leaning back in his chair, his finger running against his lip, like he was thinking. God, this was so hard.

"Well, I understand that you and Maggie have five kids."

"Four."

"Oh. Well, anyway, that's a lot of kids and as a man, you must get... um...lonely."

His brows furrowed in confusion. "Actually, with that many kids, I'm never alone."

"Right," I blushed furiously. I needed to come up with a better way to say this. "I just mean that you must not get very much alone time with Maggie."

"Well, yeah, it's difficult, but I don't see what that has to do with anything."

"Sometimes when a man is lonely, he might go looking for...comfort somewhere else."

He leaned forward slowly, eyeing me like a cat about to pounce. "I'm not sure I follow."

"I'm just saying that you might go looking for...sexual relations elsewhere and that I understand that you might be looking in my household."

He jumped up, shoving his chair back in the wall with a bang. "Uh, I think there's some confusion here. I'm not looking for anything else. I love my wife and there's no one in the world that I would ever leave her for."

"Come on, Sebastian. I saw the way Craig looked when he came home last night. He was devastated."

"That has nothing to do with me. I swear! I'm sorry if he gave you the impression that there was something going on, but there's not. I would never do that to Maggie."

"Okay. I just wanted you to know that I understand and I'm not judging."

"Look, Reese, you're a nice woman and I'm sure you're...everything a guy could want in bed, but you do nothing for me."

"What?" I shook my head, sure that I had heard him wrong. "What are you talking about?"

"I'm talking about you and me. It's never gonna happen. I'm sorry, but I've never felt anything for you and I never will."

"Wait, I'm not talking about me."

"Then who *are* you talking about?"

"Craig. Who else?"

"Craig?" he practically shouted. "Why would you think that I would... and Craig? No. Just...no. Never."

"Then, I don't understand."

"Neither do I. How about you start talking and explain to me why you would think that I would have a thing for your husband."

"You what?" I spun around to see a man I hadn't met before standing in the doorway.

"Chance, this is not what you think," Sebastian said quickly.

"You're Craig's wife?"

"Yeah."

"I'm Chance, different team."

"I assumed."

"Cap, you want to explain what's going on here?"

"I would if I had any fucking clue," Sebastian spat.

"Wait," I looked between the two of them. I was so confused. "Craig came home last night and he was insisting a little too much that nothing happened between him and his teammates."

"And you assumed he was implying that something happened with me?" Cap said incredulously.

"Well, it wouldn't be Alec. He's mad about Florrie."

"And I'm mad about my wife!"

"Well," Chance shrugged. "I could see why she would assume..."

"How?" Cap shouted. "How could you look at me and assume that I was interested in a man!"

"Well, your wife is always pregnant and you never have any free time because of those kids. She probably assumed that you were looking for a little nookie on the side."

"Thank you!"

"No! Never. That's just..." He shook his head and shook like he was wiggling something off of him or he was having a seizure. "So, you just decided that I was the most logical choice."

"Well, actually it was Brooke. I mean, she pointed out everything and it just clicked. I mean, you agreed to help me change the locks after you told me that you owed him."

"Yeah, well, I also believe that a woman shouldn't be forced into marriage. I was trying to help you!"

"But you gave up so easily."

"I still don't see how you came to that conclusion. Is it something about me? Is it the way I dress or something?"

"Well, you have been wearing a lot of ties lately," Chance said.

"Ties? I look gay because I'm wearing ties?"

Chance shrugged. "You never know. I mean, you've just never been such a fancy man before."

"I've been going around to banks to get loans so we can keep functioning. Our jobs are only taking us so far."

"Alright, no need to get your panties in a twist," Chance laughed.

"Out! Get the fuck out right now before I make you go train Maggie."

Chance's face grew serious. "That's just mean."

He turned and walked out, leaving me alone with Sebastian again.

"So, you're not bisexual."

"No!"

"Alright, geez, I just wanted to be sure."

He shivered violently and sat back down in his chair. "Now, if you would like to know what happened, I'll be glad to explain it to you."

"Please do. I've been freaking out about this conversation."

He rolled his eyes and sighed. "He was trying to get centered so he could, I don't know, figure out how to win you over. The guys hired a yoga instructor, but it turned out it was tantric yoga."

"Oh."

"Yeah. Let's just say, you're lucky you didn't walk in on what I did."

I swallowed hard. "Right."

I stood, turning for the door. I was so embarrassed. This was the worst idea ever.

"Do me a favor and kick Brooke's ass for me."

"No problem there."

She was so getting her ass kicked.

Chapter Thirty-Seven

CRAIG

"Hey!" Cap shouted. I was in the new training room, testing out my leg on the obstacle course. I looked up and saw that he was stalking toward me like he was ready to kill me. I got down off the climbing wall, careful not to put too much pressure on my foot. Yeah, I might not be totally ready to do this shit yet. Even my ass still hurt.

"What's up?"

"You need to go fix things with your woman."

"Okay. Do you mind telling me what I need to fix?"

"She came to me and told me that she understood if I was ready to move on."

I looked at him in confusion. "Move on from what?"

"That's what I wanted to know. She thought that with Maggie and I having so many kids, I would be looking for sex with someone else."

"She came onto you?" No fucking way. That woman was mine and she wasn't leaving me for a married man.

"No, she thought that I wanted you."

"Me?"

"Yeah, apparently, you looked devastated last night and rambled about not doing anything with any of us. She thought that I was trying to seduce you!"

I snorted in laughter, trying to hold it in. That was the first time that I knew of that anyone accused Cap of being gay. He was the furthest thing from being gay.

"Well, you have been wearing a lot of ties lately."

"What the fuck does that have to do with anything? Chance said the same fucking thing."

"Well, you know, they're...floofy."

"Floofy?"

"Yeah, you know...girly."

He looked down at his tie and held it out to examine it more closely. "How is this tie girly?"

"Well, not girly exactly, but something that a woman or...gay person might pick out."

"And how exactly does a gay man pick out ties differently than a straight man?"

"Well, see a straight man would probably choose black or dark blue, but you went with purple. And it has pink stripes."

"But...Maggie told me I look good in it."

"And she's a woman."

He quickly loosened the tie from around his neck and tore it off over his head. "Why didn't someone fucking say something?"

I shrugged. "I guess I thought that you were going for a new style. Who am I to judge?"

"You just fucking did!"

"Right. Well, I'm not perfect."

"Fine, no more fucking ties. No more suits." He started ripping his clothes off, his jacket first and then his shirt, throwing them to the floor. "When I go to the bank from now on, I'll just wear jeans and a nice shirt."

"Yeah, but not that blue one."

"Which blue one?"

"You know, the periwinkle one."

"Fuck, is there anything about my clothes that's okay?"

I thought about it for a moment. "You know when you're *not* dressing up to go kiss ass?" He nodded. "Those are fine."

"Honey, I'm home," I said in a sing-song voice as I walked through the door. Reese was sitting on the couch, eating a chocolate bar and watching something on tv.

"What do you want?"

"Uh...just to see my honey bunny and give her a kiss!"

"Go away."

I sat down on the coffee table, blocking her view of the tv. "What's wrong, my little sweet potato?"

"Would you knock it off? Enough already."

"What would you like me to stop?"

"Stop everything! We aren't really married. It's only on paper. You know that this is all a sham, so just give me my divorce and we'll put this all to rest."

"I don't understand. You don't want to be married to me?"

Of course she didn't. This was all a joke to her, but it was so real to me.

"Craig, I went to your office and accused your boss of being gay! You're turning me into a lunatic. This has to stop. I hate this house. I hate being married to you. And I'm really hating my life."

Wow. That really hurt. But, I was never one to give up when times got tough. Besides, Brooke had told me this would happen, so I had been preparing for this. I took a deep breath and nodded.

"Okay."

"Okay? You'll give me a divorce?"

"No. Not a chance in hell. But I'm willing to give you the time you need to figure out that we're meant to be together. And you can change the house again. I don't know what you were thinking with the decor. It's really not our style."

"We don't have a style. We aren't really a couple."

"Pixie, we're more of a couple than anyone I know."

I stood and walked out of the room. I may have to deal with this and give her time, but I didn't have to listen to her telling me that we didn't belong together. It hurt a man's pride.

I went upstairs and got in the shower, scrubbing that conversation off me. I couldn't believe that she kept asking for a divorce. It was just ridiculous. How could she not see how good we were together? I knew she felt it. Every time we made love, and that's exactly what we were doing, I could feel her giving in to me. Her body gravitated to mine at night, until she was pressed tightly against me. That wasn't something that happened when you didn't like the person that was in your bed. In fact, that wasn't even something that happened when you just liked that person.

"Craig."

I looked up and saw my little pixie standing in the bathroom, but she didn't look happy to be here. In fact, if I had to guess, she was here to try and let me down easy. Again.

"Did you decide on something different to do with the house?"

Even I could hear the anger in my tone. That's what this was turning into for me. Every time she came to tell me it was over, I felt a little piece of me dying inside.

"I'm not redecorating the house. I know that you think this is going to turn out differently, but it's not. This doesn't end any way except in divorce."

I scrubbed at my nails, making sure to get every last piece of dirt out until my fingers felt like they were bleeding. I didn't respond. I just couldn't. I was getting tired of defending myself and trying to convince her that this was real. I needed a job. I needed to get away and clear my head for a minute. But that wasn't going to happen, so I shut off the water and pulled back the shower curtain. Stepping out onto the bath mat, I watched as her eyes hungrily took in my body. That wasn't the look of someone that didn't want me.

"We...we need to be...realistic here."

"Sure."

I plucked the towel from the towel bar and started to dry myself off. She licked her lips, her eyes growing wide as I hardened. If she was going to leave, I was going to be damn sure that I got to have her one more time. I was going to give her everything, pleasure her in so many ways that when she went out with someone else, it would only be me she was thinking about.

I stalked toward her, wrapping my hand around her neck as I

leaned in to kiss her. She didn't pull back when I pressed my lips to hers. I slipped my tongue inside her mouth, stroking her cheek as my lips caressed hers. Her breath was short and sweet as she gasped against my lips. I slid my other arm around her waist and pulled her flush against me.

Her heart pounded against my chest and her nails dug into my skin as she gripped me to her. God, I could practically feel my soul reaching out to her. I couldn't live without her. My heart would break and I would lose all reason to be here. I had to convince her to stay.

Picking her up, I carried her into the other room. Her legs were tangled behind my back as I laid her down on the bed and kissed her sweet lips. I broke the kiss, skimming my lips across her jaw and down her neck.

"How can you deny this?"

I slowly pulled the clothes from her body, swallowing hard as I looked at my gorgeous wife. My heart hammered in my chest, but this was make or break time. There was no waiting and hoping she came around. This was my moment to show her how much I loved her.

"I love you, Reese. And I know you think I'm an idiot, that I just have some obsession, but I love you and that's never going to stop."

Her fingers slid into my hair as I kissed my way down her body, running my tongue over her breasts and down to her belly button. I waited, desperate to hear the words, but they didn't come.

I dragged my tongue down her body, pulling her pants down until she was bare for me. She shuddered against me as I kissed up her thighs and ran my thumb across her pussy.

"Craig," she whispered.

"Tell me."

"Why?"

"Because I know you feel it. Just say it."

My breath fanned out across her pussy. I was aching inside, needing to be in her and needing to hear those three words. Inside I was begging her to say it. I could wait forever for her if she would only say what I needed to hear.

"I do. You know I do," she finally said.

"Then say it," I urged her. I moved back up to meet her lips, kissing her hard, taking everything I could from her. "Just say it."

"I love you."

That was all I needed. I was inside her just a minute later, taking what was mine, what always would be mine. There was nothing else in the world that meant anything to me if I didn't have her. She might try to run, but I would always be there to chase her, to bring her back to me.

Her hands slid to my face. There were tears in her eyes, but I knew deep down that it wasn't because she loved me. It was because she was going to walk away again. She just couldn't accept who I was, and she would fight her feelings forever.

I kissed her once more on the lips and pulled her into my arms as I laid down beside her. I could feel her tears on my chest and it broke my fucking heart. I didn't know what more I could say to her. She had made up her mind and there was nothing more I could do.

When I woke in the morning, she was gone. It was the weekend and she didn't have work. She didn't want to be with me, so she left. I sighed and stared at the ceiling. I was shocked when I felt a tear slip from my eyes. She was gone, and I was all alone.

I sat on the couch, drinking away my sorrows. I didn't even get a note or anything. She just up and walked out of the house. When I got up, I held out hope that she had just ran out to do some shopping, although, I don't know many people that going shopping at six in the morning. But all her clothes were gone. I hadn't even heard her leave.

So, here I was, sitting in this sad, pink house with creepy animals on the walls. It was seriously disturbing. But they were my friends now. Who else did I have? Michael Bublé was crooning on the radio, singing his sad song about kissing a fool. That was me, the fool.

I tossed yet another beer bottle on the ground and snatched another from the cooler that was sitting beside me. I had made a run to the store earlier and practically bought out the beer section. Well, not quite. There were at least twelve cases of beer stacked in the kitchen. I wasn't planning on going anywhere this weekend.

"Oh my God. Who decorated this place?"

I looked over drunkenly at Alec. He was standing in the doorway with Chance, Jackson, and Gabe. They were staring in disgust at the pink walls.

"And I thought I had bad taste," Jackson muttered. "Seriously, who decorated this place?"

"Jessica," I slurred.

"Shit." Chance's eyes were wide with shock. "Don't tell Storm. He'll go running for the hills."

"Don't worry about it." I stood and walked over to the bathroom, not even bothering to shut the door. I yanked down my zipper and pissed. I washed my hands and looked at myself in the mirror. Yep, I could still see my face. It was time for another beer. I stumbled back out to the living room where the guys had already grabbed their own beer and sat down. "She only did it to fuck with me."

"Jessica did?" Gabe asked.

"No, my little pixie. Shhhhe wanted me to freak out about the scary eyes staring at me all night."

"And the wall?" Chance asked.

"Oh, that's nothing. You should see the vagina she left on the table. It came with a book and everything."

"Yeah," Alec cleared his throat, "we heard about Reese leaving you. We figured we should come over and see how you're doing."

"How'd you hear?"

Alec scratched his jaw and glanced at the other guys. "Uh...well, she moved in with her grandma and Brooke called me up to tell me. I guess the grandma is pretty happy that she's there."

"That bitch was supposed to be on my side."

"The grandma?" Alec asked.

I looked at him in confusion. "What grandma?"

"Reese's grandma."

"No, that bat hates me."

"So, who was supposed to be on your side?"

"Brooke," I shouted. It was like he was fucking deaf. Did I have to repeat everything to him?

"I think if we get drunk too, our minds will work like his," Jackson suggested.

"Help yourself. I've got a gazillion more cases in the kitchen. Bought out the whole fucking store this morning."

"So, what happened?" Chance asked.

"With what?"

"With Reese," he stressed.

"She left."

He sighed. "I know she left. Why did she leave?"

"Fuck if I know. She doesn't really love me, I guess. I mean, she told me she loved me last night when we were making sweet love, but then she was gone. Why would she do that? Why would she walk out on me when I love her? Is it me? No, it's God." I stared up at the ceiling. "Why would you do this to me? Why did you take her from me?" I shouted.

"Craig, you gotta chill," Jackson said, steadying me with a hand on my arm. "She's not dead. She's just not here."

"I know she's not here. That's what I was just fucking telling you!"

They all sat there in silence for a minute. I didn't care. I grabbed another beer and drank some more.

"So, now that she's gone, are you gonna redo the place?" Alec asked.

"Redo the place? This is where we lived as man and wife! You want me to throw that all away?"

"You've lived here about five days," Alec pointed out.

"It doesn't matter. She decorated this place for me," I cried.

"She decorated it to piss you off," Gabe said.

I threw my beer bottle at Gabe. "Don't talk about my wife like that."

Chance cleared his throat and smiled. "So, you want to hear some good news?"

"Why not? My life's over. Someone should be happy."

His smile faltered for a second. "Uh...well, I'm going to ask Morgan to marry me."

"Seriously? My wife is leaving me and you're going on about how you're getting married? That's so mean!"

"I wasn't going on about it. I just mentioned it," Chance explained. "I thought you would be happy for me, man."

"Sure, I'm fucking delirious with...delirium for you. I'm so fucking deliriously deliriated that I want to throw you a fucking wedding shower. Is that better?"

"Maybe we should just take away the beer," Alec suggested. "I've never seen him like this before."

"That's because my wife tore out my heart and stomped all over it, crushing it into little bloody pieces on the ground."

"Are we not doing this the right way?" Alec asked the guys.

"Hell, I don't know. This is what all the guys did when someone else got dumped," Gabe said.

"We need Cazzo," Chance suggested. "And Ice. They both went through this. They'll know what to say."

Twenty minutes later, my house was fucking packed with the guys from Reed Security. Or, at least it seemed that way, but I think I was really just seeing triple of everyone. It looked so fucking crowded in the house.

"Alright, listen up everyone," Cap shouted. "I've got paint for everyone. If we're all going to be here, we're going to make this house look normal again. If you don't have a roller, start hauling animal heads out of here."

"I can't believe you want to paint over my wall," I cried on Alec's shoulder.

"Believe me, you'll thank us in the morning."

I picked up my roller and slowly started painting over the pink wall. But the more I painted, the angrier I got. How could she do this to me? I was a good man and she just walked out like I meant nothing.

"Whoa, easy with that roller." Gabe put his hand on my wrist. I had been very vigorously painting the wall. "I know you're angry, but you don't have to take it out on the wall."

"I can't believe she just walked out!"

"Let it out, man." He handed me a paintbrush. "Here, write it out on the wall."

I snatched the paintbrush out of his hand and dipped it in paint. "I am a good fucking person," I wrote on the wall. "I don't deserve to be shit on."

"That's it. Get it all out, man."

I shrugged Gabe off. I didn't want sympathy. I wanted to shoot something.

"You know, it's not like I'm the only one with faults. Do you know, she grinds her fucking teeth at night. It's fucking irritating as hell, but I'm not walking away over it."

Gabe nodded and picked up a brush of his own. "I'm with you there. You know, Isa's been bitching at me about taking out the fucking trash. Like I'm the only one with two functioning hands."

He wrote on the wall *take out your own fucking trash!*

"That's right," I said in agreement. "But seriously, you should really probably take out the trash." He nodded. "But yeah, fuck that!"

Alec snatched the paint brush out of my hand. "And why the fuck does the man always have to be the one to initiate sex? I feel like a fucking rapist, the way I'm always pouncing on her."

Take some fucking initiative, he painted on the wall.

"That's right! These women, they just don't get it. We'll show them. We'll paint all our fucking complaints on the wall!" I shouted.

Chapter Thirty-Eight

REESE

I pulled into the driveway at my house. Well, it was my house for about five days. Now, there were like ten trucks in the driveway. I put my car in park and wondered what was going on. I had to grab a few things that I hadn't taken with me. Anything else could wait until another time. I got out of my car just as a line of trucks pulled into the driveway behind me. What the hell?

A woman with strawberry blonde hair stepped out and rushed over to me. "Are you Reese?"

"Yeah."

"I'm Maggie. I came to collect my husband."

"Oh, it's nice to meet you." I shook her hand and turned for the house.

"So, I'm guessing you're here to get your things."

"Um..."

"Word spreads fast in this family. The minute you moved in with your grandma, everyone knew that you left Craig."

God, this was awkward. I didn't think I would have to explain myself to people that Craig worked with.

"Of course, we all knew it was going to happen. I mean, stalking only works for a select few women."

"Is that right."

"Well, if you met Knight and Kate, you would understand."

I stopped, wondering why we were having this little chat when I'd only just met her. "I'm sorry, but I really don't want to discuss my non-existent relationship with Craig with you."

"That's fine."

"Hey!" A woman came running up, looking really excited. "Is this Reese? Oh my gosh! You're so lucky that you married Craig. I'm Claire, by the way. He's super hot. Which you already know because you married him. What's he like in bed?"

"Claire!" Maggie slapped her on the arm. Claire turned bright red.

"Sorry, it just happens sometimes."

"Anyway," Maggie said, "We're all just here to collect our husbands and we'll be on our way. Oh, this is Lindsey," she said pointing to another woman and then she just pointed around the circle of women that had joined us. "Lucy, Vanessa, Cara, Ali, Morgan, Raegan, Ivy, Lola, Emma, Isa, and you know Florrie."

Florrie glared at me, probably because she was overprotective of Craig. Maggie stepped up to my defense though. Sort of.

"Chill, Florrie. Even though she broke Craig's heart and can't see how much he truly loves her, doesn't mean that we should shit on her. It's not her fault Craig's a psycho."

"Um, thanks."

"Don't worry, you'll get used to it," Maggie said, waving me off. I wanted to tell her I wouldn't be around to get used to it, but then she started dragging me to the house. It was so weird. I was going to be entering my house with a bunch of women that would probably be more comfortable walking in there than I was. I used my key to open the door and then stopped, my mouth hanging open in surprise.

All the guys were spread out around the living room, laying on the furniture or the floor. And each of them had one of the animals that had been hanging on the wall. Actually, one of them was laying on top of the life-sized bear that I had put in the study.

"What did they do to the walls?" Lindsey asked.

"It looks like they were complaining," Emma said, stepping up to the wall to read one of the messages.

"*I don't fluff fucking pillows*," Ivy read. "Whose is that?"

"That has to be Cazzo," Vanessa replied. "Is it really that big of a deal? Do we have to have flat pillows on the couch?"

"Look at this one," Ali said. "This has to be Chris. *I just want to watch my fucking tv show.*"

"Is this normal?" I asked.

"Is what normal?" Ali asked.

"The writing on the walls and the sleepover."

"It's not the first time we've seen something like this."

Ivy walked over to the man lying on the bear and shoved him off. He flopped on the ground and then jumped up, looking around the room frantically.

"What! What's going on? I swear, I didn't do it!"

"Jules, you said you would be home last night."

"I..." He rubbed at his eyes and looked around the room at the other men. "I swear-"

"You always swear. Ivy, I'll be home to take Johnny out. But you're never home when you say you'll be."

"No," he said, a tinge of anxiety in his voice. "You don't understand. This isn't what it looks like."

"You mean, it's not all of you getting together and bitching about your wives and then not coming home to us?"

He laughed nervously. "Not at all. You see, we were doing that yoga thing the other day and..."

"And we thought we needed to clear our minds," Hunter stepped in. "With everything that's happened over the past few years, we were all feeling like there was too much chaos in our heads."

"He's right." Chance stood up and walked over to Hunter, squeezing his shoulder. "Some of us had more to deal with than others. Hunter and I were talking about how we just weren't the same as we used to be."

"Right," Hunter grinned. "So, we figured that if we did yoga to get our bodies and minds in order, then we could be better husbands for the women that support us without reservation."

I was confused though. What did this have to do with what they painted on the walls? Not that I was buying this load of crap, but I was interested to see how they tried to talk their way out of it.

"So, what does yoga have to do with all the complaints on the walls?"

"Uh…" Hunter looked to Chance for help, but neither of them had any answers.

"It's to be more at peace with…our…family," Cap tried. "You know, if you're angry about stuff that's basically insignificant, then you can't be the best version of yourself."

"So you complained that *My wife is responsible for taking care of the kids. I have a job to do*," Maggie read off the wall, then looked to Cap. He swallowed hard and shook his head.

"That wasn't me. That was Jackson."

"Jackson doesn't have any kids," Maggie shot back.

"Okay, look, I know that I complained about that, but like I said, it's to get rid of those negative thoughts and move myself into a peaceful state of mind."

Maggie walked forward slowly. I watched in awe as she snatched her husband's testicles and twisted them painfully all with her eyes. Yeah, she had some voodoo power there. I felt bad for Cap. I could feel the fear radiating off him as Maggie stepped right up to him. She leaned in and whispered something in his ear. His eyes went wide just before she brought her knee up and nailed him in the balls. He bent over, gasping for air.

"How's your state of mind now?" She looked around the room, raising an eyebrow at the other guys. "Anyone else have any creative explanations for us?"

Chapter Thirty-Nine

CRAIG

"Reese, wait!"

I ran outside in just my underwear. I didn't have time to stop and put on something decent. My wife was walking out on me. Again. I had to figure out someway to get her to understand, to just fucking listen.

"What?"

"You came back. Don't just leave."

"I just came to grab a few things."

I shook my head, not willing to believe that she was really walking away. I was so close. I knew it. She admitted she loved me, so why wouldn't she just stay and try?

"Look, just give me some time. You told me you love me and I know that wasn't a lie."

She sighed and took a step toward me. "Craig, I do love you. There's a part of me that knows what a great man you are and wants to see where this goes."

"Then listen to that part of you," I urged her.

She shook her head sadly. "There's a bigger part of me that knows that your life is not what I want."

"We've been through all this a million times. But have you gotten hurt yet because of my job?"

"Me? It's not about me. I'm not worried that I'm going to get hurt. I'm worried that you're going to. I'm worried that I'll fall even harder for you and then you'll be gone. You already told me that your company was attacked. You said that people got hurt. How bad was it?"

Shit. If I told her how bad it really was, there was no way she would stay with me. But I couldn't lie to her either. "It was bad."

"How. Bad."

I gritted my teeth and gave in. "Hunter was shot in the neck. He almost died. Ice was shot in the heart." She gasped, but I kept going. She needed to hear it. "He just barely survived. Gabe had a severe concussion. Morgan and Chance were both taken. We didn't get them back for a year."

"What happened to them?"

I shrugged. I didn't have the whole story. "I don't know for sure. Chance was tortured."

Her whole face paled and she reached out to grab the door. "And what about you? You said that something happened and nobody trusted you. Why?"

"I didn't get out of the building with everyone else," I said after a moment. "Some of the guys that attacked us captured me. I was taken for information. They didn't get anything out of me, but they tried. Storm wasn't in the building, but he saw me being taken and he found me. It took a few days."

"But they did things to you."

I shrugged. "It was mostly just beating the shit out of me. Nothing I couldn't handle."

"And what happened that nobody trusted you?"

"We had been betrayed and nobody knew where I was. It looked like I just disappeared. It was wrong, but we were under attack and I was the missing link."

"And you want to work for people that didn't trust you?"

"They're my family. Yeah, it took me a while to get over it. I was pissed for a long time, but they would have never thought that if things weren't so fucked up. And holding onto that anger, no matter how much it was deserved, would have torn me up inside. So I chose forgiveness."

"And what if that happens again? What if you get taken on a job or you get shot in the heart like Ice? Am I supposed to just accept that?"

"Yes. Because you love me and I love you. I won't ever do anything to purposely get hurt-"

"You mean like having Alec shoot you on the job so that you could win me back."

I flushed bright red. "Okay, to clarify, I didn't ask him to shoot me. But no, I'll never do anything like that again. If you just stay with me, I'll do anything to make sure that I always come home to you."

"Except leave the job that puts your life in danger."

I didn't say anything. What did she want me to do? She knew why I joined the military, and that was the same reason I was in security. It was all to protect people that couldn't protect themselves. Not every job was like that, but most were. And it was rewarding to know that I was helping others. But she wanted me to ditch all that to be the boring spouse.

"Look, I just want a divorce. I'm not asking you to change who you are. I'm just asking that you realize that this isn't going to work and let me walk away."

But I was stubborn and that was never gonna happen. "No."

Her whole body tightened in anger. "Fine. I'm going to start dating. A piece of paper that I didn't want to sign in the first place means nothing to me."

She opened her door and got in, slamming it and peeling out of the driveway.

"That went well," Alec said from behind me.

"I'll figure it out."

"Maybe you should just walk away. I know you love her, but this train has been going down the wrong track for too long. Besides, do you really want a woman that doesn't want you?"

I turned around and glared at him. "You don't know what it's like when we're together. You see this and you think I'm chasing a woman that doesn't want me. But she loves me, and if you could see the way we are when she just lets this all go, you would see that what we have is worth fighting for."

I stormed past him, but he grabbed my arm, stopping me beside him. "I've been where you are. You know what it was like with Florrie and me. Sometimes walking away is for the best."

"Reese isn't Florrie though. She won't come to her senses. She'll walk away and think it's for the best. I would lose her forever."

"Then just walk away. She's not worth it."

I jerked my arm from his grip. "She's worth everything."

Chapter Forty

REESE

I waited in the restaurant for twenty minutes before my date finally showed up. I hated waiting. Craig would never make me wait. I shook my head in frustration. I couldn't think about what Craig would or wouldn't do. If I was going to move on, I just had to rip off the bandaid. And if Craig wouldn't give me a divorce, I would just have to go out on dates until he realized that we weren't staying together.

I stood as the man approached, but he didn't seem to notice and just sat down. Feeling like an idiot for standing, I sat back down and took a sip of my wine. The man was okay looking. Compared to Craig, most men were just okay in general. He was tall and had blonde hair, but it was shaggy and that really wasn't my thing. And then there was his outfit. He put in absolutely no effort. His tie was hanging loosely from his neck and his shirt was wrinkled, like he picked it up off the floor after it had been there for a week. He also had a weird eye twitch that made my eye twitch every time I looked at him.

"So, Reyna, right?"

"Reese."

"Right. Right. I'm Steven."

"It's nice to meet you. Were you working late?"

He looked at me in confusion. "No."

"Oh." I grabbed my glass and took a huge gulp of wine. But then he sat up and it appeared that he was collecting himself.

"You're a school teacher."

"Yes. I teach kindergarten."

"Lots of germs."

"Well, you get used to it," I said with a smile. God, this was painful.

"I'm an accountant."

"Oh. Is that exciting?"

"No."

"Oh, well, I'm sure you have to be really smart to work with numbers all the time."

"Yes."

I tapped my finger on the table, trying to figure out what to say next. If I could get a response out of him that actually furthered conversation, that would be helpful.

"So, what do you do in your free time?"

"Free time?"

"Yes. Like, when you're not at work."

"I eat dinner and go to bed. I start work early."

"Oh." God, I wish I had something other to say than 'oh'.

We sat in awkward silence for the next five minutes until the waiter came by to take our orders. When the waiter left, there was just silence again. And he seemed perfectly fine with it. It was like he had absolutely no desire to speak at all.

"My little Reese's Pieces!" My head shot up in relief and anger when Craig stepped up to the table. How could he just show up here when I was on a date? On the other hand, this gave me the perfect excuse to walk away. "Brooke told me you were here."

"She did, huh?"

"Yeah." He pulled up a chair and sat down with us. "Hey, I'm Craig."

"Steven."

"Hi, Steven. What do you do for a living?"

"Accountant."

"Wow," Craig grinned. "That's sounds...exciting. Doesn't that sound exciting, my little sprite?"

"Yes," I said through clenched teeth. It was one thing for him to show up, it was another for him to be rude.

"So, Steven. Did my little woman tell you that we're married?"

"No," Steven responded with absolutely zero feeling. It was like he didn't even care. If a random guy walked up to me and started hitting on me, would he care? This sucked.

"Yeah, we've been married all of a week. And then she just up and left me. Yeah, it hurt deep down, but you know how it is," he grinned. "You either fight like hell or you move on. Am I right?"

"Sure."

I eyed Craig, trying to convey to him that he was going to have to start some kind of fight to get me out of here.

"So, tell me, Reese, what does Steven have that I don't?"

I rolled my eyes. Why did Craig have to be so dense? Either that or he was purposely dragging this out to torture me.

"I don't know Steven, so I couldn't say."

"Yeah, but let's look at this realistically. Steven, you work how many hours a week?"

"Seventy-two."

"Seventy-two. Wow, that's a lot of hours. Now, I work a lot too, but I have down time between jobs. Actually," he started laughing like he was telling a really funny joke. "I'm off for a while because I was recently shot three times. In the ass, the foot, and the leg. Talk about bad luck."

Steven still didn't say anything.

"What about guns? How do you feel about those?"

"They're bad."

"They're bad," Craig repeated. "Well, Reese, if you don't want a guy that has guns, then you should definitely go with Steven. He's the safer choice. That is, unless your house gets broken into. Then, I guess you just have to wait for someone to show up."

"I have my bat," I said testily.

He slapped himself on the forehead. "That's right. I completely forgot. And that will really come in handy if someone comes to rob your silverware." He nodded for a moment and then turned back to Steven. "So, how are you at hand-to-hand combat?"

"Craig!"

"I've never studied."

"Really? A strapping young man such as yourself? You should stop by the company sometime. I'd be glad to show you a few things."

"No, thank you."

"Well, I think this has been enlightening." Craig slapped his palms on the table and gave me a peck on the cheek before leaving. I smiled awkwardly at Steven. The thing was, Craig was right all around. Steven wasn't the man for me, and there was no point sitting around here pretending that he would be.

"I'm sorry, Steven, but I think it would be wrong to sit here with you after what you just heard. I am married. I'm so sorry."

"Goodnight."

The waiter brought our food as I stood and Steven dug right into his food, not even bothering to give me a second look. When I got outside, Craig was leaning against the building, like he knew I would leave.

"What the hell was that?"

"That was me reminding you who you're married to."

"Like I could forget," I spat back. "At least you're predictable."

"How's that?"

"You're still stalking me!"

He bobbed his head back and forth. "Technically, this wasn't stalking. Brooke called and told me you would be here."

"Of course she did."

"And she thought that as your husband, I would want to know where you were so that I could look out for you."

"So you could ruin my date, you mean."

"Oh, come on, Reese. That guy was as boring as mud. He didn't even try to have any kind of conversation with you. And he was twenty minutes late!"

I gasped. "How did you know that?"

"Because I followed you here and I've been watching from outside. Also...I may have planted a microphone on your purse so that I could hear the conversation. The way I see it, you needed the rescue."

"But you didn't rescue me! You ruined the date and then left."

"Yes, but I did mention that you were married. That ended the date and you know it."

"Fine. Let's say that he wasn't the most interesting man. What you did in there was so rude, trying to point out how he couldn't rescue me because he didn't know hand-to-hand combat. Like I need rescuing! You live in a fantasy world where there is always a damsel in distress. But I'm not one of those girls and I never will be!"

He spun me around, gently shoving me against the wall where he once stood. His knee nudged between my legs so he was nestled against my body. "Go ahead. Keep dating douchebags. I'll keep showing up and proving that I'm the better choice."

He kissed me hard, sucking me into his life with every swipe of his tongue against mine. He pulled away suddenly, and then he was gone, leaving me shaking with need against the building.

Chapter Forty-One

CRAIG

"Goddammit!" I shouted, slamming my fist into the locker.

"Problems?" Sinner asked as he stepped out of the shower.

"She's going on another fucking date."

He nodded, stepping over to his locker and grabbing his clothes. "Did you try yoga with her?"

"When exactly would I have done that? She doesn't even want to be in the same room with me."

"Look," he stepped over to me, glancing around the room really quick. "I know a guy-"

"I'm not murdering anyone."

"That's not what I'm suggesting. I think we need to do a little snatch and grab."

"What do you have in mind?"

"I know this guy that's an actor at one of the Benedum Center For Performing Arts. We snatch her real date and swap him out for this guy. He's an actor. He can play it anyway you want."

"What would we do with the guy that we snatch?"

"You know, kidnapping isn't completely out of your realm."

"No," I shook my head. "I'm not kidnapping some other dude and replacing him with an actor. She needs to see that anyone she dates is wrong for her. It has to be someone real."

"Well, it's not like I suggested you replace him with a dummy. Of course this guy's real."

"You know what I mean. No, I'll show up just like I did the last four times she's gone on a date. I don't know where she's getting these guys from. None of them are even close to her type."

I grabbed my stuff out of my locker and headed out.

"So, that's a no on the actor?" Sinner shouted.

I didn't stop and talk. I got out of the building as quickly as possible and ran for my truck. I was just about to leave when Alec stepped in front of my truck with Florrie.

"Move," I said after I rolled down my window. "I have to get to Reese."

"Is she okay?" Florrie asked.

"She's fine. She's just going out on another date."

Alec rolled his eyes. "Alright, lets go."

"What?"

"Come on, this is ridiculous. Every time you show up, you make things worse. Florrie and I will go with you and we'll spy on her for you."

"Seriously?"

"Yeah. What time is the date?"

"An hour."

"Florrie and I will grab some stuff and we'll meet you at the location. Text me the address."

"On it."

I headed right to the restaurant that Brooke told me they would be at and found a good place to park so that I could see most of the restaurant. Alec and Florrie showed up forty-five minutes later and climbed in the truck with me.

"Alright, after her date shows up, Florrie will go in and plant a bug at the table. We'll wait in here. You need to know how the date goes when you don't show up."

"Fine," I grumbled. I didn't like it, but he had a point. I needed to see how she acted on the date and use that to my advantage.

"I think that's him," Florrie said, pointing to some douchebag in a sport coat.

"How do you know?"

"Because, I talked to Brooke and she gave me the rundown. That has to be him."

"You're awfully chummy with Brooke," I pointed out. Florrie didn't get chummy with most people.

"Yeah, well, she's cool. I like her style. Besides, the only girl friend I have is Lola and we're more teammates than anything."

"So, you hang out with Brooke?"

Florrie shrugged. "I've taken her shooting."

"And? How was it?"

She grinned, sighing slightly. "It was...everything I had hoped it would be."

"Just so you know," Alec interrupted. "I'm not sharing, even if it is with a girl."

"Shut up," she said, slapping Alec. "It's not like that. Okay, I'm going in."

I turned my attention back to the restaurant. The sport coat had just sat down and Reese was smiling at him.

"That's not good. She's smiling."

"Maybe he's funny."

"I'm funny," I snapped. "She doesn't need anyone else to be funny with."

"Maybe he has a quality to him."

"Like what?"

"You know, a certain quality."

I stared at him. "No, I don't know. What quality?"

"Look, I don't know. Some guys just have something about them that makes them likable. You know, like Sinner is devastatingly charming. He can't help it. All the ladies love him. And Cazzo has that whole broody thing going on. Plus the nipple ring. Something about that just gets the ladies going. And then there's Knight. He's so dark and... something. I don't get it, but again-"

"The ladies love it. Yeah, I'm getting that. So, what's my quality?"

"Your quality?"

"Yeah, I've got to have something. I mean, I kidnapped Reese and manipulated her into marrying me, but she still said she loves me."

"Okay, well, if I had to guess I would say...you're quirky."

"Quirky? That's what you're giving me?"

"Hey, I'm not a chick. Maybe there's something else."

"Still, you could say that I'm devastatingly handsome or I'm deadly with a weapon, but you go for quirky? I'm hurt, man. Seriously."

"I'm sorry. What the fuck do you want me to say? Yeah, you're sexy as fuck and any lady would be lucky to have you. I mean, you have those really big, vibrant eyes and, yeah, you're deadly with a weapon."

I looked back at the restaurant and raised my binoculars. "It just feels like you're saying that to placate me."

"Fine, you're amazing. Alright? There, I said it. I don't get what the fuck is going through Reese's head. She has one of the best guys I know, and she's being a fool. That's what I really think."

I turned back to him and raised an eyebrow. "I wonder what Dr. Sunshine would have to say about that declaration."

His fist shot out and punched me in the eye. "Ow!"

"You're an asshole."

"Still, you didn't have to punch me. You know, I think you have some passive-aggressive issues that you need to deal with. First, shooting me in the foot and the leg, then punching me in the face. Seriously, I think you need to see a counselor."

"You practically forced me to say that shit!"

"I think Dr. Sunshine would say that you have repressed feelings."

"I think Dr. Sunshine would wonder why the fuck you're goading me."

"Hey, Florrie's at the table."

We both looked through our binoculars as Florrie approached Reese.

"Hey, Reese. Are you on a date?"

"Um...yeah."

"That's cool. I mean, I'm sure Craig wouldn't think so, but since you kicked him to the curb, I guess he doesn't have anything to say about it."

"Who's Craig?" the sport coat asked.

"Oh, her husband."

"You're married?"

Reese laughed lightly. "Ex. Well, you see, I married under duress. It wasn't like I wanted to be married. I was actually kidnapped by him."

"That is so inaccurate," I grumbled.

"Oh. Do you have a restraining order against him?"

"No. He's a good guy, just a little...inventive in his ways of getting my attention."

"But he kidnapped you?"

"Well, I mean, he was stalking me first, which led to me being kidnapped. Technically, he rescued me from my kidnapper, but then kidnapped me again?"

"So, how did you end up married to him?"

She looked back to Florrie. "Did you need something?"

"Oh! I was just coming to say hi. I was going to meet a friend, but she cancelled. So, I'm just on my way out." She turned to sport coat. "It was nice to meet you." She held her hand out, knocking over the wine glass and spilling it over the table. The man jumped out of his seat and Florrie dropped the mic during the distraction. "Oh, I'm so terribly sorry." She got down on her knees and then we couldn't see anything.

"Why is she on her knees in front of him?" Alec growled.

"Uh...I think...she's cleaning him?"

"Fuck that!" Alec burst out of the truck. I had to run to catch up to him, and then I tackled him to the ground. "Get the fuck off me!"

"No, you'll ruin my mission."

"Florrie has her hands on some guy's junk. Let me the fuck up so I can go shoot him."

He tossed me off him and moved to get up. I snatched his foot, tripping him and making him fall back to the ground. "You're not blowing this for me!" He kicked out, catching me in the face. "What the fuck, man? Are you trying to fuck up my face?"

"Get off me!"

I straddled him, grabbing his arms so that he couldn't fight back. Pulling out a zip tie that I happened to have stashed in my back pocket, just in case, I tied his wrists together.

"Now, just stop struggling. You're making it very difficult for me to spy on my girl with your freaking out." He started bucking his hips, trying to get me off. "Ooh! It's like a bucking bronco. Ride 'em, cowboy!"

I laughed, looking up to see a woman and her young daughter standing just a few feet away. I slapped Alec in the head several times, trying to get him to stop so that the woman didn't call the police on us. He looked up finally and his whole body sagged.

"Hey," I laughed uncomfortably. "We're just...playing a game of cops and robbers."

The woman took her daughter's hand and rushed off in the other direction. I got off Alec and yanked him to his feet.

"Would you relax? Florrie's coming across the street now."

Now that he was standing, he broke the zip tie and ran over to Florrie. "What the fuck were you doing on your knees?"

"I was lifting his wallet." She held the wallet up and I snatched it from her. "Now you know who he is and you can do a background check on him."

I kissed her on the mouth, pulling back quickly. "You're so awesome."

Alec grabbed me by the collar, but Florrie stepped in. "Would you relax!"

"He shouldn't be fucking kissing you."

"Shut up. This isn't about you," I cut in. "Now, what did you think about him?"

"Um, eh. He wasn't anything to write home about."

"Yeah, but she was laughing. Did he...did he seem to have a quality about him?"

"I guess. He seemed charming, but maybe in a smarmy way."

"What about me? Do you think I have a quality?"

"Definitely."

I sighed in relief. "What is it?"

"You're quirky."

Chapter Forty-Two

REESE

While the date wasn't going bad, I wasn't really enjoying myself either. Evan was nice enough and he was charming, but there was something about him that didn't sit right with me. He was too charming. Too on. It was like he was trying to impress me with all his fun stories and what he did for work. It was all a show. And sadly enough, as I did on every date, I sat here wondering why I couldn't just accept Craig. He didn't try and impress me or charm me. He was just himself, and I found myself missing that right now.

"Well, would you let me drive you home?"

"I actually drove myself."

"Okay. Well, I would love to take you out again."

He helped me with my coat and we walked toward the door. "Um..." I paused too long trying to come up with something to say. We stepped outside and into the night, but when I turned around, he looked pissed.

"I see. So, you wanted a free dinner and that's it."

"What? No, that's not it at all."

"Then why don't you want to go out with me again?"

"Honestly, I just don't think that we'd make a good pair."

He scoffed, "Right. You could tell all that by one date."

"Actually, I can. Frankly, I don't like your attitude. Everything about you screams that you're just trying to impress me."

"Isn't that what women want?" he shouted.

"No, that's not what I want."

"Is everything alright here?"

Of course Craig was here. It was so obvious when Florrie showed up that Craig was somewhere waiting.

"Mind your own business," Evan spat.

"Why don't you just cool down," Craig said, coming up beside me.

I turned to Craig, crossing my arms and glaring at him. "Why are you here?"

"I'm just looking out for you."

"I don't need you to look out for me."

"You came out of the restaurant and he was yelling at you!"

Evan stepped up to Craig, probably trying to impress me in some way. "You need to back the fuck off. Who the hell do you think you are?"

"I'm her fucking husband!"

Evan turned to me, his face contorted in rage. "You said he was your ex. You bitch!"

He lunged for me, but Craig stepped between us, grabbing Evan's arm and twisting it up behind his back.

"Apologize, asshole."

"Fuck you!"

"Apologize or I'll break your fucking arm."

"I'd like to see you try!"

Craig jerked Evan's arm and the distinct sound of bone breaking filled the air. I cringed as Evan screamed. This was not how I had pictured this going. I needed Craig to leave. Hell, I needed them both to leave. Craig was saying something to Evan, but I couldn't stand here and watch anymore. Whatever was going to happen, I wanted nothing to do with it. I turned around and walked right into another man who happened to be very handsome. Despite his concerned expression, his eyes twinkled at me.

"Is everything alright, ma'am?"

"Uh...those two are fighting and..." He walked around me, his face serious. "Uh, maybe you don't want to do that."

"Police! Break it up!"

Craig released the man and stepped back. "Officer."

"What's going on here?"

"This guy just broke my fucking arm!" Evan shouted.

"Because you tried to attack a woman," Craig shot back.

"Bullshit, you attacked me because you wanted an apology."

"Whatever's going on here needs to stop now, or we'll take this to the station."

"Whatever," Evan spat. "She's not worth it."

Evan walked away and left me standing with Craig and the officer. "Are you okay, Reese?"

"Yes."

"Reese," the officer grinned. "The name suits you."

"Thank you," I smiled.

"Oh, come on. You've got to be kidding me!" Craig shouted. "Tell me you're not flirting with this guy."

I ignored Craig and stared at the man in front of me. He seemed to be very interested, and he handled that whole situation without even pulling out his gun. I'd say that was a big plus.

"I don't suppose you'd like to go out to dinner with me tomorrow night."

Craig snorted. "Are you kidding? Of course she doesn't. Her last date just tried to attack her."

"That sounds great." I pulled out my phone and handed it to him so he could put in his information. He handed it back to me when he was done and grinned.

"Leif. I'll call you tomorrow."

"Okay," I said, somewhat giddily. It's not that I really liked him. I didn't even know him. But he was interested in me, and he asked me out right in front of Craig. It won major points with me. I smiled as he walked away. That is, until Craig stepped in front of me.

"You're not seriously going out with him."

"Of course I am. Why wouldn't I?"

"His name is Leif!"

"And?"

"And who names their kid that? Was he born from a plant? Is he a fucking explorer?"

I shrugged. "Maybe he's from Iceland. I bet he's got huge muscles."

"I've got huge muscles!"

"And he probably has the best sense of humor."

"I'm fucking hilarious!"

"You're gonna have to give me a better reason that I can't go out with him than that."

"You can't because you're-"

"Married. I know. You keep reminding me."

I turned and headed for my car in the parking lot. I could feel the heat coming off Craig as he walked behind me. He was pissed.

"Tell me what he has that I don't."

"Well, he didn't try to kidnap me yet."

"Give it time. You've only just met him."

"He also didn't try to trick me into marrying him," I smirked.

He got in front of me, walking backwards so he could still talk to me.

"Hey, I didn't try to do that until weeks after we first met."

I stopped walking. "He hasn't killed anyone in front of me."

"Alright, *maybe* he has that going for him, but he's in danger every single day that he steps out in his uniform. And that's what you told me was standing in the way. So, tell me why he's okay to go out with, but not me, when you're already in love with me."

I didn't know what to say. He was absolutely right. I was pushing him away, just for the sake of pushing him away. Maybe I wanted to see if he would still be interested if he had a chance to step away from me. It was all insane. I mean, he was telling me he loved me way too soon, and maybe he was being serious, but I was finding it all very hard to believe. And deep down, I was worried that after the charm of stalking me wore off, he wouldn't want me anymore. A man like Craig was just too big of a risk. I had too much to lose if he walked away.

"Maybe it's just because of that. I don't love him. I can go out with him this once and it doesn't mean anything to me. *You* do mean something to me, as you keep pointing out. But I don't want you to mean anything to me. You stalked me and manipulated my whole life. And as soon as you have me right where you want me, I won't be so interesting anymore. You'll drop me and move on to stalking some other woman that you meet at...a pumpkin patch! You'll shoot some pumpkin that looked like it was about to attack her and she'll fall for this whole routine of you being in love with her, and how you protected her. But I'm not falling for it, so just leave me alone!"

I walked away and he didn't follow. At least, not until I was driving down the road to my grandma's house. I watched as he parked on the side of the road and waited until I got inside. Then he drove away and I was left wondering if I was hurting myself or protecting myself from getting hurt.

Chapter Forty-Three

CRAIG

"Three fucking dates, Brooke! You told me that she would come around. You said that I just had to keep stalking her. You know what she did when I showed up at the restaurant last night? She ignored me. She pretended I wasn't even fucking there!"

"Okay, calm down." Brooke sat across from me in my living room, perfectly calm and relaxed while my fucking world was falling apart. "Listen, I told you that this might happen. She just needs to see that what's out there isn't nearly as good as what she had with you."

I gripped my hair and screamed in frustration. "She's going out with him again. Do you know what that means?"

"Um...it's their fourth date?"

"Exactly! Don't you women have a three date rule or something?"

"Oh..."

I started pacing the room. I really needed to go shoot someone or beat up a druggie. Anything to relieve the tension running through me. "Yeah, that's what I was thinking. God, I'm so fucked. If she goes home with him, I'll never hear from her again."

"Just hold on. It can't be all that bad."

"It can't be that bad? Are you serious? Does she look like the type of woman that would go screw someone else and then just come waltzing back to me?"

Brooke grimaced. "Okay, maybe you need to do something to make sure that doesn't happen. Blow up the bridge before they can cross it and get home, or go murder someone so that he gets called out."

"You want me to murder someone?"

"Well, it's not too far from what you already do." I shot her a glare, but she just shrugged. "I'm just trying to be realistic here."

"I'm not going to kill someone or blow up a bridge. I'll just have to think of something else."

"Well, you'd better hurry," she said as she looked at her watch. "Her date just started."

"Shit." I grabbed my coat and raced out of the house and headed toward town. I had to come up with something, anything to keep her from going home with him. But on the way into town, I got a flat tire and then I got pulled over for speeding, which was total bullshit. Since when did the police pull you over for going ten miles over the speed limit? By the time I got to the restaurant, they were already gone. I dialed Cap's number, praying that he would pick up.

"Yes?" he said, as if he was expecting my call.

"Cap, I need Becky to look up this guy's address."

He sighed into the phone. "I really wish I could help you, but today was Becky's last day, or did you forget?"

"Shit."

"Yeah, you missed the going away party and everything."

"Look, I'll send her a wreath or something. Just get me that address. They've already left the restaurant and this is the fourth date!"

"Ooh, that's not good."

"I already fucking know that!"

"Alright, I'll get you the address, but you have to promise that you won't go shooting anyone."

"Of course I won't."

"Alright, what's his name?"

"Leif something. He works at the police station."

There was silence on the other end. "Wait, he works there or he's a cop?"

"Does it fucking matter?"

"No, I guess not. I just need to know if I should plan on bailing you out later."

"I'm not planning on confronting him. I just need to show my face so that Reese doesn't go through with it."

"And if she does?"

"She won't. She loves me."

"Alright. Give me a few minutes and I'll text you the address."

I waited outside the restaurant, not having a fucking clue which way I was supposed to head. Frustration was mounting so deep inside me that I thought I might pull out my gun and shoot something just so I didn't go insane.

My phone beeped and I pulled up the message from Cap. I quickly found the location and sped through town to get there. I was about halfway there when police sirens sounded behind me. I hit the gas pedal and sped all the way to the house. My heart skipped a beat when I saw that Reese and Leif were just getting out of his car. They must have stopped somewhere. I pulled over, my tires jumping up over the curb. I got out and made a dash for it, but stopped when Reese saw me. I prayed that she would come toward me. I prayed and pleaded, but she just stood there.

I was tackled to the ground, my arms wrenched behind my back as the cop read me my rights. But I kept staring at Reese. I watched as she turned away from me. I watched as she laced her fingers through that jackass's hand. And I watched as she gave me one backward glance before walking into his house and leaving me forever.

"Do you know why you're here?" the officer that arrested me asked.

Yeah, I fucking knew why I was in the police station. What I didn't know was why I was in an interrogation room instead of in a cell. I should have already been processed, but instead, I was hanging out and waiting to find out what happened to me. Not that it mattered. My wife was gone, off with that douchebag, probably lying in his bed right now.

"Yeah."

"Do you want to tell me why you didn't stop when I hit my lights?"

"Does it matter? Just lock me up and throw away the key."

He raised an eyebrow at me. "Well, the way I hear it, you have a friend here at the station, and he wants to know what the fuck is going on with you."

"What's going on with me? My wife left me for that jackass, Leif. What kind of name is that anyway? *Hey, I'm Leif and I'm a Norse God.*"

The cop snorted, but then cleared his throat to cover it. "And how did that lead you to his property tonight?"

I might as well tell him. He obviously wanted to know. Besides, it wasn't like I had anything to lose at this point. "My wife was on a date with him. Apparently, she doesn't believe that I love her. She thinks that just because I was following her around everywhere and I kind of tricked her into marrying me that I don't really love her. That it's all in my head and as soon as she gives in, I'll walk away."

"Is she right?"

"Of course not." I looked down at his notepad, but he wasn't actually writing anything. "Aren't you going to write down what happened?"

"What? Oh, no, I just want to hear the story."

"Anyway, she's been seeing *Leif.* This was their fourth date."

The officer cringed, sucking in a deep breath. "Ouch."

"I know, right?"

"You know what happens on the fourth date, right?"

"Of course I fucking know. Why do you think I didn't stop when you flashed your lights? I was trying to get to her before she went in."

"You did, though."

"Yeah, but it didn't do anything. I never actually thought it would happen. I mean, I thought she was just trying to piss me off, but four dates? And then when I found out that she wasn't at the restaurant anymore, I just had to know. She was getting out of the car and walking toward the house with him. And when she saw me, she just kept walking. Right out of my life and into his bed."

"Sorry, man. That's terrible."

I nodded solemnly. "Do whatever you have to do. It's not like it matters now anyway. She's gone."

The officer stood and picked up his pad, but he made no move to take me away. "Listen, I'm not gonna arrest you. As far as I'm concerned, my radar gun wasn't calibrated properly and you thought your woman was in trouble. Let's just call it square."

"Why are you doing this?"

He leaned in so that only I could hear. "Between you and me? Leif is a dick and if he happens to walk into a few fists and he doesn't see who did it, I won't come looking for you."

I nodded to him, thankful that he saw my side of things, but it didn't change anything. Reese was gone and I was all alone again.

Chapter Forty-Four

REESE

"Did you sleep with him?"

Brooke stormed into my grandma's kitchen, where we were having our morning tea. This wasn't exactly something I wanted my grandmother to hear.

"Brooke, this isn't really something I want to discuss right now."

"Why not? It's not like Grandma's never heard about sex before."

Grandma sighed next to me. "I miss sex. Do you think it would be the same for me as it was when Grandpa was alive?"

"Grandma! Don't talk like that."

"Why not?"

"Because...you're my grandma and...you're too old to be thinking about sex!"

"Oh, please. Do you think that just because a woman gets older that she doesn't want sex anymore?"

"Well, you shouldn't. Besides, the last thing I need to think about is my grandmother having sex."

"It doesn't matter what she does," Brooke cut in. "I need to know what you did. Did you sleep with him?"

"No, of course not. Why would you think that?"

"Uh...because you went home with him on the fourth date!"

"So, what? He wanted to give me a book."

"Oh, honey, that's not all he wanted to give you."

"Well, it doesn't matter, because nothing else happened."

Brooke stared at me in confusion. "Wait, so you're telling me that Craig almost got arrested last night because you went inside to get a book?"

I shrugged. I wasn't sure what she wanted me to say. I wasn't responsible for what Craig did.

"Then why didn't you try to help him when he was being handcuffed?"

"Because Leif told me that if I interfered, I could get in trouble. I didn't want to cause any problems."

She flopped down in the chair. "I can't believe that. Craig is over at your house, completely wrecked because he thinks he lost you."

"He did lose me!"

"Such a shame," my grandma said from beside me. "He's such a good boy."

"What? You're the one that had me kidnapped so that he couldn't get me."

"Well, I may have been mistaken about him. What do you want me to say? Look at all the effort he's put into getting you back."

"He's psychotic, grandma. He had me kidnapped. He tricked me into marrying him. He sold my house out from under me!"

"Yes, all in the name of love."

"What's love got to do with it? He's a psychopath!"

"See, you've always been a little too uptight," Brooke said. "You need to loosen up and learn to go with the flow."

"So, I should just allow him to do whatever he wants to get me? I should let him kidnap me and force me to marry him? What if he decides to do something even crazier?"

"Well, honestly," my grandma said. "Can you really say that you haven't enjoyed your time with him?"

"Well, I guess not all of it was bad."

"Isn't that all you need in life? Someone that you can enjoy life with?"

"Well, yes, but-"

"No buts," grandma scolded. "Seriously, Reese, you've always been too uptight for your own good. This man is good for you. Sure, I didn't see it in the beginning, but that man loves you very much. Maybe he is a little outrageous in his methods, but it makes life exciting."

I shook my head, confused by this change of events. "But, you and grandpa were always so...normal."

"Sure, when we had kids, but before that, your grandfather had a way of making everything exciting. And just because things weren't chaotic anymore doesn't mean that we didn't get our thrills. We just had to be more careful about how we got them. It's not like we wanted our daughter walking in on the things we did."

"So, you and grandpa..."

She smiled as she looked off into space, obviously remembering something. "There was this one time at the zoo. Your grandfather had me pressed against the cage-"

"Oh, grandma! There are children at the zoo."

"We were careful. Honestly, it's not like he took me right in front of a tour group."

"Ew."

"I like your style," Brooke grinned.

"Stop it!"

"What? You should take a page from her book. She knew how to live life."

"But he's going to break my heart!" I shouted.

Grandma took my hand and squeezed it. "So what if he does? Do you really want to go through life wondering what might have happened? He may break your heart, and I can almost guarantee that he will. We're only humans after all. We all make mistakes. But isn't it better to go along for the ride and enjoy it?"

"That ride could be dangerous."

"Oh, nonsense. It's not like he's going to take you along on a job and tell you to shoot someone. He's just asking you to love him like he loves you."

I looked at Brooke and then back to Grandma. I couldn't believe it, but I was starting to think they had the right idea. I did love Craig, and we were already married. Why not give it a shot and see how it went? What was the worst that could happen? I would get a divorce? That would have to happen anyway if I chose not to stick around.

Suddenly, I felt like I had to see him now. I stood and raced for the front door. If I didn't get to him soon, it could be too late. He might change his mind and tell me he didn't want me. I jumped in my car and headed to his place, but then pulled over when I thought about what I was doing. Before I saw Craig, I had to break things off with Leif. Craig needed to know that I was serious and things were definitely over with the cop.

I turned the car around and headed to Leif's house. He wasn't working today, so I could stop in and see him really quick, tell him things weren't working, and then get over to Craig. The urge to see him was so strong that I almost called him. But this wasn't something I wanted to say over the phone. Besides, he might show up at Leif's house and make everything worse.

I got out of the car as soon as I parked in his driveway and raced to the front door. But when I knocked, nobody answered. His truck was in the driveway, so he must be home. I went around the side of his house, thinking maybe he was raking leaves or something. The door on his shed was open and I heard voices, so I headed that way.

"I told you not to bring this shit around here. I would lose my job and end up in jail if anyone ever saw this."

I stopped outside the door, praying that he hadn't heard me walking up.

"I need to get rid of this shipment. The cops are crawling all over me and you're doing nothing to stop them from looking."

"What the fuck do you expect me to do with this shit? I don't have anywhere to store this."

"I don't give a shit. Just get it the fuck out of here."

I'd heard enough. Screw telling him that things were over between us. I would just tell Craig what happened and let him deal with Leif if he ever came around. I started jogging away, but the crunching of leaves made it sound a lot louder when I was trying to sneak away.

"Reese!"

I cringed and slowly turned around. "Oh, hey!" I said too cheerily.

"I was just stopping by to say hi, but I heard you had company. I'll just catch up with you later."

The two of them looked at each other and then they were running toward me. Eyes wide, I took off running, but I could hear them gaining on me. I screamed as I was tackled to the ground, but Leif shoved his hand over my mouth, pressing down so hard that it felt like my teeth were cutting my lips. Struggling underneath him, I tried to figure out a way to get out from under him, but I had nothing. I should have let Craig train me.

"Shut up! Stupid bitch. You know, I would have kept you out of this, but now you're gonna have to disappear."

I mumbled under his hand. He moved his hand slightly so I could speak. "You won't get away with it."

"Why don't you call your husband to come rescue you? Oh, that's right. You chose me. I guess you chose wrong."

He hauled me up, gripping my arms so hard there would be bruises. "Don't try to scream, or I'll send you off with Dirk. He won't make your disappearance quite so pleasant."

I wanted to say something funny or witty, but I was terrified. I had no idea what I was going to do. He walked me to the back door and led me through the house to the garage. Along the way, I tried to think of something I could do or anything I could leave behind as a clue. Something that would let someone know that I had been here. But there was nothing I could drop besides my phone, which was in my back pocket. And that was something that I would need. The other guy disappeared, but Leif was on my side. I slowly stuck my hand in my back pocket and slid my phone out. If he checked me, he would find it in my pocket. I slipped it into my waistband under my underwear and prayed that he didn't find it.

"I really hate to do this. You would have been a good fuck."

"I wouldn't have fucked you. I was coming to tell you that I'm getting back together with my husband."

He snorted with laughter. "Yeah, you seem like the type of bitch that can't make up her mind."

He shoved me against the old car that was parked in his garage. He unzipped my coat and threw it in the corner, then patted me down. I breathed a sigh of relief when he didn't find the phone. He popped the trunk and shoved me inside. My heart kicked into overdrive when he slammed the door shut. When I was sure we were moving and wouldn't be stopping anytime soon, I pulled out my phone. I just hoped that Craig answered. The phone rang and rang, but he didn't pick up.

"Shit." I dialed again, but this time he picked up.

"Reese."

He sounded so sad, so resigned. I didn't want him to feel that way, but this wasn't the time to have a discussion about our relationship.

"Craig," I whispered. "I've been kidnapped."

"What?"

"I've been kidnapped."

He sighed heavily. "Now's not the time to mess with me, Reese. Wasn't shoving Leif in my face enough for you?"

"I'm not messing with you. I went to his house to break things off with him, but I overheard something I wasn't supposed to. Now, I'm in his trunk and he's going to kill me!"

"Right. Well, I'm sure you'll enjoy the ride."

The dial tone sounded and I stared at my phone in disbelief. Did he really think I was screwing with him?

Chapter Forty-Five

CRAIG

"Reese?" Alec asked beside me.

"Yeah."

I was hanging out with him, watching movies. I decided when I got up this morning that I was taking some time off work. I needed a break to clear my head after the mind fuck I got last night.

"What'd she want?"

"She says she's been kidnapped." I snorted, shaking my head in amusement. "Like I'm gonna believe that."

He sat up, his face scrunched in concern. "Why wouldn't you believe her?"

"Because she's fucking with me. She's just trying to piss me off even more than I already am so I'll give her the divorce."

"You jackass. Her being kidnapped wouldn't make you mad. She's not fucking lying." He tossed my phone to me. "Call her back right the fuck now."

I sat up, looking at him in confusion. "You mean...you think she's telling me the truth?"

"God, you're one dense fucker. What does she gain by telling you she's been kidnapped?"

I thought about it for a second and then it was like a lightbulb went off in my head. "Holy shit. She's been kidnapped!"

"No shit, fucker."

I pulled up her number immediately and called her back. "Reese!" I shouted when she answered.

"What the fuck took you so long to call me back?"

"How the hell did you get kidnapped again?"

"Look, I'm in the trunk of a car. Do you think you could come get me?"

"Of course, but seriously, getting kidnapped three times in a little over a month, that's gotta be a record."

"Can we debate my kidnapping record later? I'd like to get away from this guy before he murders me."

Alec and I headed out to my truck. I didn't know where I was headed, but anything was better than just sitting here. "Wait, are you sure that Leif had you kidnapped? I mean, how do we know it wasn't your grandma?"

"Do you want to wait and see if I end up dead in the morning?"

"Right. Okay, I'll get on tracking your phone. Do you know what kind of car you're in?"

"Yeah, it's a fucking car. Seriously, was I supposed to take down the details as I was stuffed in the trunk?"

"Well, yeah. I mean, how else do you expect to survive a kidnapping if you don't have these important details that could potentially save your life?"

"Will you just find me before I end up buried out in the woods?"

"Alright, alright. Geez. But when I get you back, we're gonna have to have a serious discussion of what to do for your next kidnapping."

"Whatever."

"Got it," Alec said from beside me. "She's headed north."

"Reese, we're coming to get you."

"Craig, just remember that he's a cop."

"I know. I'll take care of it."

"Alright."

"Just stay on the phone and tell me if anything happens. It shouldn't take too long to catch up to you."

"Cap is heading out now with Lola and Knight."

"Oh shit," I muttered. "Knight? Really? I mean, the guy's good, but now we're definitely gonna have a dead body. How the hell are we gonna explain that to Sean?"

"We could always *not* call Sean and then we'd just have a body to get rid of."

"He's a cop. That's not gonna just go away. Plus, Reese is involved. I don't want her caught up in the middle of an investigation."

"Turn here. We'll cut across and head them off," Alec said, pointing to the side road up ahead.

"Um, so, do I get a say in what we do with Leif?" Reese asked.

"Don't tell me that you want him to get off."

"Actually, after being shoved in the trunk and called a bitch, I'm good with burying him in the woods."

"Really? After all the grief you gave me over the past few weeks, now you're willing to throw your morals aside?"

"Hey, I've never been in this situation before, but I can tell you that getting kidnapped really sucks!"

"Well, yeah, that's why I rescued you the first time."

"Shit. We're slowing down."

"It's okay. We have your location."

"You'd better get here fast. If he kills me, I'm coming back for you and I'll make sure that you never have sex again."

"Okay, I could be wrong, but I think you're being slightly dramatic."

"No," Alec interrupted. "I'm pretty sure that the punishment fits the crime."

"Slip your phone back where you had it. We'll be there soon."

"What's this Leif guy like?" Alec asked.

"I don't know. He seems level-headed enough."

"But he took your woman because she heard something she wasn't supposed to."

"Which means that he's a wild card right now. Even if we get to him in time, there's no telling if we'll be able to convince him that killing her isn't going to help him."

"He's probably already past the point of reason. All he's thinking about right now is getting rid of any witnesses. We have to go in prepared to take him out."

"Reese warned me he's a cop."

"And when has that stopped us before?"

"It hasn't. I just thought I'd pass along the warning."

"Duly noted. Turn up ahead on the right."

I barely slowed, yanking the wheel to the right. I just kept us from going into the ditch. He picked a good spot. It was isolated out here and no one would hear her scream. I punched the gas, worry spreading through me. We didn't hear anything yet, but we still had a few miles to go until we caught up.

"Craig," Reese whispered. "We're stopped. He's getting out."

"Hide your phone. I'm coming, Reese. I won't let you down."

"I know," she whispered, just before there was a rustling sound. I heard a muffled scream right before the line went dead. I tightened my grip on the steering wheel and looked at Alec, who wore the same cold expression that I did. This fucker was gonna die.

He had her up ahead, yanking her out of the trunk of the car by her hair. I slammed the truck into park and Alec and I both jumped out the truck, guns raised and ready to fire. Leif yanked her around, holding her against him as he drew his own weapon and pointed it at us.

"How do you want to play this?" Alec asked.

I shrugged. "I could just shoot the fucker." I took another step forward, trying to figure out if he had the balls to actually shoot.

"Why take all the fun out of it?"

"I guess you're right. I mean, we could at least take him out in the woods and have some fun first."

"Hey!" Leif shouted. "Don't come any closer. I'll fucking shoot you."

"There, there," I said placatingly. "There's no need to panic. We know this is hard on you. It's a rough world. I mean, with all the shit going on in the world, it's no wonder you snapped. There's too much fucking shit to worry about. Climate change, light pollution, the wind turbines killing all the birds." I sighed and shook my head. "It's amazing that you've even made it this far in the world. And I bet it's no better at work. I bet they make you work forty hours a week. I would also guess that they don't use eco friendly pencils at work. Am I right?"

"What are you doing?" Alec asked.

"I'm bonding with him."

"That's bonding?"

"Yeah, I'm showing him that I understand his plight."

"You think you can bond with him over climate change?"

"Well, isn't that what all these snowflakes are into right now?"

"Craig, he's holding a fucking gun on your wife. Try a little harder."

"Fine. I can be fucking nice." I turned back to Leif and did my best to be nice. "So, hey there, Leif. Uh, nice weather we're having."

"*That's* your version of nice? You suck at this."

"What the fuck do you want me to do? Am I supposed to throw down my gun, all in the name of love?"

"No, jackass. Just try to appear calming and negotiable."

"You want me to appear calming?"

"Yeah, that's what I want."

"You want me to be calming?" I shouted.

"Yeah, be fucking calming!" Alec yelled back.

"I can do calming. Fuck, I can be the calmest bastard on the face of the planet," I shouted back.

"Oh, I'd like to see that."

I threw down my gun and held my arms wide. "What's more fucking calm than this?" I started walking toward Leif, arms still spread wide. "Is this calming enough for you? Am I making you feel better?"

"Just stop!" Leif shouted.

"Don't!" Reese pleaded. "What are you doing? Don't do this!"

"You're not gonna shoot me," I said with all the confidence in the world. "Just relax, Reese. He's not gonna shoot me."

I kept advancing and I could see the fear and anger in Leif's eyes. He was gonna shoot me. But not if I willed him not to. I just had to keep telling him he wasn't going to shoot me. I was only about ten feet away now.

"You're not gonna shoot me. You don't want to."

"Please," Reese cried, tears streaming down her face.

"He's not gonna shoot me. He doesn't really want to."

Leif's hand shook and he closed his eyes. I had him. And then he opened his eyes and something dark took over.

"Holy shit. He's gonna shoot me!" I dove to the side, just barely moving out of the way in time. I felt the bullet hit my arm, but it was better than the kill shot. I heard Alec fire, shooting Leif in the arm. I jumped up and tackled him to the ground, throwing the gun away. I was too pissed right now to have a gun in my hands. I might end up shooting the fucker. I punched him in the face and then grabbed him by the collar, pulling him closer to me.

"You fucking shot me!"

I threw him back down and punched him repeatedly until he passed out. When I finally got up, my hands were bloodied, but I wasn't raging nearly as much.

"Feel better?" Alec asked.

"He fucking shot me."

"So you keep saying."

"I just can't believe it. I told him not to fucking shoot me."

"Well, that's the thing about crazy people. They tend to not listen."

"Still," I said, staring down at the fucker on the ground. "He fucking shot me."

Reese came up to me and wrapped her arms around my waist. I turned in her arms until I had her snuggled up against my chest. "Thank you for coming after me."

I sighed and kissed her on the head. "Yeah, we're gonna have a serious talk about how the fuck you got kidnapped for a third time when we get home. Seriously, woman. It's like you have no sense of danger."

"Correct me if I'm wrong," Alec interrupted, "but this is your fifth gunshot wound in just a month, right?"

"Hey, it's been like a month and a half. And this doesn't count. It's just a graze."

Before I knew what was happening, Alec pulled out his gun and shot me in the same fucking leg he shot me in last time.

"What the fuck? You just shot me!"

"It's just a graze. It doesn't count."

Chapter Forty-Six

REESE

It was the last day of school and the summer was starting. I had big plans for the summer. I was finally going to have Jessica redo our house. We never did paint over the wall with all the complaints and I almost considered leaving it up as a tribute of sorts to all the guys. But then I wouldn't be able to have anyone over without starting a huge fight. The animal heads had been completely removed before I moved back in with Craig. There was no way I was staying in the house with those beady eyes staring at me.

I drove to the store to pick up a few groceries before I headed home. After loading the groceries, I unlocked the car and opened the door, but something was thrown over my head before I could get in. I screamed, but a hand clamped over my face and then I was being dragged backwards. I kicked and fought, doing everything Craig had taught me, but then there was another set of hands on me, grabbing my ankles. I was carried and tossed into a trunk. I knew this all too well from my kidnapping days.

I had learned to carry my phone on me at all times after the last time I was kidnapped. It had saved my life. Luckily, I had a tracker that Craig had insisted on putting in my arm. I thought it was a little creepy. Now I knew why he did it. I pulled the hood off my head and spit the fuzz out of my mouth. Yanking my phone out of my back pocket, I pulled up Craig's number.

"Hello, my little pixie!"

"Craig, I've been kidnapped!"

"Again? Seriously?"

"Yes, seriously! Get your ass on the road and get me!"

"Uh, that's gonna be kind of difficult. I'm in a meeting and then I have a lot of work to do."

"What?" I screeched. "Are you saying that you're not coming for me?"

I heard him sigh and say something to one of the guys. "Alright, I guess there's no way around this. I'll leave in a few minutes and catch up to you."

"I'm gonna kill you when I get home! How can you act like this isn't a big deal?"

"Well, it's just that we've already done this before. It gets tiring coming to the rescue all the time. That's why I had you take self-defense classes."

"I want a divorce when this is over."

"Yeah, I've heard that before too. I'll see you soon."

He hung up on me. That fucker. I dialed Brooke's number, fuming that my husband didn't seem to care that I had been kidnapped. Again.

"Hey, what's shakin'?"

"Brooke, I've been kidnapped!"

"And you're using your phone call to talk to me? Wow. I feel special."

"I called Craig already-"

"Oh, so I'm an afterthought. I see."

"What? Would you just listen? I called Craig and he made it sound like it was a chore to come get me!"

"Let me ask you this. What are these kidnappers like?"

"I don't know! I didn't see them."

"Well, it just seems to me that they're pretty stupid if they didn't even check you for a phone first. Did you try jumping out of the trunk?"

"I'm locked in here. How would I do that?"

"There's a latch above you. Just yank on it and jump out. Problem solved. Seriously, you don't need Craig to save you."

"And what if I'm in the middle of nowhere?"

"Well, I guess the kidnapper puts you back in the trunk. Seems pretty simple to me. Honestly, I'm not sure why you even had to call me."

"Does anyone care that I've been kidnapped?"

"Sweetie, we've already done this before. Maybe if something else happened, I mean, something exciting. Next time try for a bomb being strapped to your chest and you're tied to the tree. Ooh! Maybe you could be hanging from the side of the building by a rope. You should definitely talk to Claire. I'm sure she'd have some good ideas."

"I can't believe it. The two people that I would think would come running to my aid don't even give a fuck that I've been kidnapped!"

"Yeah, maybe you should talk to someone about that."

I felt the car slow and started to panic. "Oh my God. We're slowing down."

"Alright, sweetie. Have fun. Let me know how it goes!"

She hung up and the car pull to a stop. I didn't know what to do, but I was going out swinging. There was no way I was going to die in here. And when I got out, I was getting a divorce and a new best friend. I heard the pop of the trunk and then bright light shone in. There were two figures standing over me. When I could finally see, my mouth dropped open. Brooke shot me a finger wave and Craig grinned at me.

"Ready to get married?"

ALSO BY GIULIA LAGOMARSINO

Thank you for reading Craig and Reese's story. There's still more to come further down the line, so keep reading. The Reed Security gang will be back in A Mad Reed Security Christmas!

Join my newsletter to get the most up-to-date information, along with new content in the Reed Security series.

https://giulialagomarsinoauthor.com/connect/

Join my Facebook reader group to find out more about my obsession with Dwayne Johnson!

https://www.facebook.com/groups/GiuliaLagomarsinobooks

Reading Order:

https://giulialagomarsinoauthor.com/reading-order/

To find the individual series, follow the links below:

For The Love Of A Good Woman series

Reed Security series

The Cortell Brothers

A Good Run Of Bad Luck